S0-BER-818

Across the River

Megan Easley-Walsh

Also by Megan Easley-Walsh

Flight Before Dawn

What Edward Heard

North Star Home

Across the River

Megan Easley-Walsh

ACROSS THE RIVER

Dedicated to

Those who endure
and for Stephen, with love

There is no life and death.
There is only life.
Death is an illusion, an appearance, nothing more.
It is a fleeting shade that disappears in the light of truth.
And life, life is constant, ever-flowing like a river.

CHAPTER ONE

The English Countryside, Summer 1774

Rebecca's head rested against his chest, as Caleb lay with her beneath the star-strewn sky. The afternoon's rain had dampened the grass, but the ground was not muddied. Rich earthiness whispered against his nose, but was drowned by the scent of Rebecca. Clasping her hand with his, she leaned over him. Her cheeks, rosy from the coolness of the night, danced merrily under her eyes.

"Come away with me," Rebecca said.

He knew that look.

"Come away with you?"

She nodded, the stars conspiring with her to more intensely highlight her beauty.

"I could not bear to marry another and they are so intent on promising me to someone else."

She knew what she was doing. Merely hearing her words had cast a dagger into his heart, though he knew she had not meant to be cruel. Rebecca only meant to use the truth to make her proposition irresistible to him.

"Caleb, I could not bear to be with another man."

The softness of her skin as she held his hand stood as reminder to the sweetness in his memory, when there had been more than—

"Come away with me," she repeated.

Caleb swallowed. Oh, how he wanted to indulge her! It was all he could do to keep from agreeing. But, he had to be practical; one of them did.

"What would we live off of?"

"Our love."

She was not so naive to think this the only necessity, but she knew the power of her charm on him and she was determined to get her way.

"And how shall I pay for food when you are hungry?"

She said nothing for a moment. He wasn't supposed to object.

"Those silver plates, the ones my mother is forever having polished."

There wasn't a servant for miles that didn't dread the thought of Rebecca's mother's plates.

"Your mother would never part with them."

"Then, I shall have to take them."

"Your plan is to steal the plates?"

"It can hardly be called stealing if I am taking my own inheritance."

Caleb put his hands behind his head, forgetting he was supposed to be applying practicality and now only concerned with watching her loveliness as her mind raced forward.

"Yes, yes, that is it. I shall hide them in the river," Rebecca said.

"In the river, whatever for?"

"You ask too many questions," she said, leaning into him. Her lips brushed against Caleb's, to silence him.

"And you," he said, feeling the softness of her hair over

his arm, "make it truly difficult to concern myself with the answers."

Rebecca looked at him to remind him that yes, she was the power-holder here. She laid her hand against his shirt.

"I feel your heart," Rebecca said, "I feel it as strongly as though 'twere my own. Truthfully, Caleb, I hear your heart beat."

"You hear my watch," he said, with a laugh, pulling his watch from his pocket. The face was marred, but it shone in the sunlight as he worked, glinting at him when he clicked open its half-broken hinge to count the hours until he could see Rebecca again. She stared at him with such intensity that his laughter dried up like a brook encountering an oasis.

Temptress. Beautiful, beloved temptress.

Tiny prickles of grass pushed against his skin, like splinters in his workshop. The world was awake here, rawer, but in a pleasant way. Everything burst with vibrancy, with vitality, like a thousand trees with arms outstretched to the skies above. Pines clung in his nose, fully rooted, away from the saw and the hammer that he would transform them with into the finest furniture for miles. Furniture that someone as noble as Rebecca could even sit on, and yet furniture that cemented his place in the world as a craftsman.

"Caleb, you have kept me waiting far too long. You really ought—"

"So, this is where you wander off to." The words sliced through their shared moment, shattering all promise of what was to come.

"Richard," Rebecca said, hastily moving away from Caleb at the sight of her brother. Caleb's eyes went wide, as a guilty flush washed over him. He scrambled to his feet, pulling Rebecca up with him.

"Richard," Caleb said now, "I can assure you that I mean Rebecca no harm. I only have the best of intentions toward her."

Though caught, his honor would not be sullied.

Richard looked from one to the other.

"I know my sister well enough to know that she can only abide by her own will. I am certain that the only one who has been led here this evening is you."

"I— " Caleb opened his mouth to speak and then, realizing he could make no argument, shut it again. Yes, Rebecca had led him. Caleb, accustomed to cursing the gentry beneath his breath as he toiled for the paltry wages they offered, would bend to no man. But Rebecca, her long hair falling over her silken body, was no man.

"Richard," Rebecca said now, stepping nearer her brother and resting her hand on his arm, "we have done nothing wrong. Promise me, Brother, you will not speak of our innocent secret."

Whether she had deftly bent the truth or spoken the reality she believed was unclear. When Rebecca spoke with such sweetness of purpose, one soon found himself agreeing with her.

Richard, fond though as he was of her, was adept at navigating his way through her persuasive powers. Looking at them now though, with their eyes absent of fear and only love finding a home therein, he couldn't help but agree with her. Perhaps, he was not so immune after all.

"All right, I will do as you ask. But, Sister, do be more careful. You can hardly think that Father would be willing to overlook the state I have found you two in. Mother would have you married off or else sent away to a nunnery before the sun rose."

Caleb wondered at the validity of the threats, but Rebecca, successful in at least one dealing tonight, brushed aside his comments.

"Richard, you worry far too much."

"Even so, you must realize that if you are gone any longer you will soon be missed."

She really couldn't object to this point. Turning to Caleb

one last time, she said in a voice that only they could hear,

"Do consider what I have said, my love. I admit to wishing to sway you, but believe me, it is no whim. I have thought of nothing else for days."

"Rebecca," Caleb said. Doubt had dragged its ugly fingers across his face and she wanted to see nothing of the sort.

"Kiss me, Caleb, kiss me as though 'twere for the last time."

She threw her arms around him before he could object and Richard turned away.

"Rebecca, we best leave," Richard said, beginning to walk away from the two.

Her lips pulled slowly from Caleb's, only to say,

"Yes, I am coming."

The words had hardly slipped from her mouth, when she pushed her lips to Caleb's again.

"Go," he whispered against her. Assuredly, if he had known what was to happen, he never would have said it.

CHAPTER TWO

To satisfy Richard and quiet his concerns, Rebecca had agreed to leave Caleb. Following her brother's dark form, they returned to the sheltering—or perhaps, confining— walls of the family estate of Turrington Manor. Rebecca's restless spirit carried her thoughts to her plans she had spoken in earnest to Caleb. The only regrettable detail of her plan would be Richard's unhappy heart. His alliances lay with her; of that she was certain. He was, however, also a man of his word and, as a result, there was a certain rigidness that resulted.

"Richard," she said, as the house came into sight. In the moonlight, he was bathed in an innocence and the years of age he had accumulated fell away. From deep within her an urge rose to include him, as she had when they were young in her games and capers. Seeing him turn at her voice, the feeling in her subsided. Young though his profile had appeared, the full view of his face confirmed that their play days were long behind and no conspirator kinship could be resurrected.

No, she couldn't tell him. The thought of it broke her heart, but it also only served to strengthen her love for Caleb; yes, he was all that she now had. He was looking at her expectantly and she hadn't yet answered,

"Yes?"

"You will keep your word, yes? You will not tell?"

He looked at her, as though seeing through her. She was certain he knew. She meant to say more, but had stopped herself. There, in his eye, was the same thing that she felt so keenly now; something, unknowingly and unwelcome by both of them, had changed.

He shook his head,

"No, Rebecca, I will not tell. You are safe with

me."

⁂

Rebecca lay awake long into the night. Never one to delay in seeing a plan through, she had chosen tonight as the night to hide the plates in the river. Though she had been charming and coy with Caleb, Rebecca had laid her plans on the firm foundation of practicality. Caleb could not enter their home and without him, she could not carry all that was required to begin their life together. In truth, they would not begin alone but rather with her horse, Dandelion. Just as Caleb could not wander through the halls, neither could Dandelion. She would smuggle her life out of the house one piece at a time, beginning with the silver. When all was ready, she would saddle Dandelion and take one last look at her Palladium prison.

As her mind retraced the steps she must take to succeed in her mission, she listened to the sounds of the household. When the last voices of the servants had faded, she crept from her bed to begin. With a twinge of guilt, she realized that some unfortunate maid would undoubtedly be blamed for the theft, but she could not dwell on such matters. There was another robbery at play, that of her own life, and she was determined to gain it back.

Her plan posed little problem. Regrettably, she had underestimated the weight of the plates and only managed to conceal two under her cloak. Certainly, if she were not leaping from shadow to shadow, she could have carried more. Well, never mind, it was better to be successful with two plates than to transport all of them but be discovered.

When she was through the backdoor, she gathered her skirts in her hands, cradling the plates in the basket they made before her, and ran across the expanse to the cover of trees. She took in a deep breath, as the sweet arbor air filled her lungs. Rebecca was coming alive. Tempted as she was to repeat the whole process of recovering more plates tonight, she knew there would not be enough time. Waiting for the servants to finish putting the house to bed had taken much longer than she had imagined it would. While those inside slept, Rebecca was well aware that others would soon awaken to set about the early morning business.

As she passed back through the fields that bordered the forest and the walled gardens of the estate, a heaviness fell over her.

Turn and run.

An uneasiness gripped her. Had she sufficiently hidden the plates? Supposing someone came along and discovered them —But no, that wouldn't happen. She had chosen the right spot, under the rocks, between the reeds, near where the ducks nested in spring. The place was right. It was something else that was wrong.

A line of gray appeared on the horizon. Was it later than Rebecca realized? Surely, the dawn was not already approaching!

As she slipped through the backdoor, a clatter stopped her cold. Her mind had wandered. She hadn't been focused enough and had run into something. She held her breath, as she searched for what had fallen. Rebecca waited, certain of her imminent discovery. But no, that wasn't what had happened at all.

The gray that she had mistaken for the dawn loomed larger. Like the mighty rolling clouds over a turbulent sea, it raced toward her. The clatter that she had heard soon erupted into a chorus of frenzied voices and falling objects.

"Fire! Fire!" someone shouted.

As though giving power to the smoke that approached, Rebecca choked at the words, coughing as she pulled her cloak over her mouth. Had the kitchen fire been left burning but unattended? No, the kitchen was to the far side and the smoke was coming from the opposite direction of the kitchen. The smoke thickened around Rebecca, hanging heavily in her eyes. They watered under the presence of the smoke.

A bevy of moving people danced before Rebecca's eyes, as hazy clusters of color. The servants' faces, which she knew as well as those of her own family, hurried across the grounds. Behind them, Rebecca feared she would see the growing arms of the fire, devouring what had surrounded her each day. Perhaps, there would no longer be a home to run from.

More terrifying than she imagined, the flames lapped against the walls as ravenous dogs descend upon their prey. She stood transfixed, unable to move.

"Rebecca!" Richard's voice called to her through the billowing smoke,

"Rebecca, run!"

Try though as she might, the smoke made it impossible to move.

"Rich— " Rebecca broke into a convulsive cough, having swallowed smoke as she tried to speak.

Through the dense pockets of the shrouding gray, came a figure on horseback. With his black cloak and a band of black around his mouth, he swept down, plucking Rebecca from her spot on the cobblestones. Overcome by the smoke, she wavered and slumped against the stranger's back.

CHAPTER THREE

Shouts, as loud as thunder cracking across the sky, awoke Caleb from a deep slumber. He stumbled out of bed, pulled on his breeches and stuffed his feet into his shoes. Pulled from his house by the commotion, he joined the gathering assembly of the town's street. Stretching his back, like the cats that watched him in the cabinetry shop as he worked a piece of oak or walnut into a handsome table or bookcase, he tried to clear the sleep from him.

It had been late when he had returned from Rebecca. Sleep refused to cooperate for a long while. Her arguments had been convincing. When he finally did fall asleep, it was with the heavy awareness that she was not lying beside him. It became clear to Caleb that she really ought to be there. Nothing else seemed to make sense. Rebecca's quiet breathing and the softness of her hand on his arm no longer seemed merely niceties; they had become necessities.

Caleb, caught by the overpowering arms of tiredness, was jolted forward.

"Pardon, Caleb," the blacksmith said as he hurried past him, recovering from ramming into him more quickly than Caleb had.

"Peter, wait," he called after him. The man, whose jet hair matched the hammered metal of the forge, half-turned but continued walking. Caleb, less bulky than Peter but equal in height, soon caught up to him.

"What is it that has happened?"

"Thieves."

"Who?" Caleb said, tripping over a stone on the path, but regaining his footing quickly enough to keep up with Peter.

"Lord Turrington."

Caleb's eyes went wide, erasing all tiredness.

"Rebecca Turrington," a sweet voice from the recesses of

his memory said, summoned at the sound of her name.

"I never much cared for Lord Turrington, but if the place burns to the ground I will lose almost all of my business," Peter said.

He paused, only briefly, to lift a bucket from the stand in front of the cooper's shop. Peter thrust a bucket into Caleb's hands, as he bent to pick up another.

"Burns? Has there been a fire?" Caleb said.

"Caleb, you have been a peculiar man on many occasions, but never more so than now. You do not think we could fight off a gang of thieves with buckets, do you?"

Caleb had heard all he needed to spur him into action. Dropping the bucket, he began to run.

"Wait," Peter called after him, "you forgot the bucket."

Caught in the throng of villagers, who like Peter had financial interests at heart or else were moved by goodwill for the unfortunate nobles, Caleb fought through the crowd. Gossip sparked nearly as quickly as the flames had. The scandalous flames of fiery tongues leaped at him, as he battled his way toward Rebecca.

The smell of smoke washed over him long before he saw the growing flames. Carried by the wind it swirled around him, the oppressive chokehold becoming more intense. Swallowed by the surround of gray, Caleb slipped away from the others to enter through the backdoor. Rebecca's chambers were nearer to it. She had taken him there on one especially daring day. He had almost been discovered, but she had managed to smuggle him out. One or two servants had raised their eyebrows but, well aware that Rebecca was treated as a child though she'd been old enough to be a woman a good number of years, they had turned a blind eye.

"Rebecca! Rebecca!" he said, pounding his fists against the door. Plumes of smoke, like the bellows in Peter's forge, hung heavy in the air.

"She is not there," a bent-over washerwoman, with a rough leathery face, told him. Though elderly, she moved quickly and was already well down the corridor before he could turn to her.

"Wait," he called after her disappearing shadow, "where is she?"

She didn't stop walking and most of her words were swept away as she answered,

"—taken—gone."

"Gone? Gone where?"

Caleb took off after the washerwoman but in her escape, she had disappeared through the archway and into the open. Caleb, reckless in his search for Rebecca, turned and reentered. The fire had spread quickly. The wallpaper purchased in Paris peeled from the walls under the pressure of the heat. The walls sighed and heaved under the power of the encroaching flames.

White, porcelain-like plasterwork crumbled around Caleb. Silk hanging from the windows and delicately interwoven tapestries blazed. The heat poured against Caleb's face, as he sprang from room to room. Through the soft leather of his shoes, the tiles burned hot. Whole forests of beautifully carved wood went up as kindling. Leather-bound books, much treasured by Rebecca and occupying the long shelves of the library, lay charred in the wake of the flames.

She had wanted to leave. Rebecca, never one to beg, had practically pleaded that he go away with her.

Why did I not listen to you? Why did I hesitate? Why did I not insist that we go this very evening, in that very moment? Rebecca, oh Rebecca, I have failed you.

Her house lay in the ruins of ashen piles. Certainly, this is not what she had intended. Oh, where was she? As though the fire had entered his own body, his stomach tangled.

The townspeople had poured buckets of water over much of the house in an attempt to stop the spread. An ashen puddle pooled at Caleb's feet, as he stood in the library. Feeling desperate for some link to Rebecca, he bent to retrieve a half-consumed volume from the floor.

Tucking it under his arm, he emerged from the library into the courtyard. With buckets strewn across the yard and townspeople battling back the last of the flames, Caleb surveyed the damage. Two of the wings had been engulfed almost entirely and even the ceiling had given way and collapsed.

"Rebecca, Rebecca, where are you?"

"Are you looking for Miss Turrington?" The voice appeared at his side. In the still frothing clouds of smoke, it was a welcomed reprieve.

"Yes, Rebecca Turrington. Have you seen her?" Caleb said, addressing the thin old gentleman, who was really more of a ragged-looking fellow than anything else.

"Cannot say that I have, good sir."

"Oh," Caleb said, his voice falling.

He turned to leave, but the man caught his arm as he said,

"I cannot say 'tis much use in searching for her."

"Why not? I will search until I find her," Caleb said, feeling more confident than perhaps he ought to have.

"Then you best give up. You will not find her."

"What do you mean?"

Of course, he would find her! This silly old man had no idea what he was talking about.

"She has vanished. We searched for her and she is not anywhere."

"She has to be somewhere. She cannot not be somewhere!" Caleb said, becoming angry.

"Truthfully, I apologize, but you do not seem to understand. She is gone. She is not coming back."

"Of course she is— " Caleb said, his voice faltering.

The man looked at him sadly and shook his head. Catching sight of the book in Caleb's hand, he tapped its cover,

"I am afraid, Miss Turrington, God rest her soul, has crossed the river."

CHAPTER FOUR

Pressed against the back of the anonymous horseman, Rebecca had ridden for hours. Looking like an apocalyptic rider leaping in front of the flames, she had wondered if death himself were scooping her up onto his black horse. Had the fiery condemnations of disobedience to family obligations and dire warnings against the love she shared with Caleb cursed her? But no, God had not been the master of these lies. He had spared her and as the dawn approached, she breathed in the sunlight as though seeing it for the first time.

Judgment, to maintain her safety, had prevented her from asking who her captor was. She had looked back toward the house she had planned to escape from and seen the long wisp of smoke rising from the stones tucked among the hills. How small it looked from here! How could so small a place have had such an imposing bearing on her life? Richard was safe. She knew that much was true, since she had seen him. Her parents were not at home, having left last night. Richard's warning of her staying out too late had been for naught after all.

When she had recovered from the smoke, she had ensured that she did not fall asleep. Careful observation of all she passed filled her mind, as though she were sketching a well-laid map of the journey. They were joined by other horsemen as their ride continued. The first had emerged from the tree line, not far from where Rebecca had hidden the silver plates a few hours earlier. How long had he waited there? She had assumed her caper had been completed alone. No longer certain, Rebecca began to question her safety. The thought of being watched made her uneasy and her rescue no longer seemed so providential.

Another rider signaled to the man on the horse that Rebecca rode on and he pulled back on the reins. The horse, almost as silent as the rider, came to a stop. They were isolated, well away from any town, estate or sign of habitation.

Undoubtedly, it was the reason that they had stopped here. Rebecca, having maintained her mental observations to find her way home, now took note of any means of escape. She was a fine horsewoman, having beaten Richard in many a race on Dandelion since they were children. Her reliable horse was not present, but she had taken note of the unfamiliar steed she rode on, paying particular attention to his antics.

He was prone to veer toward the left, but would soon be set straight again when pressure was applied to his flank with the rider's heel. It was not so much rebellion as youthful indiscretion. He was not more than a couple of years old but he was a gelding, gentle and easily led. Yes, the horse would not be the problem. The problem would be distancing the rider from him.

There were five riders, not including Rebecca. Unable to turn to see them without writhing about, she got her first real look at most of them now as she dismounted. Rebecca had hoped for a moment alone on the horse to attempt her escape, but the rider had been too calculated in his plan and prevented this by telling her to get down. They were the first words he had spoken to her. Not wanting to endanger herself by facing the rider's wrath for asking too many questions, she too had not spoken.

Rebecca's first chance to speak came now, as she was handed a silver flask full of water.

"Thank you," she nodded. The high temperature of the fire and clouds of smoke had parched her throat. As she drank in the cool moisture, it washed over the damage, soothing the rawness.

The rider, who had swept her onto his horse, withdrew the black band from his mouth to take a drink.

"You—" Rebecca said. She had spent much of the morning hours wondering at her captor's identity. This she had not expected.

"Miss Turrington, your surprise wounds me," he said, in a voice that suggested he meant no such thing.

"Lord Furton, I did not realize you were so intent upon marrying me," Rebecca said.

Lord Furton was one of the highest-placing gentlemen on Lord Turrington's list of potential son-in-laws. Knowing her captor reignited Rebecca's quick wit. No longer did she fear for her safety.

"Miss Turrington, you do know that I am only devoted to you." His words bordered on sarcastic sincerity.

"You have not yet explained your providential presence as my rescuer. I am surprised that you were out at so early an hour."

"Perhaps, my dear Miss Turrington," he said, stepping nearer, "we have more in common than you realize."

"Whatever do you mean, Lord Furton?" she said, feigning oblivion.

"Come now, you do not mean to say that my eyes deceived me. 'Twas you who moved so nimbly through the forest this morning, 'twas it not?"

Before she could protest, he stepped nearer again. His face, covered in whiskers and set as stone, peered at her own as he said,

"Yes, you were surprised 'twas me. I am devoted to you, but Rebecca Turrington, you have been anything but faithful to me. Oh other girls, perhaps, have carried on a flirtation with a young lord who had a bigger fortune or was, perhaps, more handsome than I."

Her skin crawled under his words.

"Lord Furton, I never—"

He cut her off,

"No, Miss Turrington, you are quite right. You never did such a thing. You have run to a lowly cabinet maker. What could he possibly give you? Or perhaps, that is no mystery," he said knowingly.

"Lord Furton, I refuse to have my honor questioned. I am nothing but noble and pure. To suggest otherwise is demeaning to me as a lady and unbecoming to you as a gentleman. Furthermore, if you presume to know so much about me, then you will know that it will not be long before we are surrounded by my search party."

Rebecca had no intention of waiting to be rescued. Let Lord Furton think that was her plan though, and her disappearance would catch him unaware.

Feeling smug, she stood tall, as she faced her captor.

"Ah Miss Turrington, that is where you are wrong. You really do not think we would go through all the trouble of starting the fire without spreading that nasty little rumor?"

"You did *what*?" she seethed.

"Oh, you have not heard?" he said, sarcasm dripping from every word, "Do you not know, Miss Turrington? You are dead."

CHAPTER FIVE

No tears streaked Caleb's cheeks. Too stunned, he had said nothing in reply to the old man's words. He had wandered silently away, unwilling to accept this version of reality. It wasn't possible. The world was not real without Rebecca in it.

"Richard, I have to find Richard," Caleb said, when his legs had walked aimlessly for a long while.

"Please, have you seen Richard Turrington?" Caleb said, to the woman who passed him by now.

"I cannot say that I have," she said, shaking her head.

Seeing his distress, she added in an encouraging word before turning to leave,

"Chin up. There will be plenty of work for a fine furniture maker like yourself, after all that has been destroyed in the fire."

The words, meant as solace, sliced through him. The terrible image of Rebecca caught in the flames hammered against his eyes from the inside out.

"Caleb, Caleb, why did you not come away with me?"

The words seemed real enough, that he could almost feel the touch of her hand on his own. He shook his head to clear the horror away and fled the befuddled woman.

"Richard Turrington, has anyone seen Richard Turrington?" he said to every face that passed him by. Some shook their heads or said they had not. Most ignored him. A loneliness began to grip Caleb, despite his immersion in the crowd. His questions continued with the same commitment as a street vendor selling his wares. Despite his earnest efforts, there was no word of the Turringtons. It was as if the fire had not only damaged their home, but also expunged the family.

Lost in desperation, Caleb wondered at the apathy of the others. Why did no one care? It was not that the others had hearts of stone; simply, they did not depend upon knowledge of the Turringtons for anything more than their paychecks. Rebecca Turrington did not sustain them.

Caleb couldn't go home. Rebecca had been there. Laughing, she had sat at his table. Smiling, she had—

Stop it! Stop it!

Unwilling to face the ruins of the Turrington house, he confined himself to the south side of the town. He entered the tavern with the book still clutched under his arm.

"What will you have, Caleb?"

He made no answer.

"Looks like he already had enough to drink," another said, laughing. His companion joined in the joke, but the proprietor took exception to the statement.

"Mr. Haroldson hardly comes here at all. He is most assuredly with his wits about him. He is never without them," he corrected.

The other two men shrugged off the comment. Caleb seemed to have heard none of it.

"Caleb, are you all right? You are as pale as a sheet," the proprietor said, leaning in to speak.

"Caleb?"

Caleb stared straight ahead, not saying anything.

"Caleb?"

"Have you seen Richard Turrington?"

The proprietor raised his eyebrows at the question. Still concerned for the man before him, he shook his head.

"I must find him," Caleb said resolutely. He gripped the book tightly, thumping it for emphasis against the counter. Taking note of the delicate binding and obvious fire damage, the proprietor tried to coax conversation from Caleb.

"What have we here?"

The book had become an extension of Caleb's hand and he looked at it now, as though surprised by its presence.

"A book," Caleb said. Standing, he left the tavern, deaf to

the words of the others behind him.

"I still say he is drunk."

Caleb did not stop walking, until he had passed the houses and buildings of the town. The fields passed unnoticed behind him. Rolling hills concealed where he was going. He hadn't decided on the direction of his feet, but they had taken him there all the same.

Stones dotted the waving grasses. Larger clusters of the scattered few gave way to the ruins of an abbey wall. Monks had lived here, seeking perfect peace centuries before. Blinded by tears, Caleb had stumbled upon this place years earlier. Orphaned before he had accumulated enough years to be called a man, Caleb had found the stone sanctuary. Here, his prayers felt closer to God. There was no ceiling to block his words.

He sat down heavily and leaned against the remainder of a column. The sky shone brightly above. How could it have such gall? Things could not continue as normal when Rebecca was gone. He choked at the thought of the words.

And yet, birds still flew overhead, the sun shone, and in the distance the river ran.

"She has crossed the river." The old man's words confronted him. The memory took on a force of its own and seemed to pull his hands to the pages of the book. Opening it, his eyes fell upon the engraved image of a man, dressed in Grecian garb and bearing the inscription, "Charon". Beneath it, he read,

"Paying the ferryman to cross the river."

He shut the book with a thud, pushing it away from him.

"I will hide the silver plates in the river," Rebecca's sweet voice said.

"No!" He stood in an attempt to clear the awful thoughts. Rebecca with the silver plates as an offering to Charon played before his eyes.

"No! Your plates will not be the silver coins to pay the ferryman! I will not allow you! I will bring you back, Rebecca! I will bring you back!"

He said those words promising her return, until his mouth ran dry. When it did, he sat back, empty of his speech but not of his sorrow.

For a long while, he sat in silence. It was difficult to tell how much time had passed when nothing, including time, made sense. A rustle in the grass drew his attention. He only half-cared what the cause was. Truthfully, Caleb would have ignored it, had the rustle not materialized into human form.

"Caleb Haroldson?"

His own name rang unfamiliar in his ears.

"Are you Caleb Haroldson?" the voice repeated.

"Yes, why do you ask?"

"I have information."

"Why should that concern me?"

Caleb was upset and wanted to be left alone.

"You are looking for Richard Turrington, are you not?"

CHAPTER SIX

When Rebecca's captor had worn his cloak of anonymity, she had embraced the belief that her escape was imminent. When Lord Furton revealed his deep-seeded plan, her confidence wavered. He knew things that she had believed were sacred between her and Caleb. Oh dear sweet Caleb! How he must be suffering now, if he had heard the horrid rumor!

They had ridden the horses hard for most of the day. As dusk sparked against the horizon, they tethered the horses in a grove of trees.

"We make camp here," Lord Furton said to the others.

Two of the riders built a fire to fend against the approaching dark and cold of the night.

"Sit please, Miss Turrington. I would not want you to think I was an ungracious host," Lord Furton said, gesturing for her to take a place beside the fire.

Rebecca sat rather stiffly, the way that she had at so many of her mother's banquets. At least she was not constrained by her layers of uncomfortable skirts, as she had been at those dinner parties. Lord Furton had been considerate enough to kidnap her at night, when her cumbersome garments were replaced for stealth movement.

The others— she was certain now that they must be servants for they kept their distance and deferred to Lord Furton's direction— busied themselves, leaving the two alone.

"Why?" she said, looking at him through the veil of flames.

"Why what my dear, Miss Turrington?" he said, looking rather coy.

"Why would you do all of this?"

"You are a lovely companion," he said, his eyes narrowing and betraying the truth of all he said. The chill of night pressed against her back, as the flames' heat lapped against her face. He had insisted that she sit nearer the fire than she would have chosen to do so. He was no doubt playing on his power to add to her discomfort.

"Why, Lord Furton," she began again, remaining calm so as not to appear ruffled by him, "did you arrange so elaborate a plan?"

"'Twas required was it not, Miss Turrington? You were reluctant, to say the least, to keep our agreement."

"Lord Furton, my memory must be failing me. I remember no such agreement. You have spoken as though we are engaged," she challenged.

His mouth drew into a taut line. She was remaining calm, but he was not. Rebecca was moving into territory that she was well familiar with: occupying the seat of power. Lord Furton was a formidable opponent and unwilling to concede to her.

"Miss Turrington, I am a man of business. I never buy spoiled goods." The insult hit her squarely.

Let it wound you. If you do not, he will know that your mind is elsewhere.

She couldn't risk Lord Furton suspecting that her mind was still at work calculating her escape. If he underestimated her, it could be her greatest strength. She made no reply and her silence had the desired effect. Lord Furton looked pleased with himself.

Few words were exchanged for the remainder of the evening. Lord Furton, for all his pompous behavior, fell asleep quickly. The ride had not been as easily tolerated by his older muscles and had affected him more than he would have anyone believe. The others had still not spoken to her and it was only now, when they spoke together, that she realized the language was not English. The words brushed unfamiliar against her ears, quickly eliminating French and Latin that Rebecca studied with her tutor. One of the men caught her eye and she looked away, not wanting to appear as a spy. Poking the fire with a thin branch, he began to sing a low chant.

Ah, they are from the highlands. Yes, I should have known.

The fire flickered as a pleasant backdrop to their song.

Caleb would like this.

She hugged her arms around her, wishing that they were his. Her eyelids grew heavy as the night wore on, but Rebecca willed herself to stay awake. Her only chance of escape rested in the hours that the others slept.

Well into the night, the singing continued. Lord Furton did not awake and slept silently, away from Rebecca's vision in the pitch dark of the night. When the last choruses had been sung and the fire dwindled until there was only a line of smoke, as there is from a snuffed out candle, Rebecca prepared to make her move. The horses remained tethered to the trees. Between them lay the sleeping accomplices of Lord Furton.

Her muscles were cramped from holding them still for so long, as she pretended to sleep. Standing with more caution even than she had approached last night's caper with, Rebecca took one careful step forward. The leather of her shoes carried her softly across the expanse, as an animal travels unnoticed by another. Though quiet, her shoes were fashioned for dancing and sitting and being a genteel lady and not stalking through the forest. Sticks and stones pushed against her arches through the soft soles.

Rebecca held her breath, as she passed the sleeping forms.

Get to the horse, lead it away, mount him, and then ride like the wind.

The plans played repeatedly through her mind. Yes, if she rode harder than she ever had, she could be home by dawn. The thought of Caleb suffering was impossible to bear. Never mind that now, though. She would be with him soon. She would make it right and never leave again. Her father, overjoyed at her survival, was certain to agree to their marriage as well.

Everything would be—

Crack!

A branch broke loudly under Rebecca's foot. She froze and willed the others not to hear her. She waited. Nothing happened.

"Go on," she told herself, but her feet would not move.

All right, yes, wait a minute more.

Still, there was no indication that the others had heard her. Convinced, her feet moved forward. The horses were quiet as she approached. She had planned on taking the gelding that Lord Furton had carried her away on, but as she approached the horses now she could see that he was in the middle of the others.

If I did not know any better, I would say Lord Furton had planned it this way.

A mare on the outer edge, chestnut in color, seemed agreeable enough and made little noise as Rebecca ran her hand over her glossy coat. Reaching for the reins that tied her to the tree, Rebecca was extra cautious, certain that if the mare were to spook now would be the time.

But no, the mare behaved beautifully, as though fully knowledgeable of Rebecca's plan and a willing accomplice.

Get to the horse, lead it away, mount him—her, and ride like the wind. Lead her away—

Rebecca looped the reins around her head and gave a gentle tug. The mare, who had been nibbling on grass, pricked up her ears. Rebecca tugged again and began to walk away. The mare obliged, needing only an occasional urge to pull her grazing mouth from the luscious grass.

Lead it away, get to the river.

Rebecca paused. Going to the river had not been part of the plan but yes, it did make sense.

Let them lose the trail.

The river, if it were not being too generous to call it that, was really more of a large creek. They were camped a short distance from it. Rather than risk leading the mare through the sleeping men, Rebecca would take the slightly longer route through the trees, paralleling the camp.

She was forced to move more slowly than she would have liked, since a horse is not as nimble as a light-footed lady. In addition, the path through the trees, illuminated by only the marginal light of the moon, was proving more difficult to navigate through than she had imagined.

The rush of the water alerted her to the presence long before she saw the river.

"Come on," she whispered to the horse, giving her a reassuring pat.

The moonlight caught the water, making it glimmer as it crashed against the rocks. Rebecca hitched up her skirts and, deciding that getting her shoes wet was better than injuring her feet, she stepped nearer the river.

"Miss Turrington, how kind of you to water my horse," a voice sounded behind her.

Rebecca spun to face Lord Furton.

"Or am I mistaken? Why, you would not be stealing this horse now, would you?"

Before she could answer, Lord Furton drew a pistol and gestured toward something that was concealed under the trees clustered near the river.

"If you please, Miss Turrington, into the boat."

CHAPTER SEVEN

"Yes, I am looking for Richard Turrington," Caleb said. He had become despondent and felt hollow after sitting alone in the ruins for several hours. His earlier frenzied activity had disappeared.

"Follow me," the shadowy figure said. His face was concealed under a hood, further marring his appearance in the dark.

"Who are you?" Caleb said, as he stood from the craggy ruins.

As Caleb stepped from the shelter of the remaining stones, he saw the sinewy rope of the man's belt drag along the ground. With the benefit of additional light, Caleb could now see that the hood of the man was not just a cape but extended in billowing robes around his feet.

The man turned at Caleb's question to face him. He supplied no answer, instead saying,

"You seem to have left your book."

Caleb looked at him blankly.

"Your book," the man repeated, pointing to the volume that Caleb had cast aside hours ago. It was clear that the answers would not come until Caleb obliged him. He reached down, picking up the book. Earlier, it had rested unobtrusive— even unnoticed— under his arm. Now, it felt awkward and heavy. The words within it grew in weight, mocking him in his sadness.

Why could I not have taken a book of maps or love poems to commemorate you, dear Rebecca?

The man in the robes spoke few words. The occasional "this way" was the only explanation he offered. He led Caleb away from the ruins and down the side of the hill.

"Do you know where Richard Turrington is or not?" Caleb said, as the rushing grasses batted against his legs. The man turned and in a low voice said,

"Patience, please."

Caleb let out an exasperated sigh.

Do you not realize what I have been through? Do you not know—No, no, you would not know.

Caleb had almost confronted the man aloud, but the realization had stopped him. He had kept loving Rebecca a secret in her life; he wouldn't sully her reputation now.

His mind was keen to dwell upon his memories. The smallest things he would miss the most: the way her nose scrunched against the sun, the melodic whistle as she stared up at the sky above, and simply having her beside him.

Ah Rebecca, you would like this.

His mind was playing tricks on him. Despite being gone, he could nearly hear her speak those same words to him, as though carried over a great distance. His heart sobbed, but his eyes remained dry. Tears would not do her justice; they were inadequate. They were beautiful clear jewels, diamonds of emotion, but there was nothing beautiful about this. Quite simply, for Caleb, there was nothing.

The man continued walking, not toward the town as Caleb had assumed he would, but away from it. When they had walked another ten minutes and still no information was offered, Caleb said,

"Just where are we going anyway?"

The man paused, but did not turn toward Caleb this time. He continued walking. Caleb's feet sank into the ground. They must be approaching a creek or another body of water that had caused a runoff.

"Why should I follow you?" Caleb said, annoyed at being ignored for the majority of the day—ignored most of all by God who had not spared his Rebecca.

The thought jolted him, as if he had been punched hard in the stomach. A few feet ahead of him, the man stopped. Although it was dark, there was some visibility. Caleb could see nothing different here, from the terrain they had been traipsing through, to suggest any good reason for this being the dedicated location.

Caleb, you are following a fool. Blinded by your search, you will no doubt be robbed now.

The thought that should have perhaps worried him, did nothing of the sort. What consequence was money, when he was devoid of the most precious part of creation? Turning, the man said,

"This is where the path ends and where the journey begins. This way."

He bent near the earth and brushed aside branches and dirt. This spot of ground looked no different from the rest of the land around him. The robed man turned to Caleb, as though asking why he was not helping. It seemed like a ridiculous task that he had busied himself with. But when nothing made sense, why should it matter? Caleb crouched beside the man. Nearer to him now than he had previously been, he could see that the man was older than he had first appeared; his brisk pace had been deceptive. Unsure of what he was doing, Caleb continued moving away the dried leaves and bits of twigs. Were a bird present, he would have been able to assemble a fine home. Caleb's focus extended beyond the patch of land that the man had begun with, as he continued his clearing. Seeing this, the man turned to him,

"The t'ing is here."

Caleb realized that the man was not English, but rather Irish. He had not noticed the variation in accent to the paltry offering of words that Caleb had previously been offered. As the man turned back toward the patch and Caleb moved nearer to continue in the allocated space, he caught sight of a glimmer of a crucifix.

"You are a priest," he said aloud, surprised that he had questioned the motives of his guide.

"A monk," he said, not pausing in the clearing. When Caleb did not reply, the monk looked up at him. The book was still tightly clutched under Caleb's arm.

"And you, Caleb Haroldson, are you a scholar?"

"Me? No, I am a lowly cabinet maker."

"Lowly? Saint Joseph and our own dear Lord were carpenters," he said, in gentle challenge.

Caleb did not answer, but continued moving aside dirt. His hand brushed roughly against something previously unseen. It felt heavy, but soggy. The monk pushed it up. It creaked loudly on its hinges. Swinging open, Caleb was met by the smell of damp decay. A gaping hole stared back at them. The monk pulled a match from his pocket, struck it and lit a large stick.

"This way."

"You do not mean— "

"Yes, Caleb Haroldson," the monk said. Eying the title of the book on its spine he continued,

"Into the bowels of the earth, I shall be your Virgil."

CHAPTER EIGHT

Rebecca's skin bristled under her collar. The prospect of Lord Furton shooting her was ridiculous. Why had he gone through the trouble of saving her, if his intention had been to dispose of her? Still, the weapon made a persuasive argument that was not easily ignored. She expected his Scottish companions to step from behind the trees momentarily, but they did not come.

"I suppose you expect the horse to step into the boat, as well," she said sarcastically.

"Dear Miss Turrington, sarcasm is unbecoming— but you have larger, more important manners to learn so I do not expect you to realize that."

Since he had discovered her attempt to escape, it was pointless to pretend that she was wounded by the comment. What she was, was mad— livid.

"I am a perfect lady," she wanted to retort. But no, that would only provide him with further ammunition and she was not prepared to give him the pleasure of it.

Lord Furton tied the horse to the tree as Rebecca, with no other choice, stepped into the boat. He jumped in beside her and pushed off from the shore, casting his paddle into the murky waters below. With the pale glow of the moon whispering against the water, the boat ride for two bordered on romantic. It would have been, if it weren't for the wrong man present and the uncertainty of the location he was kidnapping her away to.

Well, Rebecca, you were feeling trapped within your home. You wanted to be free. You are free, my girl, under this big curtain of night. Yet, you have never been more trapped.

Lord Furton rowed in silence, which suited Rebecca fine. The lull of the gentle waves rocking the boat as a cradle, coupled with being awake for hours, pulled on Rebecca's eyelids. She woke with a start, catching herself from a nonexistent fall.

"Well now, Miss Turrington, 'twas not very nice of you to fall asleep, was it?" she expected to hear Lord Furton say. Instead though, he had not noticed or at least he did not say anything if he had.

Rebecca leaned against the seat, stretching her back. Desperately, she wanted to jump from the boat and swim to shore, but dashing her head against a rock would put her in dire circumstances. In addition, Lord Furton's pistol rested against his leg on the seat beside him. No longer was she so certain or convinced that he would not shoot. With nothing else to do, she willed herself to sleep.

"The poor Miss Turrington succumbed to a boating accident"—

But no, there was no explanation necessary, was there? He had said that the others had been told she was dead. What would her parents think? Would they be sorry they had smothered her? What would Richard think?

Ah, dear Richard.

She had thought instantly of Caleb, but how had she overlooked her brother's pain that surely he must feel? He had been nothing but good to her, nothing but loyal.

I am sorry Rich—

Rebecca's thoughts stumbled at what filled her eyes. Ahead of them, the river opened and a ship with full masts and sails flying from the rigging stood. She looked from the ship to Lord Furton's face.

"Yes, Miss Turrington. Is she not grand?" he said, his lips twitching.

"Lord Furton, you are English."

"Of course, Miss Turrington, but why should that matter?"

"We are going to that ship?" Her hand rose to point to the looming skeleton on the horizon.

"Of course, Miss Turrington." Rebecca's heart thudded in

her chest. She had planned to ride home. She could have walked home. But, sailing out to sea would not allow her to leave a trail. How could she take note of each wave, as she had watched the changing terrain? Panic brushed its icy hands over her, as her body erupted in simultaneous heat.

"I thought— " she said, all confidence and all sense of power abandoning her, "that you were taking me to your home."

"Ah Miss Turrington, once again you wound me. I would never be so selfish as to keep you to myself."

His words sliced against her, as though delivered on the edge of a knife.

"Lord Furton," she said, her voice giving way under her, "what are your plans for me?"

"Is it not clear, Miss Turrington? There is to be a wedding and you are to be the bride."

She shook her head,

"I do not understand."

"You do not understand? You do not understand? Do you hear that?" he said, waving the paddle out of the water and addressing the trees, "Miss Turrington does not understand." The paddle fell back against the water with a loud plop. Erasing the amusement from his words, he said in his most serious voice,

"Then allow me to explain, Miss Turrington. You will make a lovely wife."

"For you?" she said weakly, half-hoping the answer would be yes in light of the unknown alternative.

"No, no, Miss Turrington to someone else, to some wealthy merchant who has not seen a woman in months and is starving for a female companion. Yes, Miss Turrington, you will fill my pockets with a tidy sum of gold coins."

His eyes burned with calculated hatred. Rebecca, a woman of strength, had never swooned in her life. Now though, she gripped the side of the boat, her knuckles growing white in the moonlight.

"Why would you do such a thing?"

"You should not ask so many questions, Miss Turrington; it is unbecoming. That is your problem, Miss Turrington, you do not know your place. There is no room for women such as you in England." He stared at her as he spoke.

"Lord Furton, real men are not threatened by a woman's power. They applaud it." Well, at least Caleb did and Shakespeare wrote strong women into his plays and was beloved for two centuries now. Surely, that must have meant something.

His mind was made up and she could not sway him. If some terrible end were to befall her, she might as well remain true to herself and not back away from what she believed in. Lord Furton paddled to the side of the ship. A sailor hung over the side, whistling at Rebecca.

"Please, there is a lady present," one of the other sailors said in mock protest.

"Of course, there is. Why else would I greet a boat like that?"

Rebecca's stomach lurched forward, more from their words than the rocking of the small boat in the shadow of the ship. A rope ladder was flung down over the hull. Rebecca took one look at the ladder and then looked to the shore. Could she make it?

She had hesitated a fraction too long. A sailor scampered down the rope ladder. Lord Furton stepped behind her. Trapped between them, she had no choice but to obey as Lord Furton said,

"Up the ladder, if you please, Miss Turrington."

CHAPTER NINE

Descending into the hole, Caleb followed the monk, the self-appointed Virgil. If the monk were Virgil, then Rebecca was assuredly Beatrice. There seemed no divinity in this escapade, though, and Caleb had no inclination to enter a deeper layer of hell. Surely, the absence of Rebecca— her death— was already too great of a burden of pain to bear. Perhaps, being with a monk would only take him to Purgatory.

The hole they traveled through went deep into the ground. As they descended, a murkiness wedged itself into Caleb's nostrils. Knowing that his guide was a monk instilled in Caleb the ability to speak freely with him.

"What is this place?"

"An entrance."

"To what?"

Their voices bounced against the sides, causing a slight echo. Before the monk could answer, Caleb asked another question.

"Are these walls?"

"Stones, yes, and the entrance is to where you desire to go."

Caleb, who earlier would have become annoyed at the answers, now recognized an honesty in them. There was something comforting— small as it may be— in having a guide who spoke in such simplicity. He only supplied what seemed absolutely necessary for the moment.

"Are we— by chance—" Caleb said, stepping with a soft thud onto the base,
"in a well?"

"Yes, Caleb Haroldson."

He wondered at the monk identifying him always by both names, but he brushed it aside as nothing more than a mild curiosity.

"This way," he said, the words sounding comforting rather than annoying in this subterranean sanctuary. Caleb followed the monk's form, highlighted by a soft halo-like glow stemming from the makeshift torch. At the end of the tunnel, the monk stopped. He held his hand to a door that seemed to appear from nowhere and knocked, the sound scattering the emptiness of the dark.

The door whispered open and another hooded figure stood in the doorway, as if Caleb's guide were peering into a mirror. They exchanged a few words, spoken in hushed tones, which were too low for Caleb to hear.

The monk turned and Caleb expected him to say, "this way". Instead, he motioned for Caleb to follow him. Following the monk, Caleb began to see the soft glow of scattered candles, their pillars standing as beacons did on a coast.

From the doorway, Caleb could see that the space was small but considerably drier than the corridor he had passed through with the monk. A long table filled much of the room and tattered bits of paper were stuck to the walls, their corners wedged between the cracks of the rocks to hold the pages in place.

Along the back edge of the wall, there were two pallets made up as beds. A woolen blanket was pulled taut over the first, but the second was occupied by a form that stirred now at the sound of approaching footsteps.

"Caleb Haroldson, here is Richard Turrington."

Caleb blinked.

Richard is here?

Surprise abated and purpose set in, as he stepped nearer. Before he was able to take many steps, the monk laid his hand across Caleb's arm.

"Richard Turrington is in poor condition. Be careful with him."

Caleb nodded slowly, as the words sank in. Perhaps,

seeking Richard had been a mistake. Inevitably he must be scarred, perhaps even disfigured, from the devilish flames. Seeing Richard in such a state would only make his sorrow worse. Richard, for whatever damage he had suffered, had survived; his beloved Rebecca had not.

Sensing his apprehension, though he knew nothing of the reason why, the monk nodded as though suggesting that he should continue. Caleb gathered his courage and crossed to where Richard lay. Bending down to face him, Caleb took in the damage. Richard's face had mostly been spared, but the flames had dragged their claws across his neck and one of his cheeks, marring them in painful streaks. Perhaps, he had suffered in other areas as well, but Caleb could see only this. The rest of Richard lay concealed under a blanket.

At first Caleb wondered if Richard's memory had also suffered. Though Richard looked at him, he showed no sign of recognizing him.

"Richard," he said, in a softer tone than he had ever spoken to another man, "'Tis Caleb."

Richard looked at him, but said nothing. Caleb turned to the monk, searching for the words to say, trying to uncover what he should do. The monk's back was to Caleb, though, and so with no help available, he turned back to Richard.

"I needed to find you," Caleb said and then stopped.

Richard's eyes searched Caleb's face for an explanation. It came in halting phrases, as Caleb tried to hold back his sorrow.

"You are— my link to— Rebecca. What happened— do you know?—I— I, owe her— owe her that much at least—since —I, I—I, I could not save her. I know you have—lost—your sister, but I—I—lost—I lost—"

Caleb couldn't finish the sentence. A look of such confusion filled Richard's face that Caleb wondered, a sharp pain piercing his heart at the thought, if Richard did not know what had befallen dear, sweet Rebecca.

"She— " Richard struggled to speak as well, though the fire's lasting effects held a stronger chokehold on him than his emotions.

"...was taken on a horse."

"What?" Caleb said, his eyebrows wrinkling, "She was trying to save Dandelion when it happened?"

Richard shook his head, then winced at having moved his neck.

"I called to her, the flames were... coming."

From the pit of Caleb's stomach, an emptiness surged forward. This had been a mistake. He should never have—

"The rider... rescued her... they rode off."

Caleb's stomach doubled over, as though a heavy stream of oxygen had been forced into his lungs when he had not expected it.

"She is—she is alive?" Caleb said, not trusting the words.

"Yes."

Caleb slumped forward, finally able to breathe when he had forgot how hours before.

Richard's eyes shut for a moment; speaking the words had taken more strength than he could spare. He opened them to deliver one more message, before he fell back against the bed, exhausted,

"Caleb, find her."

When Richard's eyes shut, the tears that had not come in the emptiness of her death spilled over Caleb's cheeks. Rebecca was alive and life was real again.

CHAPTER TEN

As the sea disappeared below her, with each rung that she climbed up, Rebecca could not help but feel the imposing seal of oppression on her. She had dreamed of setting sail with the expansive white sheets rippling against the sky, but this was all wrong. Rather than providing the freedom she longed for, this ship would be a prison.

Despite the openly lewd behavior of a few sailors, most said nothing. The comments that she did hear were often not directed at her.

"A woman is bad luck at sea."

"What, has the captain gone mad?"

Counter to the opinions of his crew, Rebecca found the captain to be quite sane. His only fault rested in his apparent oblivion to Rebecca's kidnapping. Lord Furton had been thorough in his plan and assured that Rebecca had no time on her own with the captain or any other member of the crew.

Lord Furton had thanked the captain for agreeing to take aboard his dear wife and him, so that they might more quickly embark upon their new lives together. Rebecca's stomach had lurched forward, churning in disgust at the thought of Lord Furton describing her as his wife.

He had wasted no time in putting Rebecca where he wanted her.

"Captain, I am anxious to be with my bride. We married in such haste," Lord Furton said.

Rebecca's skin prickled, as though his words were poking sharply against her.

I would never be with you. You are a tiny specimen and not a man.

The captain had looked at her with a fatherly affection, as though to wish her well as she began her journey, before placing a key in Lord Furton's hand. He pocketed it as Rebecca stared so intently, that it struck her as odd that Lord Furton did not pull his hand away at the hot touch of the metal seared into him.

"If you say anything, Caleb Haroldson will be wiped from the land. No one will remember him," Lord Furton had whispered harshly against her back, as they had climbed the ladder. The words had pelted her with a strength superior to any rock he could have hurled at her.

Those words were the only reason she had not begged for sanctuary from the captain the moment she had appeared on deck. With no other choice, Rebecca would masquerade as the wife of Lord Furton, in order to protect the husband of her heart.

The ship's hull groaned against the sea, as the sailors pulled up anchor and cast off. Lord Furton followed an appointed sailor to the cabin the captain had offered. Rebecca's steps wavered, as the waves took hold of the ship and pulled her stomach.

"This is it," the young sailor's voice said as he stopped in front of a door that, to Rebecca, looked identical to those they had already passed.

Lord Furton slid the key into the lock. Rebecca's hand instinctively reached forward to snatch it away from him, but it disappeared like a flash of lightning back into his pocket. The door swung open, revealing a sparsely filled room. Her mother's maids' accommodations were lavish by comparison. A trunk, warped from immersion in seawater countless times before, stood guard at the end of a bed. The bed, barely big enough for a child, was pushed against the ship's wall.

"Well, Miss Turrington, what do you think?" Lord Furton said, stepping inside and waving his arms wide.

She looked at him, too angry to speak.

"Come Miss Turrington, you must not be rude."

Rebecca's eyes blazed hot, but still her feet remained planted outside of the room.

"Miss Turrington," Lord Furton hissed, "do not make me look a fool or Mr. Haroldson will never look upon anything again."

His words cut into her. She was unaccustomed to another having power over her. Those who assumed they had, such as her parents, often had no such control. Lord Furton, perhaps for the first time in Rebecca's life, had real power over her. She was the marionette and he had all the strings. Worse yet, they were tied to a trigger that, if Rebecca moved in the wrong way, would fire straight into Caleb's heart.

Reluctantly, Rebecca moved her feet into the room. Her body followed but her heart was absent, left on the dry lands of England. Lord Furton stepped nearer.

"Surely Lord Furton, you do not mean to stay here," Rebecca said to discourage him.

"Of course not, Miss Turrington. You are the strumpet, not I. I suggest Miss Turrington, that you use this time to pray."

Rebecca's fingers curled around each other into a fist behind her back in her unease.

"What shall I pray for Lord Furton?" she said, trying to swallow the contempt she felt for him.

"For purity, Miss Turrington. Pray that some poor fellow believes you are a pious woman, so that I am adequately paid for my expenses."

His words pelted against Rebecca, grinding her into the deck. Overcome by sickness, she could not muster the strength to turn him away. Instead, she could only pray that he would leave, that it would all be over, that the only remaining torment would be the unrelenting waves of nausea keeping time with the rolling ocean beneath her. But, Lord Furton was anything but a gentleman. He masqueraded for the place that he thought he had earned in the world.

"You have corrupted her!"

"Who?" Rebecca said, the process of forming the word

pounding nails into her head amidst the sickness.

"Molly."

"Molly?"

"Molly, yes, my sister. Do you not think I know that you had turned her out—what you have turned her into— " A rush of red consumed Lord Furton's face, as though someone had poured a glass of Merlot over his menacing features. Rebecca shook her head, urging the lies, the confusion, the desperation to fall away.

"The only Molly I know is in a tavern."

He snorted.

"Fine place for her to be. You might have offered her some charity, when she came to your door. You might have taught her to be a lady, but what did she have when you turned her black? She will burn for sure. No fire I set could singe away her sin!"

From the pit of her stomach, Rebecca felt the heaviness of every crumb she had ever consumed ready to break forth.

"I did no such thing. She never came and as I say, the Molly I know works in a tavern. She serves the drink. That is all."

Lord Furton's face flushed, his eyes blinking in rapid succession to keep time with her new words.

"You are mistaken. You must be. Molly serves her flesh."

"Lord Furton, no, you are wrong. My father has forbidden such practice in his lands."

Lord Furton either didn't hear or didn't care, as his barrage continued,

"You ought to be more grateful, Miss Turrington. You ought to be grateful for a father, for one who plans your future, not all of us can claim the bloodline, not all— "

He paused, ashen-faced. He'd gone too far. No one was supposed to know his secret shame—least of all, *her*. Rebecca, had she not been choking back the bile of her violent stomach, might have felt sorry for him. Standing there, in the crumbles of what he had said and painted in the guilt of what had been, she did pity him for half a second. Dear Caleb had lost his father. For an instance, she saw Lord Furton huddled in a corner, alone, as Caleb had been when he'd lost all. Perhaps, the terrible rumors of Lord Furton's childhood were true. He'd been disinherited, turned out, only to reclaim the title when his father had no other heir.

The day had been cold, her hands shaking, when she'd paused on her dash in from riding Dandelion to warm herself over the embers of the kitchen fire. The scullery maid's raspy voice had quieted, but she'd still heard the words spoken.

"His father found out his mother was untrue, you do know what I mean? He was not his father's son."

"Ah, no wonder he does not want Lord Furton marrying 'er." Rebecca had known that they were speaking of her, with a bent up shoulder, half-gesturing to her, but she'd been too polite to say anything. They had good hearts, but they were gossips. There was nothing to their words to have any bearing on her life. So what if Lord Furton's mother had cheated on his father? Why should marital infidelity, from forty years ago, in the parents of the man that she had no feelings for have any hold on her? It certainly did not affect her life. She'd laughed about it with Caleb later that day, as she'd been embraced in his deep woodsy scent. The fire flickered low, comfortingly so as his hands slid over her hair.

"You do know what is so wonderful about this?" he'd said. She'd not known what to say, in that half-asleep state of gentle soothing.

"No splinters," he said, a playfulness leaping into his eye. Her own eyes were shut, but she knew it was there.

She knew Caleb, really *knew* him, like the mariner knew the constellations to sail home by, and that's what made this all the worse. She knew the pain he felt now and it was more for Caleb than herself that she despised this situation. And now, it hit her, nearly as strong as the churning waves beneath the ship. It might have snapped Rebecca in two for all its ferocity. Perhaps, Father had cared, more than she'd imagined and endeavored to save his daughter from the shame, from the gossips. She'd never paid attention to the stories before to consider that the tales about Lord Furton were true. If so, he could be pitied for his mistake and all of this was her fault. She tottered at the edge of the absurdity; its strength taunting her.

Yes, Rebecca. You have done this. 'Tis your fault. You ought to have listened better. You ought not to have laughed at another's misfortune.

No wonder he'd scoffed at her piety, at her purity. He'd made her his mother, another woman who'd overstepped her bounds of marriage and shamed him. Only... Rebecca had done no such thing. She wasn't Lord Furton's wife, or even his betrothed. Now, it came rushing over, her spark, all that made her Rebecca, all that made her whom Caleb loved.

She pushed down the bile, stood firm in her resolve and tried to push herself up to Lord Furton's height, to offer some hand of encouragement, to take command of the situation, to return all as it was supposed to be. But the full force of his blackness descended over her again, as her legs conspired with him against her, shaking, unable to move forward in her sickness.

"My accounts must be settled," he said, in one final barb.

Now, well aware that it was the debts of the past and not only a bountiful bride price that he was thinking of, her hands began to shake as crisp dry leaves in a gale. She clasped them tightly together behind her back to calm their tremors. Before she could reply, Lord Furton left, locking her securely into the room and into his plan.

A heave from deep within her chest escaped when she was alone. Rebecca's head fell forward, as her hands rushed to cradle it. The ship moved farther out to sea, knocking the security from Rebecca's legs. She caught herself against the bed and then fell to her knees. Though she burned at the thought of Lord Furton, she did pray—not for purity, but for deliverance.

CHAPTER ELEVEN

"Dear sweet, Rebecca, I am coming for you," Caleb said, throwing his head back and looking at the stars above. Behind him lay another concealed entrance to the subterranean headquarters to the monks' work. The monk, who had identified himself only as Caleb's Virgil, had cautioned Caleb against spreading the name of Turrington.

"Caleb Haroldson, there are those who would do Richard Turrington harm. When I heard word of you seeking him, I had to find you so that you would not endanger him," the monk had said, moments before they had parted.

"Who?" Caleb had asked, needing to avenge the harm that had come to Richard, but more so to his Rebecca.

"We do not know their names, only that we must protect them, Caleb Haroldson," the monk said.

"Them?"

"Do not worry. Your friend, Richard Turrington, is safe here with us. Your mind can be at ease now."

"But, his sister," Caleb had objected, "Richard asked me to find her."

Caleb would have sought her without anyone asking, but the monk did not need to know this. The monk studied Caleb.

"I was not aware that Richard Turrington had a sister. I arrived only recently and was told that Lord Turrington's heir was in danger and must be protected."

Caleb's face could not hide his concern and the monk was an astute observer of human behavior.

"I do not know, Caleb Haroldson where this sister is, but I will pray that you will find her. Remember well what I have said and do not spread the Turrington name. If you do, it may well endanger her."

With that, the monk had shown him another escape route and Caleb had disappeared through it.

How can I find her, when I cannot ask her name?

Caleb's steps, slow and heavy with thought, led him toward town. He would simply have to search for her. If that meant he had to look into every face in England, he would do that; one of them must be Rebecca's.

⟿•⟾

Deciding that his ability to find her rested in being prepared for a journey of indeterminable length, Caleb turned toward home. His house was dark as he approached. Peter at times shared the premises, but often preferred to sleep in the forge. There was a loft above Caleb's own bed with a pallet for Peter when he felt inclined to live, as he put it "civilized". What this really meant was that he had too much to drink and feared sleeping by the furnaces. The urge to be "civilized" did not seem to come often and Caleb had managed to keep his love for Rebecca a secret to all, including Peter. The door stood slightly ajar as Caleb approached. Peter must have chosen tonight to stumble in. It would be inconvenient but, perhaps, Peter had passed out for the night. This would prove beneficial to Caleb. If he managed to gather all materials in the dark, then Peter could sleep through the whole thing and Caleb could escape as he had intended.

Gathering the materials proved slightly slower than Caleb had anticipated. He stumbled blindly around the room, stuffing a bag with bits of food, a knife, some rope, a hammer and clothing.

It was not until he neared his bed, that he realized it was not empty. Peter must have passed out here, too tired to make it up to the loft. In order to retrieve his blanket to take it with him, he would have to move quietly. He sat down on the bed and picked up the corner of the folded blanket. Rather than the itchy wool that he expected his hand to brush against, he was met with the creaminess of the skin of a female hand.

Rebecca, my darling Rebecca! Can it be true? Of course,

you would come here to hide.

Tentatively, he let his hand run across her hand and up the length of her arm. So vividly could he see her, despite the dark. The dream of her here had come true and his heart nearly burst at the thought of it. Too frightened to speak to her, lest she should suddenly disappear, he said nothing. Having her here was too good. She seemed fragile after having believed he had lost her and he was afraid to wake her, as if doing so would release a nightmare around him.

Instead, he let only his fingertips, barely pressing against her skin, run across her. Tempted to assure himself that she was really alive, he could not stop his fingers. Greedily they ran across her arm, over her shoulder and down her chest, searching for her heart.

She stirred. Caleb held his breath, not trusting his mind after the dramatic events of the day. Her hand moved and intertwined with his fingers.

"Rebecca? He said, barely speaking.

Just say yes and then I will hold you to me and never let you go again.

"Call me anything you like," the voice replied, lifting herself from the bed and the moonlight falling across her silhouette.

Caleb pulled back his hand, standing abruptly and knocking over a metal bucket.

"Who are you?"

"What Peter says you needs," she said coyly, stepping toward him, "He says you are never with a woman and 'tis not the way any man ought to be, especially a man as handsome as you. Oh, I have watched you, Caleb. You always look so serious."

She stepped forward again. The moonlight fell across her body and he turned away.

"Please, leave," he said firmly. She stepped closer to him

and he felt her breath against his neck, as she said,

"'Tis not right for a man to sleep alone."

Caleb moved away from her, as quickly as though he had burned his hand in a fire.

"There is only room in my bed for one woman and you are not her."

With that, he swung his bag over his shoulder and left his house.

On the street, his temper boiled. He felt guilty for having touched someone else, even if it hadn't been his fault.

Dear Rebecca, forgive me please.

His anger flared. If ever any man's love had been tested for a woman, today had been that day. With the threat of death and the presence of another woman having failed to alter his devotion to Rebecca, he took the first step into the night—determined and unwilling to stop until he found her.

"Caleb," a voice called behind him. He turned to see Peter. The keeper of many secrets, his anger was not one of them. As reply to the greeting, he balled up his hand and with a strong jab, he punched Peter hard, sending the man reeling.

"What was that for?" Peter said, holding his throbbing jaw.

Caleb turned and walked away.

"'Twas the last time I ever help you!" Peter called after him.

"That better be a promise," Caleb said, as he walked away from the life he had known.

CHAPTER TWELVE

Rebecca found herself dreaming of land. Time meant nothing to her anymore. There were hours of sleeping, interrupted by the thrashing of the sea, and there were hours of bored anger sitting locked alone in her room, interrupted by waves of nausea that coursed through her body and caused a stiff throbbing in her head. When time consists of such increments, days and nights cease to exist. All Rebecca knew was that, with the passage of time there was also the passing of miles between her and England.

She had hoped that Lord Furton had planned to sell her off along the European coast. Finding her way home from France or Spain would be possible, but as time—whatever existed of it—wore on, Rebecca began to feel the awful nagging that Europe was not the destination they were headed toward.

Huddled in the corner of the room, Rebecca buried her head in her lap with her knees drawn up to her chest. She had never been as sick as she felt now. The last time she had been able to eat was some increasingly distant memory.

From the other side of the door, Rebecca heard the key slide into the lock. As the door swung open and Lord Furton entered, she looked up at him. Ah, that had been a mistake. The deck shifted under her.

He shut the door behind him and walked to her, the click of his polished shoes drumming painfully against her throbbing head.

"Miss Turrington, are you not enjoying your journey? I have gone through such pains to arrange pleasant accommodation befitting you."

Rebecca raised her eyes to glare at him, but being sick and captured while locked up here and further confined by her sickness to this corner of the floor, it was difficult to feel as if she had any of her usual power.

"Why do you hate me so much?" she said, struggling to sit up enough to speak.

"Miss Turrington, have you learned nothing? You hold yourself in too high an esteem. You are not the daughter of a lord anymore."

"Lord Furton, please, surely if I am ill, it will not serve your purposes," she said, in an attempt to appeal to his business sense, if she could not play upon his sympathies.

"Miss Turrington," he said, through clenched teeth as he stood above her, "it is not the boat that has made you ill; it is your wanton ways."

"Lord Furton, you are mistaken. I am not the person you say I am."

"Do you deny it, Miss Turrington?" he said, leaning into her. His breath stunk of moldy cheese and rotting apples, as if his anger were causing his whole body to fester.

"I assert, Lord Furton that I have done nothing wrong."

"Do you deny loving Caleb Haroldson?"

Pulling herself up, she stood to face him.

"No, I do not."

"Then you are nothing more than the trollop I have said you are. Miss Turrington, You belong to a long line of women who have defiled themselves and their chance at being my wife."

"It is not I that you think ill of then, but rather every woman?" she said, trying to suppress the waves of nausea.

"Miss Turrington, a woman has one duty in life. When she seeks out love for herself, then she has failed in her duty. She has decided that the life her father chose for her was not good enough and she has broken the bond of male superiority. How will she ever be an obedient wife, if she is not an obedient daughter?"

"You are right, Lord Furton," she said, watching him carefully.

A slow smile spread from his thin lips, though it was rigid

and forced.

"But, 'tis not my aim to be an obedient wife," she said, feeling the sturdiness return to her legs, "I aim to be myself and my husband will love me for that."

His eyes narrowed as he stared hard at her. Grabbing her wrist, he held it firmly as he said,

"I would not be so certain about that, Miss Turrington. Perhaps, in England there are those like Caleb Haroldson, who are not real men, but in the Caribbean you will find that men are more inclined to my way of thinking."

The Caribbean?

Rebecca's surprise registered on her face and did not go unnoticed by Lord Furton. Satisfied, he left her alone once again, locking her into the cabin.

CHAPTER THIRTEEN

The old man heaped kindling on the a-frame fire. The night was quiet after the events of the fire at Turrington Manor. Bellowing, the smoke had rolled through the rooms with a ferocity that none of them could have imagined. Lord Turrington's estate lay in ruins and the household was scattered. Richard was not to be found and Rebecca had vanished, carried —as he had told the young man—across the river.

He let out a soft chuckle, as he struck his stick into a trout and held it to the flames. Its skin crackled against the pale glow of the fire, resembling the man's own crumpled hands. Age had pulled at his skin, shaping it like the contours of wadded paper.

Yes, Rebecca Turrington was no doubt long gone by now. He struck the stick against the ground, driving it in as a stake. Sitting back, with his arms behind him, he watched the smoke swirl around the meal as it cooked.

"Ah, Miss Turrington, I envy you. If I were younger, I would jump at the opportunity you have been given."

The fire popped, drawing him from his musing. The skin of the fish crackled as the fire crisped its edges. Removing it from the stick, he shifted the fish from one hand to the other in an attempt to not burn himself. When he was satisfied that the air had sufficiently cooled it and when the wafting of its delicate aroma became too powerful to ignore, he sank his teeth into the rich buttery flesh.

Yes, unlike the slight wobble in his steps, there were some things that age could not deteriorate; the taste of a succulent fish was just as delicious as it had always been. Perhaps, it was even more so, because in his youth he had not yet known those times of great hunger when the pains had gnawed at his stomach. But, those times were long past and—

A noise, soft like footsteps but more deliberate, caught his attention. Who would have stumbled upon him? He was tucked away into a cozy alcove among the trees. If it were a robber, he had no money to give and the thief would have to content himself with half of a roasted fish.

Picking up his carved walking stick from its place on the ground beside him, he hoisted himself up to his full height. He took a step forward, peering into the darkness. As he walked away from the fire, he more keenly felt the presence of the night and his eyesight was no longer that of the sharp marksman it once had been.

"Show yourself," he said into the darkness.

There was no reply.

Was it some assailant waiting to attack or, perhaps, a whole gang of them?

"If you mean to rob me, I have only a bit of roasted fish but you are welcome to it." A soft clomping sound emerged from the undergrowth. Sticking out with two large eyes and two steaming nostrils, a head appeared.

The old man began to laugh. First, it was a slight chuckle, but soon a whole flush of belly-shaking hilarity erupted. Grabbing his stick to keep from falling over, he addressed his supper's interloper.

"No, I suppose *you* would not want any fish, now would you? Honestly, I do not know which is more absurd— thinking that you would rob me or asking you to share my meal!"

As reply, the guest nuzzled against the ground and began to graze among the dew-lined grasses.

"Yes, you are right. Grass is much tastier for a horse."

For awhile, he watched as the horse nibbled contentedly. The animal, sturdy and beautiful, was mostly concealed by the branches and underbrush. Wild ponies roamed the countryside, but the man had seen more as a child. Often, the only equine creatures that he now saw were the saddled companions of the gentry or the harnessed helpers of the laborers. The horse, finished with the patch of grass it had buried its nose in, emerged from the foliage.

"Oh! You are not wild at all," he said, taking note of the trailing reins on the ground. The man stepped forward.

"Did you have a harsh master that you ran away from?"

Ignoring his words, the horse continued to eat. The man approached and patted the side of the animal. She stopped briefly, as though to acknowledge him, but then continued unconcerned.

The horse continued to eat, stepping nearer the man and also further into the light to reveal herself.

"Well, you certainly do not seem frightened. Perhaps, you have left for some other reason then, eh?"

The horse pawed the ground lightly and then lifted her head. In the firelight, her glossy coat shone. It was clear that whoever her owner was, the horse was well taken care of, perhaps even loved. Gentle and almost docile in her appearance, the horse looked up at the old man. The two stared at each other for a moment, the man admiring the horse and the horse indulging the man.

"Yes, admire me. I know I am beautiful," she seemed to say. The man tilted his head to the side, as though contemplating something.

"Why—I know who you are. You are Dandelion, are you not?"

Hearing her name, the horse pricked up her ears.

"Dandelion, yes, 'tis you," he said, petting her nose.

He bent to pick up the reins and tied them around a sturdy tree.

"You can stay with me now. I am afraid, Dandelion, that you will not be seeing Rebecca again. Yes, Miss Turrington would not have left you unless not coming back."

He pat the horse again, reassuring her.

"Fear not, Dandelion. Everything is going to be just fine."

Leaving Dandelion to enjoy the remainder of her meal, he sat back beside the fire. Reaching into the leather satchel, which held his modest belongings, he pulled out a leather-covered book.

The pages were yellowed and made his fingertips, which ran across the words, appear young in comparison to its own age. When he found the place he was searching for, he reached back into the satchel and took out his quill and ink. Dipping the nib into the deep walnut black, he blotted the excess and then penned,

Rebecca Turrington
Born: 1750
Crossed the River: 1774

CHAPTER FOURTEEN

Rebecca's initial shock at her discovery of the Caribbean as their destination had subsided. In its place stood only the desperate yearning for land—any land—even if it meant that tropical link of triangular trade.

Lord Furton who had ignored her for so much of the trip, only giving her attention when he wanted to gloat, now expressed concern for her. Perhaps, a pale bride was not what men of the islands would want.

No, Rebecca was not eating enough. She was too sickly, too discontented. That spark that had burned so dangerously in her was missing. With it extinguished, no longer did she seem so appealing. But no, Lord Furton could not admit to such things. He would not fall for such a woman. Other men succumbed to temptation, not the pious and proud Lord Furton.

When Rebecca's resolve had dwindled to an unrecognizable point under the weight of exhaustion and sustained hardships, her reprieve came. Sitting on the rough boards of the floor, an unexpected jolt pushed her against the bed. Her knee banged uncomfortably against its wooden post. In the past weeks, there had been the turbulent tossing of the waves and brief periods of a tranquil sea, but so deliberate of a jolting had not happened until now.

Scuttling feet and excited voices carried down the length of the corridor.

Was something wrong? Had they struck something?

Chills, induced by nausea, had spread their icy fingers over Rebecca many times on the journey, but now an altogether new chilling fear gripped her.

Would they leave her here as the ship sank? Would she drown?

Rebecca's heart raced as dread embedded its nails into her, pinching her nerves and holding her captive.

"Let me out! Let me out!" she said, as loudly as she could as she pounded on the door. Her fists ached at her abusive treatment of them, but there was no other option.

"Help me! Let me out!" she shouted at the unsympathetic door. Rebecca continued to beat against it. Drowning out all other noise with her shouting and pounding, she heard nothing else.

Startled, the door in front of her disappeared and in its place stood the formidable Lord Furton.

"Quiet," he hissed, "do you want to alarm the whole ship?"

She stared at him with a look that said yes, that was exactly her intention. With her hand still raised, Lord Furton said,

"Now, behave properly, Miss Turrington. You would not want Mr. Haroldson to suffer some terrible demise, now would you?"

Rebecca's hands dropped to her sides, like lead-weighted cannon balls aboard similar ships. The men who rushed past the opened door were busy and absorbed in their work. The scene between Lord Furton and Rebecca didn't receive as much as a look. Rather than the panic Rebecca was certain she would see on their faces though, there was only concentration.

"Come. We are here and your new life awaits," he said, feigning charm as he slipped from the scoundrel into the role of doting husband. Only when they were well away from the captain and crew would he arrange some backroom payment for his precious cargo.

They were here? They had not crashed? No, no, it had not been an untimely obstacle in the ship's path. Instead, they had arrived at their charted destination. It was the anchor that Rebecca had felt.

Wait—they were landed! Lord Furton's control over her would surely wane outside of the ship. He could threaten her with Caleb's safety, but if she were no longer there, what power could his threats have? Yes, she had to escape—for herself, but also for Caleb. It was the surest way their safety was guaranteed. Without Rebecca threatened into following Lord Furton's orders, Caleb would be left alone. Without the satisfaction of seeing his power over her, Lord Furton would have no motive to hurt him. To go after him for no reason was sloppy and pointless and not Lord Furton's style.

Lord Furton stared at her and Rebecca worried that the seeds of her plan had registered in her eyes.

Do not discover me. Do not discover me.

"Just be grateful, Miss Turrington, that your behavior was muffled behind this thick door or you would have to pay for this impertinent outburst."

He hadn't suspected after all!

Rebecca, think quick, but do not let him realize that you are.

"Hurry up, Miss Turrington," Lord Furton said, "Honestly, as much of a nuisance as you were for the whole crossing, I do not understand your reluctance. I would have thought that you would want to see land."

Lord Furton had furnished her with a few items of necessary clothing that she crammed into the small case now. Following him down the corridor, she took stake of the situation. There was no way to plan an escape route when the terrain was unfamiliar. Her legs, cramped from long hours with them drawn up to her chest as she huddled on the floor, protested at the sudden lunge of paces.

She had no acquaintances or friends on this side of the world to call upon for help. Well, that didn't matter so much. Rebecca was accustomed to solitary escapades.

Lord Furton's back surely must have burned from the hole she bore into it, as she stared at him in anger.

Money would also pose a problem. She had none and no

means to buy food or anything else, including a way to get home to England. Still, there really was nothing that she could do to change this situation.

Strange land. No friends. No money. That was the sum of it.

As Rebecca stepped onto the deck, the fresh air hit with its welcomed comforts. It filled her lungs as wind fills the sails, giving them body and purpose. The crew, busy at unloading the first of the cargo, were occupied and paid little attention to her.

She could see the gangplank below. To her left stood a few huts and beyond that a grove of palm trees leading to a strip of white sandy beach. To the right stretched a town. Around her, several boats of varying sizes were docked in the harbor. The trees could provide shelter, but were too far to run to and remain free. The town appeared to offer greater opportunity but, if Rebecca were surrounded by others whom had been employed to search for his lost bride, Lord Furton would have an immediate advantage.

No, it was better to escape by way of the other boats. A few sailors were already returning in the boat that goods were being ferried across in to the other side. Lord Furton held out his hand, to help her step into the awaiting boat. She bristled at the touch of his hand on hers. When she was seated in the boat, she held her breath as they sailed away from her maritime prison.

Her jailer said nothing, as they rode with the others to the land. Rebecca waited until the shore was nearly in sight, resisting the urge to jump from the boat while the waters clustered heavily around them. As tempting as the thought of jumping to an awaiting boat was, she would surely be caught and overcome before making it.

Or would she? Some faraway tale, of hearing that sailors often couldn't swim, trickled through her mind. Was it true? She pressed her memory as the waters beckoned to her, in an attempt to remember the source of the information. Richard had said it!

He would be true to her. As the realization hit, she stood up in the boat.

"Miss—uh—Madam, what seems to be the trouble?" Lord Furton said, in an attempt to preserve appearances and get her to sit down.

"Now Rebecca! Do it now!" everything screamed inside of her. She jumped into the crystal sea. The waters swirled relatively warm around her and her body did not suffer the shock she had braced herself for. With great strides, she pushed through the water, clearing it from her path.

"After her! Save her!" Lord Furton shouted, but the sailors did not oblige. For all his calculations, Lord Furton had overlooked the important information that Richard had told Rebecca. By the time he realized that he would have to follow her himself, Rebecca was pulling herself up over the side of a small abandoned rowboat. She picked up the oars, throwing her tired limbs into the power of the boat.

Lord Furton shouted at the others, as he tried to swim toward her, to turn the boat. Their boat was larger than hers, though, and lacked the agility to change direction with speed. It was after all, a simple means of transport and not designed to track down runaway women.

Rebecca paddled through a line of anchored ships, pausing to look over her shoulder only when certain that she had escaped. Lord Furton's exasperated cries had long since dwindled, when at last she gave into her burning arms. She took in her surroundings, suddenly feeling very alone. Rebecca was free, but she was drifting in a rowboat somewhere in the Caribbean.

CHAPTER FIFTEEN

"Caleb, kiss me," Rebecca said. Her hair brushed against his cheek, as she leaned in to claim her kiss from him.

"I love you, Rebecca Turrington," he whispered against her.

Her body stiffened at the words and she drew back from him. In that tone that said she would not tolerate anything she did not want, Rebecca said,

"You have allowed me to depart. If you truly loved me, that never would have happened."

As she spoke the words, she slipped from his reach.

"Come back. Rebecca, do not leave me. I do love you. I promise I do!" he shouted after her, but the only reply was the deafening roar of the waves as he watched Rebecca's form, now seated in a boat, dwindle on the horizon.

"Rebecca, please Rebecca," he said as he woke with a jolt. He opened his eyes to the first stars displaying themselves above him. Embarked upon a journey of indeterminable length, he had forgone the luxury of renting a room on all but the most necessary of occasions. His search dictated that he travel extensively among the towns.

Small towns could be sifted through in a day, some in only a matter of hours. When Caleb came across such places, he could often be on his way again by evening and camp out under a tree as he was now. Larger cities required more time, when there were more faces to search in earnest. The words of the monk's warning prevented him from spreading the name of Turrington. He was happy to oblige, if it meant he were protecting Rebecca, but it did slow his progress considerably.

Caleb was reduced to relying on his own eyes and even they were not adverse to trickery. How often had he seen the back of someone and reached out his hand to set on her shoulder, only to have her turn and not be Rebecca? Then, his hand as well as his heart would fall. Languishing in disappointment, though, was neither an option nor a practice for Caleb. He would recover swiftly and carry on, convinced that the next woman could indeed be his Rebecca.

"Do not be cross with me, Rebecca," he whispered into the stillness of twilight, "I will find you. I promise."

He gathered his belongings, which had slipped slightly from his bag, as he had reclined on it as a pillow. Waiting for dawn was something he was unwilling to do. Sacrificing sleep always won out over prolonging his reunion with Rebecca.

The land was dry underfoot, without the delaying hold of muddied grounds on his boots. In his pocket, a pouch of coins jangled with each stride. Food and the necessary nights spent in rented rooms to avoid thieves were depleting his resources, but there was still enough in his pockets to jostle reassuringly together.

The night was cool, but not unpleasant. Only the occasional mournful song of an evening bird gave any indication that he was not entirely alone.

"*Caleb Haroldson, you are forever chasing impossible dreams,*" the far-off voice of his father said. He had been young and told he would someday be apprenticed to a blacksmith. Caleb had disagreed, insisting that he was not a simple tradesman. Perhaps, the barb had wounded his father, but if that were the case young Caleb had been unable to discern. Sent away, Caleb had departed his father. When the time had come, he had indeed become a tradesman but rather than the cold and unfeeling iron, he turned the wood, a living piece of embraceable earth.

It was one of the few memories that he had of his father, before the illness had claimed his parents. The memory was not happy, but then nothing dictates that all that has come before must have been kissed with the golden glint of sunshine.

"*'Tis a happy ending that people are concerned about, not*

a perfect beginning," Rebecca had told him long ago.

"Must we wait for the end for it to be happy?" he had said to her, when her chances of escaping her parents' wishes seemed so slim. But now, she was free of all of that. Free, but also lost to him.

At least she is alive.

He reminded himself of this, when the doubt hung as a millstone on his neck and the words of his father and Caleb's impossible dream haunted him.

"But, she is not an impossible dream," he said aloud, to clear the muddied thoughts.

Caleb trudged on, committed as a soldier in battle, but more acutely feeling the pull of his cause. Clouds played across the awakening moon, shifting their shadows as they too journeyed on this star-studded night.

"I just want to go away. I would leave all of this behind for you," he had told her. Perhaps, he had spoken the words too broadly and summoned them into action as a wish would. He ought to have been more specific and said that he would go away with her and—

Caleb's steps slowed. Over the hill, a thin wisp of smoke danced skyward. It did not appear as though it were a town he was stumbling upon. No, there were no buildings or other structural silhouettes that he could make out in the pale light. Caleb squinted across the expanse of land, urging the clouds to move aside so that the moon might offer some glimpse of illumination. It did not oblige and Caleb, rather than the clouds, was required to move to better see where the smoke came from.

His feet carried him quickly toward the smoke. The thought of Rebecca making her return journey by night, when no one could find her, was too appealing. It was all he could do to keep from running to her. But, he was no fool. The fire might just have easily belonged to thieves. Who knew how many there might be and falling prey to them would only hamper his rescue mission. Being forced to stop to work and replenish his resources was not part of his plan. At least, it wasn't part of the plan for a long while still. No. He pushed the thought away. He would find Rebecca and he would do it soon.

The smoke carried from a greater distance than Caleb had first imagined. A clump of trees with arms outstretched beckoned to him, offering a cloak of anonymity to progress closer to the fire from. He took the trees up on their offer and slipped among the branches, as nimbly as any woodland creature might.

"Well, what did they want her for?"

Caleb froze.

The cover of the trees had carried him nearer to the fire than he had realized.

"How should I know? But, he went after her all right and he got her too."

Caleb's heart quickened.

"Where did they go?"

"Where do they all go? Across the river, of course."

CHAPTER SIXTEEN

Although she had lost sight of Lord Furton and the sailors, Rebecca did not allow herself the freedom of believing she was safe for too long. Rowing deeper into the ocean was, of course, unwise and could prove dangerous. If she came ashore, though, then surely Lord Furton could find her again. Her only hope seemed to rest in finding land, but not this land.

The task ahead of her seemed daunting, but she would not be deterred. Acting on faith, she rowed along the edge of the land. Ships had become scarcer, as she pulled away from the harbor and she no longer felt the security provided by a forest's worth of ship masts with sails unfurled.

For awhile, she let the current carry her. Her arms and back were grateful for the break. Her eyes did not stop working for a moment, though, as she scanned the shoreline, searching for any cove or inlet that might willingly oblige to be her sanctuary.

An uncomfortable stickiness wrapped its oppressive arms around her. The unrelenting humidity was unlike anything she had experienced before. "Smoldering" was the word the cook had used to describe baking day in the height of summer at home.

Home. The word fell against her with the abrasive sweetness of a thorny rose. The heat of the manor's kitchen was no match for the sweltering temperatures Rebecca found herself surrounded by now. Dampness, as though someone had splashed a bucket of water on her without any of the refreshment, covered her face. Under the itchy wool of the dress Lord Furton had supplied for her, her skin burned. She wanted nothing more than to throw it off and be rid of the wretched thing.

Just when she feared she would sail endlessly as a roasting lobster, she spotted it. She had barely seen it, but yes, there was an indention where the land gave way to water. Picking up the oars, she paddled across the current to travel closer to the shore.

Her arms ached with such intensity that she feared they would fall off. Rowing became an easier task when she was no longer battling a begrudging wall of water. Here, the land was rockier than it had been beside the harbor. No large ship would be able to dock. A high craggy wall led up from the spot, cutting it off from the rest of the island. Quite convinced that the only way to enter was the way she had come, she paddled the last few feet into the lagoon.

Almost immediately, a cool breeze swept across her. In contrast to the heat under the sun on the open waters, it offered the shelter that she sought. A thin line of grainy sand bordered the waters. Rebecca jumped out of the boat, as the overhang of rocks loomed closer. As she stepped onto dry land for the first time in weeks, her body experienced a sense of relief. The water, cooler here from being in the shade, pooled around her feet and lower legs.

Bits of shell and rock imbedded themselves into the soles of her shoes, as she neared the shore. Extreme tiredness and days of endless swaying made her feel as if she were still moving.

She sat down, plunking herself into the sand. The prospect of planting herself in the land and not moving for a long while was tempting, but also impractical. Already, the rowboat had begun to drift. If she hoped to ever leave this cove again, her escape depended on the boat. With no rope, Rebecca's imagination had to be stretched.

Stretched! Yes, that might work!

Taking off her shoes that the water had sunk into, making her stockings slushy, she pulled up her skirts. She peeled the wet stockings away from her legs. When they were off, she wrung them out and tied them together. Pulling on each side, she tested their united strength. Satisfied, she tied the end of the stockings to a small loop of rope affixed to the boat. The rocks, although amiable to her purposes of concealment, complicated her ability to anchor the boat. With no obvious post to tie the other end of the stockings to, she sat back for a moment to think.

The golden sands caressed her bare feet, providing the first sense of comfort she had experienced since leaving her house. She leaned back, allowing the sand to more fully cover her feet.

"Of course!" she said, sitting up. Venturing back into the water, she drew the oar out of the boat. Tiny pebbles poked at her feet, as she hopped from one foot to the other returning to the shore. Rebecca picked up the free end of the stockings and tied it around the oar. She let it rest against the sand, sitting on the handle to prevent it from moving, as she cleared away piles of sand. Burrowing into the sand until she hit where it was wet, under the sun-dried layers on top, she carved out a hole. When Rebecca was pleased with its depth, she picked up the oar and struck it in the sand. Holding it in place, she pushed the uncovered sand into the hole with her feet.

When the sand was in place, she stamped it down. It squished between her toes, light and powdery to her touch and so unlike that of the English soil. Rebecca let go to test her plan. The oar stayed firm and the stockings were holding the boat, keeping it from drifting. So long as no gusting wind or fierce storm blew in, it should hold just fine. For now, the air remained still and the sea mirrored its tranquility.

With her boat in place, she turned toward the land. The strip of beach stretched, perhaps, six feet. Yes, it was about the length of Caleb's height. At the thought of him, Rebecca's heart slipped. The prospect of being thousands of miles from him was too much to contend with. She pushed aside her thoughts and concentrated on the immediacy of her surroundings.

Rebecca was forced to duck, as she stepped under the rocky overhang. Saturated salt burned in her nose, accosting her with its years of collection from the surrounding seas, as she entered. Inside, the space opened and she could return to her full height. She found herself surrounded by an enclosed space that seemed to be entirely made of rock, much like a cave. The entrance was quite large allowing the lighting inside, although dim, to provide enough clarity and distinction between objects. Seaweed, carried when the tide rolled in, littered the front of the cave. No pools of water glistened to her in the dim light and she felt assured that the spot would be protected as the sea rose.

"Well, it seems I am home— at least for now," she said aloud to the cave. Her voice echoed against the walls, but not as much as she had guessed it would. Investigating further, she walked deeper inside. From above, a stream of light filtered through the rocks, supplying a small window in the roof. Turning around, Rebecca's eyes followed the line of the light. In the corner, stood a banded chest. Someone had been here before.

CHAPTER SEVENTEEN

Peter paused in his hammering and wiped the sweat from his brow with the back of his hand. Working over the boiling furnaces poured steam onto his skin. His face, rough and toughened from years of bending over the fires, felt sensitive under the heat since Caleb's encounter. As the days passed, the pain had subsided. He had not realized how hard Caleb had walloped him until later. He had been so shocked by the hit that it had taken several minutes for it to wear off and the pain to set in.

"Try to help a friend," he muttered to the furnace, as he picked up his hammer and brought it down heavy against the metal he wrought. It answered with the reassuring clang.

Yes, work and objects were more faithful than people. They were reliable, predictable, and unwavering. A piece of metal would not let him down. It would twist and turn, shaping itself under his guidance, giving in to his whims. When he hammered a piece of metal, it reacted how he expected; there were no surprises. Years of working the pieces of the earth had taught him that. People, no matter how long he knew them, could alter in an instant.

He hadn't seen Caleb since that night and, as much as he resisted the thought and hated to admit it, he missed his friend. Caleb was serious and thought too much. He always seemed preoccupied and enjoyed none of the comforts of life. And yet, he was there—loyal, dependable like a piece of sturdy iron.

His hammer beat the piece of metal, forming it into the desired shape. At least, he had been. Before.

The center of the metal burned hot, as he held it to the flame. Under the pressure of his hammer and the heat, it bent. He worked the metal. His strength emerged more than he had intended and the metal moved beyond where he had wanted it. Well, perhaps, Caleb was like the metal after all.

"Uh! You think too much, Peter. Caleb has influenced you," he said, annoyed. He set down the iron rod and hammer, pushing them aside and wanting to be rid of cumbersome tools and malleable friends. Walking away from the forge, he allowed the fire to burn. He would soon return when his head was clear and life was certain and simple again.

"Peter," a voice called after him as he walked toward the tavern. He turned and saw the reason for his still tender jaw. Nodding at her, he continued walking.

"Is your jaw better?" she said, catching up to him and lifting her hand to trace the contours of his face.

"'Tis fine, Molly," he said, though in reality her feather-like touch had caused a dull throbbing.

"Where are you going?" she asked, smiling at him with an innocence that a woman of her character ought not to possess. Well, perhaps, that was her fatal charm; she lulled men in appearing soft, when really she was a temptress. But no, that didn't seem right.

You are thinking too much again, Peter.

"To get a drink," he said in reply.

"Oh good, you are taking a break. You do know, I think you work much too hard," she said, running her hands over his arm.

He knew no such thing, but he couldn't argue with her admiring touch. He turned to her and said,

"Do you want a drink as well?"

She nodded, the sunlight catching the golden flecks in her red hair as she tossed her head.

The tavern was crowded when they entered. There were far more people here than on any ordinary afternoon. Molly took hold of his arm, as the crowds pressed in around them.

A group of men, all dressed in clothes that were too rich for any worker of this town, sat clustered together near the back of the room.

"Who are they?" Peter asked the assistant of the tavern proprietor, when their drinks had been brought to them.

"Strangers. Rode in at dawn and they have been asking questions all day," he said with a shrug.

"What sort of questions?"

"About the cabinet maker mostly—what is his name again? Charles something or other? He does not come in often."

"Caleb," Peter said.

"Caleb, yes, that is it."

In place of his curiosity, Peter now felt concern for the man who'd walked away from him. Caleb had seemed out of sorts that night. Suppose, he had done something in his disgruntled state. Suppose, he had got into some sort of trouble.

"Caleb Haroldson," Molly said, with that sweet smile in an honest attempt to be helpful. She had spoken too loudly, though, and her feminine voice in a sea of men drew the attention of the group at the back.

The words had barely left her lips, when two of the men sauntered up to the counter.

"Excuse me, madam," the taller of the two said.

"Me?" Molly said, not accustomed to be addressing by such a title. Men who came for a pint or a smile just called her Molly.

"Yes, that is right. You know Mr. Caleb Haroldson?"

"I know who he is, yes."

"And do you know where we might find him?"

She shook her head.

"No, I have not seen him for a few weeks now."

"Really?" the shorter man asked, leaning into her.

There was something in the way he said it that alarmed Peter.

Looking at Peter, Molly read his concern. Among men such as Peter it was difficult to interpret what they were feeling. But Molly knew men and, more importantly, she knew Peter.

"But, 'tis not so unusual. I never spoke to him really. I just see him about sometimes. He does not come for a drink often."

Good girl.

"What about you, sir?" the taller said now, turning his attention to Peter.

Uncomfortable with the situation and unwilling to supply information to strangers, Peter worked his fingers into a ball under the counter.

"I cannot say that I know him," he said, taking a drink of cider so he wouldn't have to look into the man's face as he answered. He couldn't lie, but the man that he had last seen by the name of Caleb Haroldson wasn't the Caleb Haroldson that he had known.

"Well, I thank you, madam. If you do see him, do tell us. Will you? We will be staying here at the tavern."

When Molly had said that she would, they departed not only the counter but the tavern as well, no doubt to continue asking questions. Perhaps, he shouldn't have said what he had about not knowing Caleb. There was a whole town that could say that he did know him. Peter had nearly convinced himself that he was the wanted man, until he realized the mysterious gentlemen did not know his name. He unclenched his fist under the table. Molly was looking at him with eyebrows raised.

"Why did you lie?" she said, in a low voice into his ear.

"It did not seem right," he said simply.

"If you ask me," Molly said, still speaking in a whisper but masking it in a veil of flirtation for benefit of onlookers, "I think he has run off with Rebecca Turrington."

"Rebecca Turrington? What has she got to do with all of this?"

"Did you not know? He is in love with her."

"What?" he said, feeling more shocked than when Caleb had hit him.

"Truthfully, I have seen them together, once or twice. 'Tis obvious, if you know what to look for."

"But, I do not understand. And if you knew this, why did you do as I asked of you?" he said.

"Because, you asked me," Molly said, "Yes, Caleb is handsome, but I did it for you."

He looked at her, feeling as though he had been blind to quite a lot for quite a long time.

"But wait, Rebecca Turrington is dead," he said.

"They never found a body," Molly said with a shrug, "maybe she is not."

Peter shook his head, trying to make sense of it all.

"Well, whether she is or she is not, I tried to push another woman on him. He is really in love with her, eh? No wonder he hit me."

Molly looked at him sympathetically.

"What do you suppose they want with him, Peter?"

"I do not know, but I do not think we ought to let them find him, wherever he is."

CHAPTER EIGHTEEN

Caleb debated with himself if he had made the right decision for most of the morning. He had concealed himself in the cover of trees, while the men had spoken by the fire. Perhaps, he ought to have emerged from the shadows and confronted them. In the early hours of the day, it now seemed obvious that he should have done it.

With the dark crowding around him, the opposite alternative had seemed the smartest decision. Remaining unseen afforded him power, or at least a sense of it. He had become a spy on a clandestine mission.

Maybe, that power hadn't been in his hands after all. It certainly didn't feel like it, as he followed them from a distance and then subsequently lost them in the crowded streets of the town. Caleb was annoyed with himself for losing the men. His plan had been to question them casually in the light of day, preferably surrounded by others. How he would do this and what he would say were not firmly in place. Not that it mattered now anyway, when he could not find them. The dim light of the campfire had revealed few distinguishing characteristics. It had been so dark that he was not even certain how many there had been.

The backs of heads and line of clothing of the other men in the town lacked any uniqueness. Any passerby might equally have been a magistrate or one of those assembled by the fire. Worse still, at least when he sought Rebecca, if he were caught staring he could deceive the lady in question into thinking he was merely admiring her. Scanning men proved frustrating and might well land him a punch in the nose, to match the hit he had given Peter.

He had offered no explanation and left no note explaining his forthcoming absence. Caleb had merely walked away.

I wonder if anyone has even noticed. Peter must have.

Well, unless he is still angry with me.

No, Caleb Haroldson would not be missed. The only one who had ever really noticed him, he was in pursuit of now. He had thought Peter had been a friend, but having that woman show up in his bed clearly showed that he knew nothing of Caleb. No one paid Caleb true attention aside from Rebecca and his name meant nothing to the outside world. Everyone knew the name of Turrington and he would not speak it, but mentioning that he was Caleb Haroldson wouldn't turn a single head.

The town was larger than many of the others Caleb had passed through in earlier days. Men and women pressed in around him. Their faces were different from the residents of his town, but they wore the same hurried expressions. Noticing the details of others was something he had little time for before. The wood had always demanded his time and when he looked into a piece of oak or beech, a form would emerge from it. He was able to read what it would become. Situations provided no such assurance of firm outcome.

I will find her.

Even as he thought the words though, his heart shifted uncomfortably. How could he be certain that he would find her, when he couldn't even keep track of the men he had seen hours before?

Caleb walked briskly through the streets, avoiding the carts of vegetables and the piles of horse manure. Trees dotted many of the yards of the town. Their forms cried out to Caleb, offering the familiar faces of a prospective chair or a potential shelf. The faces that he sought of the men, or better yet Rebecca, though were not forthcoming.

He had stayed awake as long as the men had, but they had said nothing useful. Only the curious mention of the phrase "across the river" offered any hope that they might be connected to Rebecca's disappearance. It seemed too coincidental that the old man the morning of the fire had used those words. Or maybe, it only meant something to Caleb. He was guilty of a crime of a man truly in love, in that he saw Rebecca everywhere and connected all to her.

A horse, led on a well-aged rope, passed in front of him as the road Caleb walked along came to a fork. Yes, his thoughts were far too tainted by Rebecca. If he didn't know better, he would think that the horse was hers. Of course, that was ridiculous. He was miles from the manor. Still though, its gait was uncannily similar and the soft bay color might have been an identical match to Dandelion.

Ah Caleb, not everything is related to Rebecca.

He turned away and continued walking. Something would not allow him to let go, though, and he turned back toward the horse.

"Hey, watch it!" a gruff woman, with arms overflowing, said as he stumbled into her.

"I am sorry, madam," he said, nodding toward her.

"I ain't no madam," she said roughly, as though he had unleashed an insult rather than a courtesy. She hurried on her way and he turned to the horse. It had moved on and was no longer in sight. Unwilling to lose sight of yet another possible link to Rebecca, his pace quickened as he followed in the direction he had last seen it.

The horse had not walked as quickly as he had imagined it would and Caleb drew to an abrupt stop to prevent from overtaking it. His foot sloshed into a puddle, which his eyes had been too busy to notice. Mild irritation soon passed, as he stared at the cause of the slow-walking horse. He was close enough now to see that the man who led the horse was the elderly man from the manor.

Unable to resist the impulse any longer, he approached the man. Rather than address him, Caleb said to the horse,

"Dandelion?"

The horse pricked up her ears and turned in the direction of Caleb. The man spun.

"We meet again, good sir," Caleb said, not knowing if the man were good or not, but affording him the courtesy nonetheless. In the man's eyes a spark of recognition registered, but his words declined any such thing.

"I am afraid I do not know you," he said and turned away with a slight tug of the horse's bridle, urging it to follow.

"If I do not know you, then how does Dandelion know me?" Caleb said to the man's back. Hearing her name, Dandelion stopped and turned toward Caleb. The man urged the horse on, but unable to call the horse by her name and admit that Caleb was right, Dandelion was reluctant to budge.

"You are mistaken," the man said, trying to move Dandelion.

"Dandelion knows me," Caleb said again, realizing that the more he said her name the greater advantage he had.

"And you know me too," Caleb said, "you spoke to me the morning of the fire. I am Caleb Haroldson."

The man, who had busied himself in trying to lead Dandelion, now turned his attention to Caleb. No longer was he too busy for the man who stood before him.

"You are Caleb Haroldson?"

CHAPTER NINETEEN

As Rebecca's eyes fell across the chest, her interest was instantly piqued. The ground under her feet was rockier, as she progressed farther into the cove. She stopped long enough to put her shoes back on, the wet leather resting roughly against her bare skin.

Crossing to the chest, she knelt in front of it. There was a lock bolted to the front of it, which had long since rusted under the damp conditions. Barnacles clustered against the wood, like long strings of gnarled pearls.

Rebecca's mind raced forward at the possibilities of what she might find hidden in the box. Stories of pirates, such as the notorious Blackbeard who had sailed on his ship the *Queen Anne's Revenge* along the coast of the American colonies of the Carolinas, had always interested her. Her grandfather had once recalled the tale of Captain Kidd on display for all of London to see to young Rebecca. Her mother had been horrified that he had told so impressionable a young girl such a story, but Rebecca had clapped her hands gleefully at the adventure and begged him to tell her more.

On the other side of the world, she had buried her own treasure of silver in the river. Now in the Caribbean, she tingled at the prospect of uncovering some long-hidden treasure of the sea. Rebecca pulled at the lock, but it would not budge. Disappointed, she sat back and pushed the chest away with her feet. In so doing, the leather band that held the lock fell away. Though the lock remained intact, the strap had given way under the unforgiving weight of time.

Creeping forward, she pushed aside the lid. How fortunate it would be to come face-to-face with gold and jewels to finance her voyage home! Yes, that's what she would do. She would wait for a few days, until convinced that Lord Furton had tired of searching for her. Then, she would paddle back to the harbor and offer a captain a high fee for her passage. Tempted by the riches, he would be unable to resist. A crew's protest that a woman on board was unlucky would soon be quelled by an extra ration or some rum.

So convinced was she of the simplicity and brilliance of her plan that, she stared in sincere surprise at the contents of the chest. As Rebecca pushed aside the heavy lid, there were no strings of pearls or piles of gold. Only coarse material, crumpled and laying in loose piles, filled the box. How should she finance her journey home with fabric?

Well, perhaps, he had just been an incredibly careful pirate. This clothing might only be a ruse. Under the top layer, gold and silver might abound. She pushed aside the material, but underneath it her hands were only met by more of the same. As she reached the bottom of the chest, she was favored by a bit of good fortune. It was not a coin or a pendant she came across, but rather a flask.

Upon seeing it, Rebecca became aware of her parched throat. How long had it been since she had drunk anything? It must have been several hours. For all the merits of this cove, a supply of fresh water was not one of them. She picked up the bottle and hoped that its contents had not evaporated.

Rebecca unscrewed the cap and moved the flask from side to side. Something sloshed at the bottom. Tilting it, she let the contents descend into her awaiting lips. Aware of the scarcity of her provisions, she forced herself not to be too greedy. As the liquid hit her throat, her own rationing became easier to enforce. Her throat burned at the years of fermentation.

Convinced that there was nothing else in the chest, after thoroughly checking it for any hidden compartments, Rebecca sat back and rested her chin in the palm of her hand.

"What kind of a pirate would lock away clothes like buried treasure?" she said aloud, annoyed at its lack of utility.

Realizing that she had merely hoped to find riches and

had not been guaranteed them, Rebecca began to reexamine the situation. If she had no means to pay for her return voyage, then what were her options?

Not figuring that there would be any high demand for tutelage in Latin, French, or classic poetry, she considered how else she might earn money.

Suppose, Lord Furton was right.

The thought hit her with such force, that an acidic protest rose from the base of her throat. Agreeing with him felt like she had become a traitor to herself, but his point of men paying for a wife rang too clear for her to ignore. Oh, she had no intention of actually marrying anyone, but she could hire out her services of cooking and cleaning. Never mind that Rebecca had no practical experience in such tasks. She had seen the cook and maids do enough things to know something of it. Yes, it couldn't be so hard.

"Good, then that is what I will do," she said aloud to her surroundings. Though it had seemed like a good idea in her head, giving voice to it had convinced her that it would not work. Lord Furton would surely find her, if she were required to wait for as long as it would take someone earning a maid's wages to pay for a return journey. Offering pittance to a sea captain removed all leverage Rebecca had hoped to have.

If only there were some other way. If I could—

Inspired, Rebecca sat forward and rummaged through the chest. Pulling out the cast-aside fabric, she discovered a pair of pants, a couple of shirts, even a hat and a tattered jacket. The material moved through her fingers and she felt an uneasy thrill of anticipation. There had been no gold, but Rebecca was now convinced that she had found a treasure that was much better. She had been given an opportunity to hide in plain sight. Pulling off the itchy woolen dress and underskirts from Lord Furton, Rebecca changed into the clothing from the chest. The material swathed her in bagginess, but she decided that the loose-fitting clothing would only better serve her purpose.

Rebecca pulled on the tattered coat. Something weighed heavily in its pocket against her leg. Reaching into the pocket, she pulled out a blade. Taking handfuls of her hair, she cut through the thick tresses. As they fell to the floor of the cave around her feet, a smile slid across Rebecca's face. She had found her way home.

CHAPTER TWENTY

"Yes, I am Caleb Haroldson," he repeated to the old man. The man looked at him with an odd sense of peculiarity and interest.

"How do you know my name?"

The man looked away, unaccustomed to lies and struggling to invent an answer.

"Your reputation precedes you," the man said, turning his attention back to Caleb. Vagueness was the only answer he had been able to produce. Dandelion pawed at the ground, stamping her hoof against the road. She had tired of the city and was anxious to return to the luscious grasses of the country.

"You know my name because of my business?" Caleb said. It was plausible. He was known for his fine craftsmanship. Yes, of course, that's what it must be. He had heard someone mention Caleb's name when they were in the town beside Turrington Manor.

He nodded.

"You might say we are in the same line of work."

"You are a craftsman as well?" Caleb said. His eyes took in the figure before him. Feeble is how he had looked amid the ruins and ashes. Obviously, though, he was stronger than he appeared. He had, after all, come this great distance.

"Yes, that is right," he answered.

"Your work has brought you here?" Caleb said.

"Yes, that is right," the man said again, "And what about you? When I saw you last, you were greatly distressed."

He realized immediately the mistake that he had made in admitting to knowing Caleb, when he had denied it before.

"So, you do remember me?" Caleb said, peering intently at the other man, so that this time his shifty gaze could not return and mask his answers. Unable to avoid Caleb's eyes, a smile passed across his face as he said,

"My memory is not what it once was. Sometimes, it takes a minute."

Slippery fox. You are concealing something, but what?

"Perhaps," Caleb said, "we ought to go somewhere to get a drink."

"Oh, I thank you, but I am really not thirsty," the man said, his squirming tactics returning.

"I think the horse is," Caleb said, in a tone that suggested to the man he ought to listen to him.

The old man looked at Caleb, read in his eyes some inescapable thought and then looked to Dandelion.

"She seems fine to me."

The more the old man tried to escape, the more convinced Caleb became that there was something he was trying to hide.

"Allow me to buy you a drink. I insist," Caleb said.

He reached out to put his hand on Dandelion's reins, punctuating the point.

Looking trapped, the man turned to Caleb, a flash of scorn in his eyes. He was uncomfortable and unaccustomed to the contemptuous nature of youth. With no real choice, he obliged Caleb with a nod of his head.

On the way to the tavern, Caleb walked close to the man. It seemed unlikely that he would decide to make a sudden sprint for it, but Caleb was unwilling to let any link to Rebecca or potential clue escape.

A fountain of questions bubbled up inside Caleb, alerting him to the reality that only the truth would quench his thirst. He could wait no longer and so turned to the man and said,

"Why did you tell me that Rebecca Turrington had crossed the river?"

The man looked at him, his eyes narrowing in thought.

"'Tis an expression. You should know it from the title of the book you clutched in your hand that morning."

"But, 'tis an expression that relates to death and Rebecca

is alive."

"Is she now?" the man said, his eyebrows rising slightly. Was he surprised to learn this or just had not expected Caleb to know the truth?

"Yes, that is right and taking her horse hardly seems like the gentlemanly thing to do."

"Well, then, I am glad of it and the horse will be returned, if you say it belongs to Miss Turrington. I merely found her and did not wish harm to come to the animal."

He paused to tug at the reins, to coax Dandelion along before turning to Caleb to say,

"You have seen her, then?"

"Well—no," Caleb said.

"Then, how do you know?"

The man had taken the position of power. His question planted a seed of doubt.

Richard told me.

Of course, he could say no such thing.

"I—I just know."

He had assumed Richard had been right. Caleb had taken him at his word. What if—what if it weren't true? Maybe Richard had been mistaken. And why did a horse and rider carrying her away convince him that she were alive? The questions pounded against him, assaulting his senses and hammering bonds of tension like a helmet around his head.

You would know if she were not all right. You would feel it.

The words rose from his heart, but even when truth burns brightest, doubt has a way of dimming it with its curtains of distortions and lies.

The old man was staring at him. Caleb fought back the waves of arrows that pierced his resolve.

He felt the paleness pour over his cheeks.

"You look poorly," the man said.

"I am unharmed," Caleb said, struggling in his steps.

The old man stopped abruptly. Caleb stumbled against him, catching his balance on Dandelion who whinnied her own protest.

"You love her, 'tis not true?"

Caleb blinked. His throat felt parched and words were not forthcoming.

Looking at Caleb, he secured his answer.

"Someone help me!" the old man called out, "This man is trying to rob me!"

CHAPTER TWENTY-ONE

Rebecca's hand passed over the remaining hair that she had not lopped off. Long tresses lay around her feet.

"Well Caleb, I may return looking more like you than myself, but I shall return."

Bending down, she picked up the hat from beside the pile of hair on the floor of the cave. She pushed it down on her head, letting the wide brim fan its protective benefit over as much of her face as she could manage to cover.

Would it work? Was she convincing enough?

With no mirror, she could not test the disguise of the costume on her appearance. Unless—Rebecca left the cave and felt the immediate weight of the oppressive heat.

Do not swoon, Rebecca. A gentleman would not swoon. A gentleman? I look more like a pirate. Well, then for goodness' sake, definitely do not swoon. A pirate would never swoon!

She scrambled among the rocks, feeling the freedom that came from a lack of encumbering skirts.

Ah, here was what she was looking for. She peered into the small reflective pool, which the tide had created among these rocks. The water here was crystal clear, unlike the murky mire of the river at home. Upon seeing herself, she nearly jumped back for fear of a stranger having appeared over her shoulder. But no, there was no one present but her. It was not a perfect transformation, but yes, it would do quite nicely. Rebecca had metamorphosed. She would not pass for a man. Her face, smooth and beautiful, would not allow for that. But, if she subtracted eight or even ten years from her age, she might pass as a teenage boy. Were there such young pirates?

Well, yes, there had to be, she convinced herself. She knew that young boys were sailors and so it only stood to follow that young boys might also be pirates. She would have to keep her hat on at all times and her voice would surely pose a problem. Perhaps, she could be mute. But no, that wouldn't work. How could she tell a captain that she wanted passage home if she could not speak? Writing down her messages didn't strike her as a viable option either.

If her plan were to succeed and she was to become a crew member aboard a ship, such as the one she had just been on, then she would need to not be viewed as a burden. At the thought of the ship, her stomach lurched forward. Even if she passed as a boy, how could she pass for a sailor? A seasick sailor! Who had ever heard of something so ridiculous?!

Well, now was not the time to think of such things. Whether Rebecca was a boy or a lady, she would have to return home by boat. There were simply no other options.

A seagull squawked from some far-off post. If only she might have the ability to fly like one of the birds! No, it was too fantastical a thought.

Rebecca, you are growing delirious.

To her annoyance, the voice in her head sounded very much like that of her mother's.

Making her way back across the rocks, she watched her steps to keep from slipping on the smooth wet algae. It was odd to see her leg encased in the coarse material of a pair of pants. Only her feet, tucked into the dainty shoes, were familiar.

Oh dear! That would definitely not do!

The smoothness of face could be attributed to youth, but no sailor of any age wore the soft kidskin dancing shoes that surrounded her feet, making them look only more diminutive.

"Why did I not wear Richard's shoes?" she said in disgust but quickly forgave herself when she realized that her plan had been to sneak through the halls of her house unheard, not to be kidnapped by Lord Furton or transported across the world or be marooned on a tropical island wearing the discarded clothes of a pirate.

No, she really had done rather well for herself and

mustn't be discouraged.

"I know!" she said, inspiration hitting, as she returned to the cave. Rebecca dug into the chest and pulled out some scraps of fabric from it. She wound them around her shoes, disguising the slippers and bulking up her feet.

Rebecca's stomach grumbled, supplying its own suggestion of what she ought to be thinking about. She had become used to being nauseated and her appetite had long since abandoned her. Now though, for the first time, she felt the odd familiar pangs of hunger. She had seen no fish in the pools surrounding the cave.

The prospect of eating barnacles or algae didn't appeal to her much, even though her stomach had become ravenous in the quest for food. An image of fishing boats filling the harbor, where her escape plan had been hatched, flashed across her memory now.

Yes, there would be plenty of fish there and lack of money would be no hindrance to her need for nourishment, if she plucked her dinner straight from the sea. Rebecca had no pole, line or net, but she had already found both a waiting boat, as well as a trunk of clothing and a knife. Finding a fishing pole to use seemed like a small task in comparison.

Rebecca dug the oar out of the sand and untied it and the boat from her stocking rope. Jumping into the vessel, she pushed off from the shore. Emerged in a sea of people, rather than reflected in a pool of water, her disguise would soon be put to the real test.

CHAPTER TWENTY-TWO

Caleb fell forward into the cell, aided by the guard's assertive push.

"Horse thief," he muttered in disgust, as he inserted the key in the lock and clicked Caleb securely into place behind the doors.

"I am not a horse thief," Caleb protested. Drawn up to his full height, he stood in challenge to the guard. His tufted hair had fallen across his eyes in the scuffle. Caleb's satchel had been taken from him.

Seated at a rough wooden table, a second guard rifled through the contents of the bag.

"Perhaps, but you are clearly a thief."

He had taken a leather pouch from inside the bag and weighed the contents in the palm of his hand. Caleb watched as the guard pulled the strings loose that had held the bag taut. Anger boiled from the pit of Caleb's stomach, as he watched a stream of silver coins spill from the pouch and flow through the guard's fingers.

"I am not a thief," Caleb said defiantly, his hands wrapping around the wall of bars that held him. The guard looked at him, clutching a coin as he said,

"Then, how do you explain this?"

"I earned it."

"Earned it? Ha! Is that what you call assaulting old men and relieving them of their burdens of money?"

"I did no such thing."

Resisting the urge to shake the bars, lest it should only serve to complicate matters, Caleb allowed his hands to drop to his sides.

"Then, how do you explain what happened?"

He had not yet released the coin. Seeing it in his hand and the admiring covetous glances he cast on it, stirred up an overwhelming discomfort in Caleb. The silver was intended to bring Rebecca home. It felt as though the guard was reaching out to Rebecca, as he caressed the silver's edges. It was her fingers that the guard was intertwining with his own.

Leveling a steely gaze at the guard, though the guard's eyes were downcast on the coins, Caleb said,

"The man and I are from the same town. I recognized the horse. He knew my name and then he turned on me and suddenly accused me of robbing him."

"That is what happened?"

He asked if I loved Rebecca. Then he called the guards.

"Yes, that is what happened."

Too stunned by what the man had done, Caleb had been unable to move in those short few seconds before guards had appeared and seized upon him. As Caleb had struggled with them, explaining that there had been some mistake, the man slipped away with Dandelion. The old man had paused only once to look over his shoulder. Confused, Caleb had stared at him. Only a shrug of his shoulder was offered as explanation.

"If that is really what happened, then why would he say you robbed him?"

Caleb watched as the guard spun a coin on the table. As it tottered, he grabbed it up roughly.

Do not touch, Rebecca. Do not lay a hand on her.

The guard shoved the coins back into the pouch and raised his eyes to Caleb. He was waiting for his answer. A question had been asked and now Caleb was required to offer some rebuttal. Only—he couldn't.

His anger, at being locked away and prevented from finding Rebecca, had been overshadowed only by his confusion. Almost as though the old man had panicked when he had read Caleb's love for Rebecca on his face, he had reacted in haste.

"Difficult to think of a lie quick enough, is it not?" the guard said. He stood from the table now for the first time and

Caleb was surprised at how short he was.

So, you have to berate others to make yourself feel bigger, to be more of a man. Is that it?

He was wiser than to repeat such things aloud.

Caleb said nothing. It would do him no favor to annoy the guard.

"You better think up something better than the hogwash you told me before the trial."

Trial?

Caleb groaned inside. He had convinced himself that the truth would emerge, because he was innocent and that all would soon be made right. If Caleb had to go to trial, then everything would be impossibly dragged out. His search for Rebecca could be delayed by weeks, even months. Suppose they found him guilty of this fabricated crime. He could be locked away and hindered by years! It was too much to think about. Anger bubbled over into a sickening disgust.

If only I had not—

Hadn't what? What was it that he had done to land him here?

Maybe I ought to have followed those men last night. Well, so much for being cautious!

He began to pace.

"Caleb, what is wrong? You only pace when angry," Rebecca's faraway memory voice said.

"I was cheated in a payment," he would invariably say.

"'Twill be all right next time. Next time, you will get it," she would say.

"Well, what about this time? This time they got it."

Yes, this time they had got him.

"Caleb Haroldson?"

From the door, he heard his name. His cell was deeper

back and he could not see who had spoken his name. Footsteps echoed down the corridor. There were no other prisoners being held in this small jail and so Caleb, even without first hearing his name, knew their intended destination.

"When is the trial?" Caleb heard himself ask.

He was certain that the footsteps were here to take him away. A man, concealed under a dark cloak and wide-brimmed hat, stood beside the guard. His face was hidden and Caleb did not recognize his strange appearance.

"There is no trial," the guard said, sounding disappointed as he delivered the news.

"No trial?" Caleb said, trying to make sense of it all.

The guard slipped the key into the lock and pulled the door open.

"Keep up, man. You are free."

"Free?"

"Why you care about him is beyond me," the guard said, looking from Caleb to the concealed man, "I think he is dense."

The man said nothing, but turned to walk away. Caleb stepped from the cell, held out his hand to the guard for his satchel to be returned, and looked up to see the back of the mystery man.

Caleb drew in his breath. He was one of the men from the campfire.

CHAPTER TWENTY-THREE

As Rebecca paddled toward the harbor, she began to doubt her plan. She may have been dressed in a man's clothes, but she was still a woman. Perhaps, she would stand out even more in such a guise.

Not trusting the breeze to keep her secret, she pushed the hat down farther over her ears with one hand. As her hand found itself once again on her paddle, she frowned at it. Like her feet, it too was small. To further betray her, it was of the creamy porcelain complexion of one who spent most days sequestered inside. At least, they no longer looked like they belonged to someone who never worked. Gripping the oars and scrambling over the rocks of the cave had aided her appearance, by depositing dirt and grime under her fingernails and leaving scratches and red marks on them.

This will work. It has to.

Rebecca paddled on, the water falling away as a quiet companion. The masts of the ships stood proud, as she approached. Searching for the ship that had brought her here, she soon found it. Lord Furton would still be here. Little time had passed since her escape. As keen as he had been to sell her off and punish her for his misunderstanding, he would assuredly not yet have abandoned his search.

Maybe, waiting it out would have been the better option. But no, that would not have worked. Giving him enough time to find her and trap her in the cave provided no chance of escape. Having lost her once, he would undoubtedly ensure it would not happen again. He had already locked her away from the world on the ship. Rebecca shuddered to think what taking extra precautions might entail. Besides, she had very few supplies and could not last long without procuring first daily sustenance and second, but more importantly, her passage home.

Rebecca spotted a place to dock her boat. After paddling

it into the location she found between two larger boats, she stuffed her stocking rope into her pocket to disassemble and pull back onto her feet later. A coil of discarded rope wound around itself like a snake. Rebecca stepped from the boat and began tying it in place with the rope.

Too dainty. You should leap from the boat.

The harbor was lively, as it had been earlier this morning. Rays of golden sunlight filtered through the sky, casting long shadows across the land. A chill in the air signaled that night was not far off.

The thought of soon being emerged in the dark was both an uncomfortable as well as a welcomed thought. Her appearance would be under less scrutiny without the sun highlighting the details of her face. Shadows loomed larger and danger grew beneath the moon, though, and an already grim situation held the promise of further challenges.

Rebecca tested the strength of the knot. It would hold. Taking a deep breath, her feet moved forward.

A sailor, who looked to be about her age, approached as she walked up the dock. He would be her first test. Barely acknowledging Rebecca with a brief nod of the head, she had passed. A sense of safety was not yet achieved. Not everyone would be so distracted.

Rebecca walked stiffly, holding her arm against her leg to prevent the too large trousers from falling down. As she stepped from the pier, a surge of people pressed in on her. Surrounded by crates, barrels and both the tanned bodies of the sailors as well as the dark bodies of the slave labor, Rebecca walked among life in the Caribbean for the first time. She had considered herself erudite, but now it was as if she had stepped into her books and become part of an exotic tale.

"Watch it!" someone grumbled roughly, as Rebecca stepped into his path.

"Apologies," she said and then felt herself pale as she

realized she had spoken aloud.

Rebecca, what have you done?

He had hurried on his way and, this time, her mistake had gone unpunished. Rebecca watched, mesmerized, as a man hoisted barrels onto his broad shoulders. His body glistened. Rebecca felt herself staring at his dark complexion. She had never seen someone like this up close before. His teeth and eyes seemed to blaze brilliantly white against the blackness of his skin. His appearance had so dazzled her that only now did she realize that his shirt was removed and that she, as a lady, was not supposed to be watching him.

He caught her eye. Her heart beat against the walls of her chest. Pride, dressed in sorrow, filled his eyes. Rebecca felt the urge to go to him and to speak. He turned away, breaking the bond and returning Rebecca to reality.

A swirl of vibrant colors came at her, contrasting strongly with the night. How muted the colors of home looked compared to the vivid greens, oranges, reds and purples of the fabrics and flowers!

"Squawk!" Her attention was drawn to the most colorful bird she had ever seen. Bright feathers dressed him in a cloak of many colors, which would have rivaled Joseph's.

What a wonderfully strange place! Parrots and Africans and so much color!

Just when Rebecca was convinced that her senses could be delighted no further, a wave of perfumed air tingled her nose. Spices and the dark velvety molasses and rum encircled her, wrapping her in their warmth.

Lulled into a sense of safety, she allowed herself to enjoy the walk. She had come ashore, wanting nothing more than to leave as quickly as possible. Now, Rebecca felt the strange allure of building a life among these delights.

Caleb, if only you were here.

Would he like such a place? Surely, a cabinet maker would

be needed. It seemed that there was even more that would need to be stored away with all the exotic offerings around her. Surrounded in unfamiliarity, she sank into her own new appearance, no longer fearing if she would pass a test or be recognized. With each step, it seemed there was something new to experience. Rebecca turned. Her heart froze. Lord Furton stood, not ten paces from her, waving his arms and saying loudly,

"Her name is Rebecca Turrington."

CHAPTER TWENTY-FOUR

As Caleb followed the back of the man out of the jail, his stomach twisted into a hundred questions. Why had the man freed him? Who was he? What would happen now?

The clothing, dark in color, gave away little about him. As they left the building and emerged into the sunlight of the early morning, the man turned.

He was older than Caleb, by perhaps ten years. He had a ruddy stubble beard and piercing blue eyes that studied Caleb.

"You are Caleb Haroldson."

It was not a question, but rather given as a reverse introduction.

Caleb nodded slowly.

"And you are?"

"A friend," the man said.

Caleb's confusion prompted further explanation,

"Would you not agree?"

"You have freed me, so how could I not?"

The man looked at Caleb from under the brim of his hat.

"You do not trust me."

Again, it was not meant as a question.

"Not that I do not, rather that I do not know why I should."

"Because, I freed you."

The words sounded logical enough. Something in the way that he delivered them raked against Caleb uncomfortably.

"And, because," the man lowered his voice now as he spoke, "you seemed willing to trust me before."

Caleb shook his head.

"What do you mean?"

"Only that you seemed to value my words before."

"But, I do not know you. How is that possible?"

"You do not know me?" He paused, looked directly at

Caleb and said,

"Do you regularly spy on strangers, Mr. Haroldson?"

The words spun around Caleb, dizzying his mind. His night in the cell had passed uncomfortably and Caleb had slept little. It was not that he was ungrateful to be free, only that he deplored the gnawing in his stomach at feeling caged.

"Perhaps, you are confused by my profession. I am no spy. I am a cabinet maker, a simple carpenter."

The man reached into his pocket, pulling out an apple. He dusted it off on the front of his coat and then offered it to Caleb. He had eaten little, but food hardly seemed important at such a time. Caleb shook his head and the man shrugged. Biting into the apple, he turned back toward Caleb. Crunching loudly, he said,

"Funny, is it not, Mr. Haroldson?"

"How is that?"

Before replying to Caleb, the man paused long enough to tip his hat to a woman whose path they had crossed.

"Funny that a mere cabinet maker, as you do say you are, would find himself so far from home."

"A craftsman sells his wares," Caleb said, though an uneasiness had rooted itself in his stomach. How did this stranger know so much about him?

"What you say is true, Mr. Haroldson."

Caleb breathed an internal sigh of relief.

"But, is it not customary to bring the wares you intend to sell?"

Caleb's stomach plummeted at the words. His inclination had been right. This man was no champion of freedom; he was still trapped.

"I build to individual specifications," Caleb said, not allowing the other man to see his discomfort.

Of course, with all you know, you will probably think my next thought for me.

Seeing that Caleb was eager to supply a retort to every

question, the man curbed the conversation.

"Mr. Haroldson, you were so interested in my words. Would you not like to meet my companions?"

"Your companions?"

Dear sweet, Rebecca, send me a prayer that a band of thieves will not be my undoing.

"My associates."

Caleb's legs felt heavy with each step forward. Had he escaped a trial, only to bypass the judge and face the executioner prematurely?

As though answering his question, the man said,

"Mr. Haroldson, 'tis time to cross the river."

CHAPTER TWENTY-FIVE

Rebecca urged herself not to panic.

Stay calm. He has not seen you. And, even if he has, your appearance shall deceive.

Perhaps, if it were Caleb or Richard looking at her, her disguise would not hold. The veil would prove too thin and the layers of deception would peel away. Lord Furton did not know her as they did. He would not be able to tell it was her. At least, that's what she kept repeating to herself.

Turning slowly, so that she faced away from him, Rebecca busied herself with the wares on the stand in front of her. Her eyes roamed across the baskets of tightly-clustered yellow jewels of bananas and the long flute-like bodies of the sugar cane.

Just blend in. Just blend in.

Lord Furton's voice grew louder,

"I want her found! Now!"

"Yes, sir!"

The hurried scamper of feet, from the dismissal of the sailor, fell fainter on her ears as he left in the opposite direction. Lord Furton continued toward her. The heavy clomp of his boots, which had drummed against her head so often on the crossing, drowned out all else in the crowded market. Their memory had seared the sound into her mind, enlarging the vibrations as she heard them now. Many of those around Rebecca walked barefoot, which only further intensified the sound of the boots.

Please, oh please.

The familiar feeling of fear that she had momentarily escaped, when first walking through this tropical wonderland, returned. Her heart beat like the drums of the slaves, as Lord Furton came ever nearer.

"How did she get away from me? I will make her sorry," he muttered to himself. For her to hear the words, she knew that he must be very close. Rebecca didn't dare turn to confirm her suspicion.

His icy demeanor emanated from him, making his hatred palpable to her.

"And, to think that they wanted her! I knew better. I knew better."

Knew better? Who wanted me?

Rebecca felt her world push in on her, as Lord Furton's words reduced its size. She had assumed that avoiding Lord Furton and ridding herself of him would gain her the safety she craved. No longer did she feel the truth of her assumption.

Say something else, but oh, be gone, be gone!

Conflicting thoughts of needing some further clues competed with her need to turn and know that Lord Furton would not be there.

Lord Furton stepped closer. His boots echoed painfully in her head and his proximity drew up a memory of nauseating waves. Rebecca struggled to push them back. Lord Furton continued walking. Within seconds, he would pass. The anticipation bore a hole through her stomach, like a deep cave.

Rebecca's skin tingled cold, as Lord Furton's cloak brushed her back. Every fiber of her being screamed at his grazing touch. Willing them to keep their silence and not give her away, Rebecca held her breath. He was not a portly man, but his cape seemed endlessly long as it dragged across her.

Rebecca felt each thread of his cloak burn against her. The air in her lungs felt stifled, as she struggled not to move. Mercifully, Lord Furton did not stop. The last material of his cape lingered for a final moment before he walked away from her, severing the infernal bond.

As the clomping of his boots faded away, Rebecca turned to leave as quickly as she could. She soon remembered that the other sailor had hurried down this road and the prospect of meeting him, though less terrifying than facing Lord Furton, still rattled her.

Darting down a side alley, Rebecca was soon surrounded in a dark version of this island. How different it was here, just a few feet from the enticing spices and colors of the market street! Here, tobacco smoke clung to the air, accompanied by the heavy fragrance of rum. Loud singing spilled from opened windows and men stumbled out of the doors. Women draped themselves over the men and some looked at her suggestively. At least, to someone her appearance was passing the test!

"You are a cheat!" she heard someone growl, as he kicked another man out of the door in front of her. The man fell in a heap; cards spilling from his pockets seemed to suggest the accusation had not been unfounded. Rebecca leaped out of the way, to avoid being run into.

Perhaps, it had been a mistake to come tonight. Only a murky underbelly was on offer here. There was no hope of a room, a bit of food and a chance to talk with a captain. No, she would paddle back to her cave and wait until the morning.

Rebecca could see the masts of the ships soaring over the roofs. If she followed them, she would soon be at the harbor. Her legs carried her swiftly on her way. Her hands flexed, ready to grab hold of the oars and paddle to her makeshift home. The alley, after her encounter with Lord Furton, had planted an uneasiness in her that the shadows of night watered. Never one to dally, her feet felt the overwhelming urge to break free and run.

Just stay calm. If you run, you will attract unwelcome attention.

Although the words made sense in her head, her feet tried their best not to obey. The houses were becoming less frequent here. No longer were the buildings grouped so tightly and Rebecca was able to breathe freely once again, as the crisp saltiness of the sea washed over her.

For a moment, she stood still, allowing her breathing to

return and her panicked heart to quiet itself. Paddling back to the cave would be no easy task, especially because the late hour had raised the tide from what it had been earlier. There would be more layers of water to paddle through. Her work would increase, as she would also have to carefully watch for the cave. There would be no light to lead the way. She hadn't considered this before. Suppose, she couldn't find it. Suppose, she drifted out to sea, never to be heard of again.

Or, suppose, she stayed on this safe shore only to fall into Lord Furton's hands. Suppose, she were sold to become like the beautiful proud man she had seen in the market. No, there really was no competition between the two. Rebecca's eyes traveled over the boats, searching for her rowboat. The sails rattled in the breeze, as the wind darted between the sheets raising them in a game of chase.

There. To the left, perhaps a hundred feet away was the boat. Thankfully, it had—

Rebecca's body froze, as a hand landed on her shoulder.

CHAPTER TWENTY-SIX

Caleb felt a chill at the sound of the words.

Across the river.

A faint rain began to fall. Large drops landed on the man's hat, sliding off like a waterfall on the side of a mountain. Similar drops splashed against Caleb's face, pooling on the tip of his nose and blurring his vision.

Buildings blocked a hasty escape. With the arrival of the rains, people and horses crowded under the overhang of the roofs. A church bell sounded over the din of scampering feet.

Do not toll for me. Do not toll for me.

Caleb was a man of strength and dignity, but those three words had a bewitching power over him. In strength, their power was not unlike that of Rebecca's love. That was where the similarity stopped. Rebecca's love was welcomed. He would happily give in to her, but he felt a terror that he'd not previously known at the sound of those words. They moved through him, as though dressed in a shroud.

Across the river, across the river.

Trees gawked at him, as he walked the gloomy streets.

"*You have carved us for so many years. Now, you are the one whose life will be shaped,*" they seemed to say. Helplessness was not a status well-played by Caleb.

"What do you want with me?" Caleb said, pushing aside the claustrophobic burden those words had created. The man continued walking but said,

"Mr. Haroldson, you know that answer."

What do you mean I know that answer?

Caleb restrained from asking the question aloud. He would not give the man the satisfaction of seeing him beg for crumbs.

"Where are you taking me?" Caleb said, trying a new question when he was unsuccessful with the first.

"I told you, Mr. Haroldson, across the river."

The words edged in on his nerves, begging to unleash their vexations on him again. Caleb denied them the opportunity and struggled to push away the calculated strains of the man's voice and the power harnessed in those words.

Perhaps, Caleb had imagined the sinister nature. This man had released him from jail, after all. Still, he was unwilling to wait around to find out what the stranger's plans were. Unknown motives only made them all the more susceptible to bad intentions.

Caleb looked to each side. The road was widening and the man was leading them away from the town and back toward the direction of the place where they had camped. Taking the advantage provided by knowing this terrain, Caleb's mind rushed forward into a plan. If he could distract the man for long enough, he could make a run for it. But, what could he use?

Do not overthink it. Just do it. Now!

Caleb reached for his gold watch, which had once been his grandfather's and was in his pocket.

"Truthfully, Caleb, I hear your heart beat."

"You hear my watch."

It would be a sacrifice to part with it, but Caleb's survival was more important.

He reached into his pocket, took hold of the chain and tossed it a few steps in front of the man's feet. His aim was to make it appear as if he had dropped it. Placing it in the man's path would force him to bend to pick it up, giving Caleb the perfect window to escape through.

The man paused. Stooping down, he said,

"You have dropped this, Mr. Haroldson. You ought to be more careful."

With a swift kick to his back, Caleb repaid him for his words. A loud "omph" escaped through the man's lips, as he fell flat on his stomach. Caleb planted his boot in the man's back, just long enough to keep him down. The watch would have to be left behind. Bending to pick it up would prove too costly. The man could be recovered to his feet by then. No, he had to go now. Thoughts were wasting precious seconds.

Caleb sprinted away as the man, dumbfounded, remained sprawled on the ground.

"I will not cross your river!" he yelled to the man covered in dust. Caleb was well on his way, as the man scrambled to his feet. He made no attempt to follow Caleb. Doing so would provide little success. Instead, he addressed the now absent man,

"We will find you soon enough, Mr. Haroldson. There is no place in this world where you can truly escape."

CHAPTER TWENTY-SEVEN

Rebecca could see the towering figure of Lord Furton. Each wrinkled line of his sordid face was visible. She had not yet turned, but there was no point in doing so. She knew what she would find when she did. It was an unwelcome proposition. Rebecca stood very still, trying to convince herself that if she wished hard enough he would disappear. The feeling of his cape on her back had not yet left her memory and she anticipated it and his words abrasively falling against her momentarily. Seconds, perhaps only fractions of seconds, had passed but for Rebecca time seemed to stretch endlessly.

Gathering her courage, she turned. If this were to be her fate, she could not escape it. Besides, she could always try something later. She had managed to escape once before. Even as she thought the words, they seemed feeble, implausible and rang untrue.

Rebecca fully faced him now, prepared, as much as she could be, to find out what would happen next. Only—he wasn't there. A girl stood before her.

"Oh you are a young one," she said, with a flirtatious smile, "Worry not. I can teach you."

Rebecca was so shocked that it was not Lord Furton in front of her, that it took her a moment to remember that she was in disguise. This woman before her thought that she was a man. Rebecca recognized her now as one of the girls in the alley, hanging off the arm of another man.

"What troubles you? Do you not talk?" the girl said, leaning into Rebecca. Rebecca was relatively tall and this girl was of small stature, so she seemed not to guess that Rebecca might be anything other than a man. For a fleeting moment, Rebecca wondered if she might confide in this girl. Having a friend, or at least an ally, could prove beneficial. On the other hand, just because she was also a girl did not mean that she would be willing to assist Rebecca or even to keep her secret.

The girl stepped closer, looking intently at Rebecca.

"Pray, what troubles you? Can you not hear me?"

She hadn't dared speak, but now nodded her head to confirm that she could hear.

"You can hear me," the girl repeated, "but, you cannot speak?"

Rebecca shook her head no.

With a sadness in her eyes, the girl leaned yet farther into Rebecca.

"Ah, 'tis all right. Shall I give food to you?"

Food. The offer sounded so tempting in Rebecca's ears.

"Perhaps, some meat. You are as paltry as a starved cat."

Rebecca's mouth began to water at the mention of meat. It had been weeks since she had any to eat. As delicious as it sounded, her still shaky stomach began to protest. The memory of nausea appeared on her face and the girl misinterpreted it as being insulted at being scrawny.

"Oh, but you are handsome. I did not mean you were not."

Rebecca nodded to acknowledge her.

"How about we go in search of some of that food?" the girl said, batting her eyes at Rebecca.

The thought of having to leave to obtain the food sent a wave of panic over Rebecca.

She shook her head.

"Oh, you are shy?"

Rebecca shook her head no again, lest she should have to endure a conversation to coax her into being more personable.

"Oh," the girl said, a knowing smile playing across her lips, "you desire to be alone."

Rebecca nodded. Well, it was better for the girl to think that than for Rebecca to be plunked in among the others and risk discovery. She waited for the girl to leave, but something was preventing her.

"Well— " the girl said, conveying that whatever the delay was didn't exist as a mystery to her.

Rebecca looked at her, waiting for an answer.

"You will surely kiss me, for your gratitude? You will remember your manners."

She looked at Rebecca expectantly. Rebecca froze. She was caught.

Walk away. You will find some food another way.

Before her feet could oblige, the girl reached up and moved her hand over Rebecca's chest. Rebecca tried to turn away, but it was too late. The girl's eyes went wide, as she pulled her hand back.

"You are not a man."

CHAPTER TWENTY-EIGHT

Caleb panted as he came to a halt, pressing his body against the first tree he came to. The bark pushed back against him, scratching his skin. Nothing was reliable any longer. Even his own judgment weighed questionable on his mind.

He had made a decision to rid himself of the man who had set him free. In so doing, he had also distanced himself from the only credible lead he had on Rebecca.

Have I been a coward? A fool?

"Psst, psst," a low whistle interrupted his thoughts.

Startled, Caleb turned. A woman bent-over and dressed shabbily stood before him. As though she had materialized from a pile of leaves, she spoke in a crackling voice to match.

"Fear not, boy."

I am not a boy and I am not afraid.

"Who are you?" he said, only half-thinking that he would get a satisfactory answer.

"Marion," she said.

Well, at least you did not say you were a friend. I certainly do not want any more of those!

Those who had identified themselves as such as of late had acted in a conflicting manner on so many occasions.

"And you are?" she said, when he made no attempt to introduce himself. Reluctance to supply her with any information showed on his face.

"Well, 'tis of no consequence. I only endeavor to be friendly. If'n you desire not to give your name, then you have your reasons and I will grant you a name. Adam. There, 'tis agreeable?"

He nodded his agreement to the stranger naming him.

"You appeared, suddenly," he said, not really sure at all what to say to this mysterious woman of the woods.

"I did not appear," she said with a steady smile. The lines

of her face cracked, again reminding him of crunching leaves. Caleb didn't know what to make of her answer.

"You did not?" he said.

"No, I live here."

"Here?"

She laughed, a deeper and heartier laugh than Caleb had heard in a long while.

"'Tis correct, Adam. 'Tis agreeable to the squirrels and to me, as well."

"Was there something you wanted to ask me about?" he said, not wanting to seem rude, but the strange characters that had streamed through his life dizzying him.

"Come, Adam. Have tea with me. It is so infrequent that I have any visitors."

Tea?

She seemed harmless enough, but so had the old man. Well, at least there was no one to overhear her yelling false accusations, if she turned on him without warning as the old man had.

"Fine yes, I will have tea with you."

He stood, waiting for further instructions. It was not obvious where to sit, when they were surrounded by only leaves and branches.

"Please, Adam, sit down."

She gestured to a stump and he did as she instructed.

"Now, here is your tea," she said.

He saw nothing in her hands and wondered where she would get it from. Her hands, withered with age, formed the shape of a teacup. She passed it to him, literally drawing it from thin air.

Good heavens, she is crazy. I am not going to sit here in the woods drinking imaginary tea.

"I thank you, but—"

"You know, Adam, I hear much in these woods."

Voices in your head, no doubt.

"I heard that man you were talking with, with his friends."

Man I was with?

Could she be his link to the group? But, how credible was a woman who invited him for imaginary tea?

"They talk about strange things, they do. People not being dead who have died."

Caleb's ears prickled in excitement.

"Have you ever heard such strange things, Adam?"

"Once," he said, warming to her.

"Oh?"

She took a sip from her imaginary teacup and motioned for him to do the same. He didn't drink from the tea, but he did offer a contribution to their conversation.

"A girl was said to be dead, but was alive."

Marion cocked her head to the side and smiled slowly.

"You love her."

Caleb swallowed, though no drink filled his mouth. Was his love and devotion so obvious to all?

Unlike the old man, she did not react unpredictably when she realized the truth. Instead, Marion accepted the realization and moved on.

"More tea, Adam?"

Caleb would have stood and left right then, if it weren't for the uncanny similarities he had found in her words with his own reality. What harm could pretending with her do, if she were able to supply him with information?

"I thank you, but no, Marion. This 'twas fine."

"Running a bit low on belief, Adam?"

He looked at her, unsure of the question but, feeling a need to answer her.

"I just hope that I can—that I am not too late."

She paused from the conversation long enough to take

another sip of invisible tea.

"Adam, I will help you. Will you help me?"

"Help you?" he said, sitting forward.

"Help me find those who disappeared."

CHAPTER TWENTY-NINE

Her secret discovered, Rebecca said nothing. Then, realizing that the disguise could not hold up any longer, at least to the girl in front of her, she spoke,

"Yes?"

"Oh? So you can speak?"

"I apologize. I did not desire to deceive you."

Still surprised, the girl didn't know quite what to say.

"Why have you dressed in such a fashion?"

"I— " What should she say? The girl had not yet confirmed that she would be loyal or could be trusted.

Seeing the apprehension in Rebecca's face, she said,

"Oh, you are seeking escape from someone, are you not?"

Having guessed the truth, Rebecca felt the girl knew too much of her story. Before she could turn to leave though, she said,

"'Tis of no consequence. I understand. Men can cause a heap of trouble. If you mean to escape, you must have a good reason. I suppose 'tis why I follow after the young fellows. They have not a wicked bone in their bodies. I like to teach them what to do, how to treat a lady, before someone else—some rough sailor does."

Rebecca nodded, feeling a burden clear away.

Then, concern transfixed the woman's face. Lady Turrington had looked like that once. Well, she must have looked like that more often, but Lady Turrington was reluctant in her affection and hasty in her reprieves. Now that Rebecca was older, she understood. Lady Turrington had so little control over her own life; it was only her nature to assert her authority over Rebecca. How she must have broken her mother's heart, when she turned away, no longer needing to hold the hand that had kept her steady and fully able to stand on her own two feet!

"Did he hurt you?" the woman said, stepping nearer,

peering into Rebecca's face and transporting her across the miles and years, planting her firmly back into the Caribbean soil like the banana trees and sugar cane that had saturated her senses in the market earlier today.

"No," she said, shaking her head, "Just my pride and my plans. I was kidnapped, but am unhurt. He is, thankfully, a man who praises piety above all else."

"Kidnapped?"

Now, the woman's eyes went wide.

Rebecca swallowed. She'd vowed to say so little, but that vow was made as the silent male sailor. Her voice and her truth had emerged, as the disguise had slipped as steadily away as the golden sun had sunk into the aqua sea earlier this evening. It would return, but for now had retreated. The question blazed as brilliantly as if it were still noon with the sun high overhead in the woman's eyes now.

Rebecca nodded.

"Who was it?" the woman said.
She threw her hand over her mouth instantaneously, as though trying to push the words back in.

The waves lapped against the moorings of the harbor, beating as a steady metronome against her mind. The air, now cooling with the waning moon from the oppressive mugginess of earlier today, encircled Rebecca and purged her of concealment.

"Lord Furton," she said, "He was a suitor who was turned away, but it seems that he faulted me for more than that. He thought that I was not pious and that I had turned his sister into a—"

Harlot. But I cannot say that, because you are—

Rebecca let the words fall, like dropped stones between them.

The woman blinked. Everything in Rebecca screamed out. Had she alienated the only friend that she had in this strange new land? She'd said too much; had Lady Turrington rebuked her now, she would have been fully justified.

"He has accused you of that and yet, he came to me," the woman said, the shock tumbling out with her words. Her mouth twisted into a smile, as though on the verge of laughing. Only the surprise, still registering in her eyes, contained it.

"Lord Furton was with you?" Rebecca said, "But he—surely, he did not come to you, seeking assistance?"

"He came to me months ago," she nodded, "paid the price, but just sat there crying in my lap all night, lamenting his sister's poor predicament, saying that he was unable to save her position, that the accursed Rebecca Turrington had turned her away and forced her into sin."

Rebecca shook her head, trying to make sense of what the woman before her said.

Molly.

Lord Furton's sister was Molly, whom she'd seen with Peter the blacksmith. Only, as she'd assured Lord Furton on the ship, Rebecca had done no such thing and Molly only served ale.

"I do not know what to say, but this is not true, none of it."

The girl nodded.

"I say," she said, "he has a possession in him, some tormenting obsession that dwells within him."

Rebecca nodded.

Yes, an obsession with me and with piety and with undoing the past.

She shook her head again, trying to clear the thoughts. She didn't dare consider what would become of her if Lord Furton found her again, knowing how greatly he wrongly blamed her. The girl peered at Rebecca, trying to determine if she were all right.

"You are in want of somewhere to stay?" she said now.

"I do not intend to remain long," Rebecca said. She allowed the words out only sparingly, not wanting to be overheard by any spies of Lord Furton.

"What do you need then? Your disguise is good, but be warned not to allow a woman too near to you."

"You were fooled? Truly?" Rebecca said, hoping to gain whatever help she could procure to aid her success.

"I thought you were a boy, yes. Thinkin' about it though, you do walk in a peculiar fashion. It must have been your gait that drew my attention."

"How should I walk?" Rebecca said, not wanting to leave any detail amiss.

"Well— " the girl said, stepping back on one foot and planting her hand on her hip, as she thought.

"Do I walk too softly? I did try not to be too dainty."

"No—no, I do not think 'twas that," she said, shaking her head.

"Here, walk for me and I can tell you."

Rebecca hated to wait around, wasting time. Somehow, though, she knew that the more believable her walk was the higher chance of success she had and it seemed an agreeable use of time. Feeling self-conscious, Rebecca took a step forward. Her feet clomped against the ground, as she struggled to overcompensate for her feminine feet.

"No, no, you are thinking about it too much now. Just walk like you were." Rebecca did her best to try not to think, as she walked in unfamiliar clothes trying to look like a man but also trying to look like she wasn't trying.

"There, you have it now."

"Well?" Rebecca said, after a few steps more.

"You need to look more confident."

"Confident?"

"If I am bold to say, you are awfully pale and you are not from here. I do not know how it is where you are from, but here men are certain of themselves. They have to be."

"Confident," Rebecca repeated, trying to summon all the

inches of her height as she straightened her shoulders.

"There, yes. 'Tis better," the girl said. Rebecca tried out her new stride.

"Oh, but you look like you care."

Rebecca turned to her, a question in her eyes.

"I do not understand."

"You have to look confident, but that you do not care."

Rebecca concentrated, threw back her shoulders and stepped forward in faith.

The girl walked around her, hand on hip still, evaluating her student's performance.

"Yes, I think 'tis just about right."

As she said the words, her eyes fell to Rebecca's feet.

"You will have to do somethin' about your shoes, though."

"They are all I have," Rebecca said, as she looked down at them apologetically.

"Well, I think I can get you a pair," the girl said.

"Could you?" Rebecca said, her eyes filling with hope.

"I think so," the girl nodded, "do you have any money?"

Rebecca's shoulders dropped.

"Regrettably, no."

The girl shook her head. Rebecca's chance had been lost.

"Must be mighty hard off without money. Well, never mind. I will give you what I can."

As she spoke the words, the girl drew out a pouch of coins hidden under her skirts.

Rebecca's eyes went wide. As the girl motioned that she should hold out her hand, Rebecca did so in disbelief. The tide was changing! Waters could only rise in desperation for a limited time and then the waters had to rush back out, and this time the tide waters would not be allowed to return. When the girl had returned with the promised boots and food, she gave Rebecca one final word of advice.

"I do not think I would be far off in my thinkin' to say that you hope to pass as crew on some ship to sail away."

Rebecca nodded, still feeling hesitant to show her hand. Surely, though, this girl had proven her loyalty.

"Well, if that is the case, then you would be better to find yourself near the back of the island."

"Oh?"

"The young ones gather there to sign-on. 'Twill help you blend in more."

"Shall I walk there?"

The girl tilted her head to the side in thought, as she stood with her arms crossed over her.

"I would think 'twould be better to paddle 'round the other side. There are some mighty thick trees on this island to muddle through. I guess you will have to do that," she said, casting a doubtful eye over Rebecca, as she was unsure if she'd make such a demanding journey.

"I have a boat," Rebecca said

"Do you? Then, by all means use it!"

Rebecca drew close to her cove, as she paddled near the shore. By now, the moon was high in the sky and it cast long silver curtains over the water below. When she had spotted the cove, she pulled the boat ashore having decided that a night's sleep would serve her best.

Wadding up some of the extra clothing from the trunk, Rebecca made a pillow and curled up to sleep. Lulled to slumber by the soft roll of the sea against the sand and a steady drip of water falling from the cave's ceiling, Rebecca slept long into the night. She stirred rarely, but woke long enough once to feed her ravenous stomach with some of the food the girl had supplied her with. Rebecca had been too exhausted to eat anything when she had first returned. When she'd eaten, she fell asleep more soundly.

Only when the black of night had been wiped from the sky did Rebecca awaken. It was not the light streaming into the cove, though, that awoke her. It was the sound of a boat that startled her awake. Rebecca's eyes went wide at the sight of the man standing in the mouth of the cave.

CHAPTER THIRTY

"Those who disappeared?" Caleb said to Marion.

"'Tis right, Adam," she said, nodding her head. Gray lines of hair spilled over her shoulders as she did.

"I do not understand. Who disappeared?"

"Oh lots of people, Adam. You are certain you will have no more tea?"

If he obliged her, would she offer answers with the beverage or would they be as nonexistent as invisible tea?

"Perhaps, a bit more, thank you," he said.

She sat, looking at him, and he began to wonder what was so enticing about his appearance until she said,

"Your cup, Adam."

"Oh yes, I am neglectful," he said, forming his hands around the air so that she might have something to fill.

She smiled,

"I see you have chosen a larger cup this time. Your appetite is growing."

"My appetite?"

"For truth," she said, as though it were obvious to all but him as she filled his cup with her brew from the air.

"Marion, who were these people who disappeared?" he said, hoping to coax answers from her.

"Oh young ones, old ones, men, women, friends, strangers."

He might as well have asked her if it would rain this day next year. The answer would have been just as vague and unsatisfactory.

"How many were there?"

"Oh dozens maybe. No, twenty-three. No, seventy-eight. Hmm, perhaps, ninety-one."

He looked at her, not believing this caricature he was seated with.

"What is it that you want me to do?"

"Find them, Adam. Bring them back."

He stood abruptly.

"How do you expect me to find people I know nothing about?" he said, agitated.

"Adam, you should not have done that. You have spilled your tea all over you," she said, shaking her head.

"Marion, you need help. You should go to town and see a doctor," he said, turning to leave.

"I am not ill, Adam. Besides, you are wrong. You know everything you need to know about the people. They are missing. They need your help. Their names, ages, even how many there are does not matter. What matters is that they need you."

The words hit him squarely in the chest, but he was too angry to admit that she had made perfectly logical sense. As he walked away, her words burned themselves into him, burrowing into his conscience.

When it came to these nameless strangers, Caleb was concerned with numbers and answers. If there weren't practical solutions, then the task seemed unable to be done. Yet, when it was Rebecca, he would do the impossible. Logic didn't matter when it came to finding her; it had been discarded, thrown against the wind, abandoned fully.

All he knew about Rebecca was that she was lost. All Marion had said about these people was that they were lost. But no, it wasn't that simple. He loved Rebecca.

But someone loves them too.

Caleb clenched his teeth and compressed his hands into fists. Cursed with the cloak of integrity, he knew what was required of him. As angry as he was that this could serve to further delay his reunion with Rebecca, it had fallen on him to find them—all of them. At the very least, he had to investigate further.

If finding Rebecca, when he was cautioned not to speak her name, had proved difficult then this seemed impossible. How could he find someone when he didn't know whom he was looking for? He wrestled with the question for most of the hour, as he wandered over the countryside. Returning to the town seemed the logical destination, but he was reluctant to return to where he'd been falsely accused, arrested and where he'd been threatened with that ill-fated journey across the river.

"Then I shall be your Virgil," the words pushed themselves through his muddled mind. Yes, a guide was what Caleb needed. With a heavy heart at the thought of wasted weeks, he turned toward home.

CHAPTER THIRTY-ONE

The man at the entrance to the cave stood well over six feet and his frame filled most of it. He was dressed in luxurious fabrics: damasks, velvets and silks, but his face lacked the grooming of a gentleman. A full dark beard and long cascading barrel curls made his already large face seem even bigger.

Seeing him, Rebecca scrambled to her feet, jamming the hat back down over her ears and hoping he had not noticed that she was a girl. From the look on his face, though, his concern was not that she might not be a boy but rather that she was here.

"I see you have lifted my clothes for your own," he said, in a deep voice that bellowed through the cave.

Rebecca's heart quickened as a wave of unease spread over her. She had no way to escape and no weapon to defend herself.

"I apologize. I did not know," she said, trying to deepen her voice as much as she could. Silence didn't seem like an option in this situation.

"Well, whose did you think they were? You have to have known they did not belong to you."

"Yes, I do apologize. I certainly did not think they belonged to someone who dresses as fine as you do."

"Hmm, flattery and a light touch of another's goods. You remind me of myself when I was a lad. How old are you, anyway?"

"Sixteen," Rebecca lied and then held her breath to see if it were a suitable answer. She had failed to ask the girl how old she looked.

"Sixteen," the man repeated, stepping forward. He nodded, as he saw Rebecca closer.

"Yes, you are the age I was when I began my career." He placed emphasis on career, as though implying that he meant something else. Rebecca breathed. She was fooling him; it was working! As the tension eased from her shoulders, under the realization that she did not seem to be in danger after all, something else became clear to her as well.

"You are—a pirate," she stuttered, amazed both by the fact that she was standing in a cave with a pirate and secondly that she had not realized that he was one until now.

"To whom do you attach the name 'pirate'?"

For a moment, she feared she had made some awful mistake that would prove costly to her ruse. Instead though, he spoke again convincing Rebecca that he was exactly whom she had suspected.

"I am a gentleman of the sea. I merely put what belongs where it belongs."

Oh, he was a pirate all right but, to Rebecca's surprise, she felt more at ease in his presence than around many others.

"Besides," he said, "George is a bigger pirate than I shall ever be."

"George?"

"Why King George, of course. At least he calls himself king." He drew out a sword as he spoke, cutting the air in half and suggesting that he would like to unseat the monarch.

"Do you not agree, Mr.— you did not mention your name."

"Haroldson," she said.

Well, at least she wanted that to be her name.

"Mr. Haroldson," the pirate echoed, "And your Christian name is?"

"Richard," Rebecca said, without first having considered it. As she spoke her brother's name, it felt right. Yes, she would forge a new identity based on the two men closest to her and with the intent to quickly be reunited with them.

"I am Phillip Trent," he said with a theatrical tip of his hat. His diplomacy struck her. He was obviously wealthy, but put on none of the airs that the gentry at home did.

Philip was looking at her and she realized that she had not yet answered his question. No one had ever posed such a question to Rebecca Turrington. Everyone knew the Turringtons were loyal servants of the king. Such talk was treasonous! Aside from that though, only Richard Turrington was bothered with matters of politics. No one cared what Rebecca thought on such matters. Her opinion was not even supposed to exist, save on the china patterns and lace designs of the tablecloths. Phillip did not seem to notice, though, and instead said,

"Exorbitant! Exorbitant!"

I never knew a pirate could be so elegant.

"Yes," she nodded.

Philip looked Rebecca over, so thoroughly that she feared he might cause his clothing she had taken to fall away, revealing her secret.

"So, how did you happen to find my hideaway?" he said, at last.

"It— well, it just kind of appeared," Rebecca said, not really sure what to say.

"Just appeared— haha! You speak in our manner already."

Philip turned his back on her and paced for a moment, before turning around to say,

"What do you say? You already make a fine match for the cut of my clothes. Will you also attach yourself to my crew?"

CHAPTER THIRTY-TWO

Sunlight shone through the boxes created by the spaces between the rungs of the ladder. Peter leaned it against the side of the wall. Testing its strength and sturdiness, he shook the ladder. When it held, Peter stepped onto the first rung.

Before climbing higher, he reached for the twisted metal he had fashioned into a weathervane. He had spent several hours crafting the delicate features and smoothing the metal until it shone. It contrasted with the roughness of his hands. Balancing the weathervane in one hand, he climbed the ladder with the ease afforded a man who did this many times before.

The sun caught the gleaming metal as he ascended toward the roof. He averted his eyes to avoid the blinding light. As he did, he looked down on the townsfolk below. They scrambled like birds for crumbs under his feet. Lacking education and wealth, a sense of power surged through Peter as he perched on his ledge high above the action below.

"Is that— "

Peter stared hard at the figure of a man walking quickly toward him. The man looked as though he were in a hurry and his arms swung at his sides as he walked. From this distance, Peter could not make out his features. Clouds of twirling smoke, coupled with the heat of the flames, had taken their toll on his eyesight. Years passing swiftly also did his eyes no favors. He thought the man's shape seemed familiar and he stopped at the top of the ladder to watch him approach. As he passed beside Peter now though he saw that no, this was not the man he thought it had been.

"Caleb Haroldson, you are pushing me to madness," he muttered under his breath. Since deciding to protect Caleb from the nosy newcomers to town, he had been convinced that Caleb was everywhere. The group of men that had appeared had left town, but they repeatedly returned to check-in on the whereabouts of native Caleb Haroldson.

Speculation leaked through all the streets and flowed liberally from the mouths of gossips to explain their interest in Caleb.

"I always thought he was a dull sort of a chap," Sam, the baker, had remarked.

"What has he done, anyway?"

As readily as the questions and suppositions flowed, there were no answers—at least, none that satisfied Peter. As the days passed and the men who sought him were still in the area, he began to suspect that Caleb must have become entangled in some dangerous business.

Perhaps, Rebecca Turrington is not dead after all. Perhaps, he has run away with her.

"Honestly Peter, be serious. You are like Molly and her gossiping friends."

Despite his muttered admonishment to the scandalous thought, it did not abandon him entirely. Instead, it rooted itself in his mind and an idea, no matter how unlikely it first seems, can be watered by the drought of answers. A hope for information can be clung to like a desert oasis and then anything becomes plausible.

Caleb Haroldson was not the sole topic of discussion for the busybodies of the town. Rebecca Turrington's death had been widely circulated through the streets. Just what had happened, though, to Richard Turrington? Lord and Lady Turrington had been away at the time of the fire, but no one had since seen them return. Surely, they would have wanted to see their son. Their absence had been explained by the inability to face what had become of their daughter. In Peter's mind, where doubt about Rebecca's death had now fully taken root, this explanation no longer made sense.

I have to find Richard.

"Ah Peter, why are you getting tangled up in such

things?" he muttered to the weathervane, as he secured it to the roof. As he let go of the spinning instrument and it held its position, he was well aware that he could not so easily distance himself from the strange goings-on of the Turringtons and Caleb Haroldson. The wind would not decide what direction he would face; a fire had decided for him.

As he descended the ladder, a voice behind him said,

"Do you know of somewhere I might stay?"

Peter turned to face the stranger.

"Are you speaking to me?"

The man nodded.

"Yes, do you know of some place I might stay?"

"There is a tavern down there."

"I thank you heartily. I will buy you a drink later."

"Yes, fine," Peter said, lost in his own thoughts— somewhere he was not accustomed to being— and brushing the man's words aside.

"Good. Just ask for Caleb Haroldson."

CHAPTER THIRTY-THREE

"What do you say, Richard Haroldson?" the pirate said.

"Yes."

The word flew from Rebecca's mouth like an escaped bird from a cage, before she could give his offer consideration.

"Well then Richard Haroldson, welcome aboard."

Philip thrust out his hand and she stared for a second.

Shake his hand!

No one had ever shook Rebecca's hand before and it felt unnatural to clasp her hand into that of a stranger's.

Oh goodness! Do not realize I am a girl.

Her silent plea came, as she felt the smallness of her hand in his own. A look of amusement played across his face and, for a moment, Rebecca thought her fear had been confirmed.

"Now, we best go. This port has grown suspicious of those like us and we are no longer as welcome as we once were," Phillip said. Only when he turned his back to Rebecca, did she let out a relieved sigh.

Having passed her most difficult test yet, Rebecca knew that this was only the beginning. Her ruse would have to stand firm as she worked alongside many men—who knew how many there could be?—while proving her worth as a sailor.

As a sailor.

The words jolted her. Already her knees felt shaky and threatened to buckle under her. She had barely managed to survive her last crossing and now this time she would have to not only tolerate the nauseating effects of the sea, but hide them as well. Ah, but on the other side of those tumultuous waves she would be rejoined with Caleb. This thought, far superior to the last, applied itself to her worries as honeyed salve.

"So, where do you come from, anyway?" Philip said, as he left the cove. Rebecca followed and watched as he untied a rowboat that was larger than her own. She stood beside Philip to help him push the boat off, as she said,

"England."

Rebecca thought it a funny question. Couldn't he see that she was pale and not tanned like those who were of the Caribbean? Well, perhaps, he couldn't tell. He might have poor eyesight, which would account for her appearance going unquestioned. The thought began to gnaw at her stomach, working its thorns into her.

Phillip was shaking his head.

That is it. He has realized.

Pointing to the other rowboat, he gestured for Rebecca to leave his side.

What have I done? Is he upset that I come from England? Or, has he realized my secret?

Whatever the reason, he was clearly dismissing her before she had even received an adequate chance to prove her ineptitude.

"Best bring that one along, too. Can never have too many supplies, eh?" he said.

"Yes— uh, yes," Rebecca stumbled in her words.

Pushing off from the shore and paddling close behind Philip's own boat, she was struck by the civility of his words. He was certainly a man of status since he had spoken of the crew as his and yet, he lacked any of the loftiness that swirled around the lords at home.

Home. The place seemed so far removed, and not just by distance, that it sounded out of place in her thought.

Rebecca, do be sensible!

On the horizon she fixed her eyes, expectantly searching for the ship. Rebecca watched, as Philip deftly raked through the waters. He must have been at least as old as her father, but he embodied none of the stodginess that Rebecca associated with men of his age. Nothing, save the rusty lock on Philip's chest, seemed to age in this tropical version of life. Leaving behind the sordid streets and threats of Lord Furton, Rebecca was again lured by the color that she had only dreamed of before. Tropical plants stood as sentinels along the rocky coast. It was not until they were within a couple of minutes rowing from it that Rebecca saw the ship.

"Oh!" she said aloud, without intending to. As though it had materialized from the air surrounding the land, a ship larger than she had expected rose from the waters. From the mast, a flag fluttered bearing the emblematic Jolly Roger.

Rebecca swallowed, as she saw it.

Rebecca, what are you getting yourself into? Home, you are going home. Just remember that.

"There she is," Philip said, with pride, as he turned to call over his shoulder to her, "Mr. Haroldson, would you not say 'tis a fine vessel to carry us to America?"

CHAPTER THIRTY-FOUR

Peter jumped off the last rung of the ladder and sprinted to catch up to the stranger. He put his hand on the man's arm, catching him and forcing him to stop.

"What is your name?" Peter said. The man's brow creased at the abruptness of Peter's behavior.

"I told you, Caleb Haroldson," he said calmly.

Peter shook his head.

The man tried to free himself from Peter's hold, but still he held the man's arm.

"What is your name?"

"Caleb Haroldson," the man repeated, becoming annoyed.

"No," Peter said, "you do not understand. I know Caleb Haroldson and you are not him."

"Do you not think more than one person can have the same name?" he said, pulling his arm free of Peter's grip.

The question caught Peter off guard. Perhaps, he was overreacting. But, then again—

Peter shook his head, to free himself from the entangling web of thoughts. The mind's trickery and penchant for casting doubt proved a more cumbersome load to bear, than the crates of raw metal he transported.

"What is your business here?" Peter said, unwilling to distance himself from this man he viewed as an imposter.

"Just passing through," the man said. His voice had remained calm as he had spoken the words, but he had made a mistake that had not gone unnoticed by Peter. He had looked him straight in the eye, when before his vision had wandered. Overcompensating for his lie, this man had revealed himself as a fraud.

Peter stepped closer, feeling the full power of his muscular arms and strong back that contrasted with this slip of a man.

"Both of us know that you are lying," he said, in a low voice, "Now, I suggest that you tell the truth in haste if you intend to leave this town."

"Are you making threats to me?" the man said, puffing out his chest, but looking rather like a spaniel matched against a pit bull.

"I am paying you the courtesy of letting you choose what happens to you," Peter said, his hand balling into a fist at his side. His fingers ached to stretch the truth from this man, the way that he bent the metal to his liking. Violence had never accompanied Peter as a leading trait, but his friend was in danger. After the pain Peter had inadvertently caused Caleb, he would not tolerate that.

The man looked at Peter, narrowing his eyes. Frustration clustered around his temples and he looked as though very little was preventing him from lashing out against Peter. The stormy disposition had settled over him, as quickly as a sun-filled day can turn cloudy in spring. If he had known Peter's true character and reluctance to act on his threats, he may have hit Peter squarely in the jaw as Caleb had and left him alone with only questions. This man did not know Peter, though, and decided that his safety was the pressing concern.

"Perhaps, I am not the only man to use the name of Caleb Haroldson that is not as he seems," he said, in a low voice.

"What do you mean?" Peter said.

"Just that, truthfully you would fare better if you were wiser in the company you keep."

The man was speaking in circles and Peter felt his patience disappear.

"Speak plainly," Peter said, gruffly.

"Speak plainly," the man repeated, dancing on the edge of coyly playing with Peter and knowing that he must tell him the answer, if he were to remain safe.

"Tell me," Peter said, his nose flaring as he spoke through clenched teeth.

"Fine. Here it is. Caleb Haroldson has dangerous friends."

"You speak the truth," Peter said, pounding his fist into his palm.

"You?" the man said, with a laugh, "No, you are nothing compared to these men."

"What men?"

"Traitors."

"Traitors to what?" Peter said, his voice becoming louder.

"To the king. Caleb Haroldson is a traitor to England."

CHAPTER THIRTY-FIVE

America?

Rebecca's hand froze on the paddle, as she stared at Philip in the rowboat and, beyond him, the mammoth pirate ship. Its masts that had at first risen so majestically, moments before, certain to speed her safely home now raised their arms like a cage ready to entrap her. She would be carried away, not to her home but, farther from it.

"Ah, if only I could spend all my days there," Philip said.

Rebecca's fingers twitched on the paddle.

"We will not stay in America?" she said.

"Alas no. They are not as friendly as they once were to us. Though, with these rumblings of rebellion, we might prove useful once again." He spoke the words, sounding cheerful near the end.

Rebellion?

Rebecca had no idea what Philip meant, but his tone had once again conveyed welcome.

"Of course, you can stay in America, if you wish. My crew is free to stay or leave at liberty, provided we are not betrayed."

"Oh, I would never betray you," she said hastily, finding comfort in the freedom of his words.

"If I had suspected you would, Mr. Haroldson, I would not have invited you to join us," he said, with a laugh.

The icy shock of the destination cracked and Rebecca's hands were free to paddle after him again.

They drew nearer to the ship and a rope ladder was flung over the side for them. An eeriness prickled over Rebecca's spine, as she recalled Lord Furton's raspy voice,

"Up the ladder, if you please, Miss Turrington."

Today, there was no coercion. There was no prompting from Philip or the others. No hand was forcing her journey, as so often had happened before. With pride and a surge of independence, Rebecca stepped onto the first rung of the ladder.

The others looked at her as she boarded. Only one or two stared a few seconds longer than, perhaps, they would have when meeting a more masculine-looking new member of crew. Confidence enrobed her and she soon found herself nodding to those assembled around her.

"Now, Mr. Haroldson, will you swab the deck for us?"

Swab the deck?

She could hardly pass for a sailor, if she knew none of the jargon.

Furton, you are a fiend. You prevented me from hearing the sailors speak!

Another sailor, looking close in age to Rebecca's adopted persona, appeared with a bucket and mop and held them out to her.

"Yes, I would be happy to," she said.

The others set about on their own business and no one paid her much attention. Rebecca concentrated so thoroughly on her task that she did not realize that they had set sail, until she looked up and found herself surrounded by blue. The mild swell of waves quickly swallowed the shrinking coastline.

When they were at sea, many of the men who had busied themselves with tying the sails and pulling up the anchor now wandered on the deck. In an odd sort of way, Rebecca felt as though she were watching her father and his friends drink Cognac and meander through the parlor as she stood concealed behind a pillar. Now, in place of her pillar, stood the mop. The conversation flowed freely between the men, as it had so often in her own home, but something struck Rebecca as entirely different.

Her father's friends spoke of hunting but these men spoke of the places they had been, of the dreams they had for their lives, of politics and of the unfolding world. Oh, assuredly her father and his friends must have spoken of politics, but not like this. This was so unlike anything that she had experienced before. The variation in accents alone was enough to hold her attention and required her to force herself to remember to continue with the mopping. Yes, that's what it was. More than the variety of the conversation, it was the assortment of men that struck her. Spanning several generations, their skin ranging from the palest white to the deepest black, and their clothes coming from every style, fabric, and bracket of wealth, Rebecca felt herself standing amongst a microcosm of the world. Two thoughts spun her mind in directions it had not previously been.

So this is what you meant of democracy, Mr. Plato. Hmm – I wonder if Caleb would be agreeable to signing on with me for the life of a pirate.

CHAPTER THIRTY-SIX

Caleb came to the edge of the tree line, where he had walked with Rebecca so often before. Returning weeks after he had left, without Rebecca, made him feel the sting of defeat. He had no other options, but to start over. Just exactly what Caleb hoped to gain from the Irish monk, he could not be certain. Perhaps, the offer to be his guide had applied only to entering the hole and descending into the chamber where Richard had lain. Still though, with the uncertain tide of being caught in an unstable netherworld, seeking out his Virgil was the only spark of hope.

Branches cracked loudly under Caleb's feet, as he walked through the forest.

"*Would you like another cup of tea? How about some invisible people to go along with it?*" Marion's voice taunted him as a persistent wind darted between the limbs, rattling the leaves and his senses.

A noise drew Caleb's attention to a hollowed stump. A russet squirrel peeked its head out, but seemed uninterested in Caleb and scampered away again.

If only I might so easily run away.

He shook his head to clear it of the thought, ashamed of himself. Shirking his responsibility was neither a habit nor an option.

"Think," he said, aloud. Only a hazy stream of discombobulated characters, who had paraded through his life these past few weeks, stood as answer. They reeled backward through his mind.

A crazy woman who entrusted me with a mission to find those that have disappeared. The man who sprung me from jail, but then spoke of crossing the river. Dandelion's new companion, the old man, who pretended not to know me and then had me arrested when he realized I love Rebecca. The men beside the fire. The Irish monk taking care of Richard. Rebecca, my dear sweet Rebecca. I feared you were lost, but then the hope that you are still alive appeared.

The ground under Caleb's feet seemed unfamiliar as he sifted through his memories to not only make some sense of all that had happened, but to find the hidden passageway to the tunnel. When he had first followed the monk here, he had not trusted the stranger who had appeared at his time of grief. Believing that he had lost Rebecca, Caleb had been utterly distraught. Taking note of which tree stump he had passed or how far into the forest he had walked had not been his priority on that night. But on this night, oh how he wished that he had paid more attention!

It had rained considerably in recent days, further complicating his success. Pools of water washed out what little variation there was between a deliberate clump of dirt and an inconsequential rock pile.

"Where are you?" he said in desperation, aloud to the trees.

"Whoo who?" The mournful cry of an owl answered him.

A scamper in the leaves drew his eyes to a bare patch of ground. The squirrel had returned, but then darted away again. Yes, this looked vaguely familiar. Caleb sank to the plot of land. The moist ground soaked through the legs of his pants as he knelt. Scooping up the dirt, the mud oozed between his fingers. Heavy in his hands, the mud slowed his progress as he struggled to reach where the dirt no longer lay. In anticipation, he clung to the hope of feeling his fingers fall against the door that concealed the tunnel.

"Come on, where are you?" he muttered, clearing more mud away and dumping it in a pile beside him.

Rain began to fall in soft drops on Caleb's neck, as he bent over the mound of earth. The weight of the water soon increased, until giant drops catapulted themselves against his skin. Amassing in expanding pools, the rains swept the dirt back across the land he had cleared. A muddied river flowed over his hands. In vain, Caleb tried to hold back the flood but he was unable.

"Something else that is beyond me!" he said, pounding his fists against the land and sending puddles sloshing over him.

Heaviness, which could only be from the weight of another person, pressed against his shoulder. Caleb tried to turn to see who it was but a jab to the back, most likely from a knee, prevented him from doing so.

"Who are you?" Caleb said. As answer, a band came across his mouth. There would be no speech. Caleb struggled to stand, but the weight he'd first felt on his shoulder pushed him back down. Squirming to turn his neck resulted only in a blackout of all around him. A heavy band had been wrapped across his eyes as a blindfold. Caleb felt the oppression of a group's persuasive power, as another set of hands confined his own with a coarse rope. Blindfolded, gagged and bound, Caleb's attackers pulled him to his feet.

CHAPTER THIRTY-SEVEN

"So, what is your story?" a sandy-haired, bronzed skin sailor said to Rebecca. She looked up from her mopping, to see him pulling in a thick rope from the side of the boat. After Philip had paired her with the mop yesterday, she had been unsure if she were expected to continue in the duty or not. No one had assigned her the task, but it was a job that she knew she was capable of doing. Passing for a sailor was sure to prove much more difficult, if she were asked to complete something that she knew nothing of but that a sailor would be competent of performing.

The men around her, young and old, seemed to ooze with strength. She found herself watching as the sailor pulled in the rope. The muscles of his back pushed against the fabric of his shirt and his arms seemed to heave with life of their own.

Rebecca, stop staring!

Feeling an inward blush at studying the man in so many details, she realized his question had gone unanswered.

What is my story?

A glimmer of panic prickled against Rebecca's spine.

What shall I tell him?

The rope slid through his rough hands, coiling like a snake at his feet.

Just tell him the truth.

The thought struck her with such force that it nearly sent her tumbling backward. She grabbed the rail of the deck and plunged into the story, regaling him with a condensed version of the truth.

"My father and I did not see eye-to-eye on the position I ought to take in the world."

"A runaway." The sailor nodded, not sounding at all surprised. With a tug, he pulled up the end of the rope. A flailing fish squirmed on the floor as he pulled a knife from his pocket and, with one quick movement, brought the shining blade down. It pierced through the fish, cutting off its life and spilling the rawness of the sea onto the deck. Slicing through its skin, the sailor severed the head from the fish.

"Did you run away, too?" Rebecca said, watching his movements to learn what she could. Perhaps, striking a friendship with this man could prove beneficial to her acquiescence.

The sailor shook his head, as he lopped off the tail and the fins of the fish. His hands moved quickly, as if the action were something he had been born doing.

"I cannot say that I have. John Prentice has been many a thing, but never a runaway."

"Is that your name?"

"'Tis true," John said, as he wiped his forehead with the back of his hand. Blood from the fish dripped over his fingers.

"Richard," she said, sticking out her hand. Philip had shaken hands with her and she wanted to blend is as best as she could. John did not look up, though, as he continued to cut away pieces of the fish and she dropped her hand to the side. Perhaps, only captains shook hands. There was plenty she still had to learn.

"Well, Richard," John said, as he looked up now, "you are the first Richard I have ever known who was on this side of things."

"How is that?" Rebecca said, trying desperately hard not to scrunch up her nose as she asked the question. It seemed a most un-pirate thing to do.

"All the Richards I have known have been sons of some wealthy overseer. Not the life I would like to live," John said, looking up again as his blade flashed over the fish, scraping away its scales.

"Nor I," Rebecca said, the claustrophobia of the Turrington estate with its endless line of suitors, such as Lord

Furton, crossing through her mind.

John raised an eyebrow, but resisted asking if this were the life that Rebecca had run away from.

"Do you know how to make a hammock?" John said, eying Rebecca as if the answer might be hidden in her clothing.

Am I supposed to know how?

She had hesitated a fraction of a second too long and John had received his answer.

"I can show you how."

"I would be obliged, if it does not trouble you greatly," Rebecca said and then felt overtly female for the remark. But no, she had worried over nothing. John did not seem to consider anything out of the ordinary as he said,

"'Twill be more comfortable than sleeping on the deck."

Rebecca blinked. She had spent the night in a corner of the deck, nestled against barrels, rather than venturing below deck to find a wooden bunk where the others had bedded.

"Unless you desire a bunk below deck, of course."

No, she certainly didn't want that. A repeat voyage from last time, confined without any air, was something she was going to avoid if she had a choice.

"I would rather stay up here, if 'tis all right with everyone," she said, hoping she had not said the wrong thing.

"Pay it no heed. Philip lets us sleep wherever we wish. I sleep out here myself sometimes. 'Tis nice to lay back and look at the stars. There is more air up here too. Do you know what I mean, to help with the seasickness?"

Rebecca looked at him. Had he discovered that she was an imposter? Was he baiting her like his fish?

He looked up, but none of the malice she had imagined was present in his face.
She nodded,

"Yes, the fresh air helps."

"*That* is my story," John said, plucking the fish up from

the deck and standing up, "freedom. Seems to me that men ought to be free to take what is theirs for the taking."

He held the fish up for illustration.

"Yes, sir, I shall be glad if this war starts. We will be able to take back what belongs to us."

Rebecca nodded slowly. She was confused, but John interpreted the nod as agreement.

"Despite your accent, I figured you had left that life behind."

My accent? Should I be masking my accent, as well?

The thought had not occurred to her before in her dedication to concealing all else. Suddenly feeling careless, Rebecca watched as John bent back down to spear the head of the fish with the blade of the knife.

"Old King George will be surprised when he finds himself in such a state, no?"

CHAPTER THIRTY-EIGHT

Prodded by a heavy elbow in his back, Caleb moved forward. With no use of his hands, no vision and an inability to speak, he was completely at their mercy—whoever they were. Branches rubbed abrasively against his skin. Scratched by brambles and thick undergrowth, Caleb was pushed forward.

Knock them out, then run! And do what? Fall in a tangled heap!

Caleb's mind sought for a plan to whittle away from the stump of the problem, but no options were forthcoming. Searching for a means of escape was proving useless and so his thoughts turned toward the possible identity of his captors.

The likelihood of the men beside the campfire going through the trouble of tracking him down didn't seem to make much sense to Caleb. Wouldn't it have been better to attack him before? The old man that had been with Dandelion might have had a throng of assailants as his accomplice. As Caleb considered this, though, it too seemed unlikely.

The ground under Caleb's feet grew uneven. His knees bent at the shift in slope of the terrain, but the men around him did not slow their steps. He stumbled against the back of someone, for which he was given a strong jab from the man's elbow into his ribs.

"Uhh!" Caleb groaned heavily, but the gag blurred and muted the involuntary reaction. Half-expecting someone to sharply reprimand him for it, it was then that he realized that the gang around him was silent. No one had spoken a word to him.

A burning seized his body from the blow to his ribcage. With each step forward, it roared in unnamable pain. Under his feet, the dirt became small pebbles.

The river.

He knew where they were.

"I shall hide the silver plates in the river," Rebecca's

faraway voice said. He clung to the memory of the words, caressing them in his mind, as though he were holding her in this moment.

As confirmation to his realization, his feet felt the slosh of the waters rush over him. The leather of his shoes overran with the river's water. His stockings sopped up the moisture, emerging his feet in the soggy chilling waters.

Fear gripped Caleb, as a terrible thought played over his mind; did they intend to leave him here, to discard him without knowing his name?

Without knowing my name.

Did they even know who he was? He had assumed that they did. Now, though, he felt confusion mix with the fear. Why should they go through so much trouble for a stranger? It didn't seem to make—

Bam! Caleb stumbled backward at the abrupt jolt to his leg. Rather than water, the last step had knocked him against something solid. Had he run into a boulder? But no, that didn't seem right. There had been a difference in texture and hardness than stone would have provided.

"Step in." The words startled Caleb, who had become accustomed to the silence.

Step in? A boat! Yes, it must be a boat.

His legs bent awkwardly, as he attempted to climb into a boat that he couldn't see. Without use of his hands to feel the boat's outline, he pressed his knees against the sides to try to determine how big it was and where he should move. The idea of climbing into a boat seemed easy enough. The practicality of doing it, when so restricted, was proving impossible.

Impatient at his lack of progress, the men decided to move Caleb themselves. Gruffly, their hands closed around his limbs as they lifted him into the boat.

Kick them!

Caleb knew the idea could prove risky, but it seemed

some small option had been provided. He struggled to break free with his leg, but the men held him tightly. Writhing was accomplishing nothing, other than intensifying the pain in his ribs.

The restrictive hold of the men pushed Caleb down toward the floor of the boat. With a thud, he landed on the boards. Tension converged across Caleb's neck, gripping his muscles more tightly than those of the fleshy hands of the men. His body ached at the rough treatment, but his growing concern was rooted entirely in his mind.

Will I be left here?

Being held captive seemed the better alternative than being left alone, bound at the bottom of a boat. With no one paddling, the current would have its way and carry him farther downstream. As the river widened, the boulders grew larger and would rise from the water as taunting columns of disaster. Without benefit of sight, Caleb would not see them in time. He would have no knowledge of them, until the boat was pounded against their jagged bodies. And, if by chance or some miracle, the boat happened to navigate safely around these obstacles, he was faced with the prospect of drifting out to sea as the river merged with the ever-expansive waters.

Caleb tried to swallow, but the gag prevented him from doing so. No, there would be no means for him to suppress what would come.

CHAPTER THIRTY-NINE

"Where is Caleb Haroldson?" Peter said, grabbing the man's arm.

The man shrugged and turned to walk away. Peter took hold of the man's shoulder, closing his wide hand over him.

"The plot thickens—" he said, with a devilish glint in his eyes. Despite recognizing Peter's persuasive power, it was proving difficult to change from his teasing way.

"What are you speaking of?" Peter said, growling like a tiger tracking its prey who is too busy laughing to notice.

"You not knowing where the other Caleb Haroldson is suggests that he is missing and it is a most interesting development."

Peter stepped forward and his towering presence over the man drew the attention of onlookers.

"Perhaps, though, if you insist upon further conversation we ought to do it someplace private. We seem to be drawing a crowd."

"Why should you want to get me alone?" Peter hissed, speaking in a low voice.

The prospect of so slight a figure suggesting that he wanted to rid himself of the protection of the town either meant, the clever expression he wore was merely a ruse or there was a trick at hand. Peter had not left this unnoticed. A veil of the smugness, which the man had worn, transferred to Peter's face now.

"You should not look triumphant at your deduction or even surprised at my suggestion," the man said, not taking kindly to the idea of someone else looking so pleased with himself, "Really, 'tis quite simple. We both want to find Caleb Haroldson, the other one that is."

"The real one," Peter corrected. The man did not reply, but instead he began walking away to show that he had made the decision for them. Peter hated the role of follower, but supposing this man were not baiting him to a dead-end but did indeed have information, following his lead was unavoidable.

The buildings of the town soon fell away and were replaced by thick congregations of trees. Silver splashes of the river, which beckoned to him to cast in his fishing rod, now lay placid beside them. In the distance the river widened and grew in ferocity, as it cascaded over the tightly-grouped rocks. A man would have to ride for several hours until he came to a place where it slowed to a luring pace again before sweeping into the welcoming sea. The man continued to walk and Peter felt a growing discomfort. Just where were they headed, anyway? Any threat to their privacy had been left far behind.

A soft babble of water whispered to Peter, as they approached the river.

"I think that is far enough, do you not?"

The man turned and shrugged,

"As you wish."

"Why did you bring us out so far?" Peter said, his eyes moving over the landscape to seek out any possible threats.

"If you are looking for men to jump from behind the trees, there are none," the man said. With a flush of foolishness descending over him, Peter retrained his gaze on the man.

"No, I merely thought it would be pleasant to sit beside the river. I passed it on my way into town. It reminded me of the Thames in an odd sort of a way. Have you been to London?"

Peter shook his head, "Tell me who you are."

"Someone you ought to trust."

"Why is that?" Peter said. His cuffs of his sleeves chafed against his skin uncomfortably, as though the fabric were vexed with each stalling word of the imposter.

"Because, I am protecting England," he said, drawing something from his pocket. It was a watch that he clicked open, examined the time and then clasped shut again. Rather than clicking into place, though, the watch remained open.

"Truthfully, 'tis— " he said, turning away from Peter.

Peter's eyebrows rose. Taking the man by the arm and spinning him back around, he said,

"Where did you get that watch?"

"I bought it," he said, pulling himself loose from Peter's grip, "truthfully, if we are going to work together, I must insist that you refrain yourself."

"Who did you buy it from?" Peter said, taking hold of the man again. The man's forehead creased at the destructible nature of Peter.

"Some peddler," he said, trying to break free of Peter's grasp once again.

"What peddler?" Peter said, taking the man by the shoulder this time.

"How should I know his name? Do you ask the name of every man you buy something from?" he said. Then, tilting his head to the side, he added, "Well, you do, I suppose? Speaking of names, you have not told me yours."

"Caleb Haroldson," Peter said.

The man's eyebrows rose,

"Parents are not very creative around here with names, are they?" he said dryly. He looked at his arm as though considering pulling free once again. Then, half-shrugging to himself, he decided that it would prove pointless with Peter still here to grab him again.

"That watch," Peter said, "belongs to the real Caleb Haroldson."

Surprised amusement splashed across the man's face, but Peter saw none of it. His interest lay solely in the thought that had planted itself in his mind. A flash of anger transformed his face into a mounting storm.

"You killed him. Speak the truth," he said, grabbing both shoulders of the man now. The man's eyes darted up at the rough treatment.

"You killed him and took his identity."

"Please," the man said, sobering at the treatment and attempting to appeal to Peter's logic, "Why would I want to find him if I did that? I promise you, I did not kill Caleb Haroldson."

"Why should I believe you?" Peter said, shaking the man. His size dwindled in Peter's rough embrace. A passerby might have noted that it looked as though a bear were shaking a small frightened leaf.

"Because, it is the truth," the man said.

"Tell me what happened. What have you done?" Peter said, shaking the man again.

"Please, I did not hurt Caleb Haroldson. I never even saw the man before."

"Then why are you so interested in him? Why are you here? Why do you have his watch?"

"The watch is merely coincidental. I know, 'tis odd but 'tis true. As for the rest—" he said, his voice lowering, suggesting that he really did not want to disclose the information but recognized he must.

"As for the rest, what?" Peter roared, closing the gap between the man's face and his own.

"I—I was sent to watch a group he is known to be associated with."

He paused.

"Sent by whom?" Peter said, sensing that there was more.

"By the king. I am a spy for his majesty."

CHAPTER FORTY

Caleb felt the boat push away from the land.

Rebecca, I love you. I am sorry I failed you.

He waited, not at all prepared to accept his certain fate, but knowing it would come. He feared its imminence but hoped, that if it must happen, it would be over soon.

I thought I would have had more time. My years were not enough for a life.

Blackness closed around Caleb and the thoughts began to erode whatever remaining shreds of hope he had. Rotting thoughts began to decay the resolve he had clung to, since beginning his search. Being thrown in jail, strange conversations, none of it mattered anymore. Even the ominous threat of *across the river* rang hollow in his ears. Perhaps, he should never have run away from it. But, none of that mattered now. He had played his cards; he had made a choice and he would lose. It was not going across the river that he should have feared, but rather going down it. That's where his destruction would reside.

Sloshing waves lapped against the boat, sending a spray of water over him. This would be it. The waters must be rougher here to cause the churn-up of the river. The rocks, invisible to his eyes, taunted him. Despite not being able to see, Caleb shut his eyes tight and waited. He made some feeble attempt at a prayer, but the words would not come. It seemed useless to pray for safety, when his outcome was guaranteed.

"There!"

The voice broke through Caleb's panic and took him by such surprise that he felt stunned to have heard it. A tightness knotted itself in Caleb's chest. Overwhelmed by the prospect of life, if indeed he were not alone in the boat, he felt tears moisten his eyes.

His heart thumped wildly, enthusiastic at the idea of pumping for several more years. Attempting to control it, so that he could quiet the rush of blood in his ears, Caleb lay as still as possible. He listened for some sound, to confirm that his mind had not played some monstrous trick on him.

Only the sound of the water, growing in intensity as he moved farther downstream, poured against Caleb's ears.

Please, let me hear it again. I have to live! I have to!

A surge of renewed vigor sprang from him, as he heard the sound of a shoe scraping against the bottom of the boat.

"There, yes." The words rang as the most beautiful he'd ever heard. Life had not given up on him.

Caleb's back banged against the side of the boat. Surely, the men had not been so careless as to allow it to crash. The rocking slosh of the waves gave way to the bumpiness of a boat being dragged across a pebbled shore. A commotion of docking the boat and strong arms half-pulling and half-prodding Caleb along resulted in the feeling of ground settling comfortably under his feet. Tempted to celebrate that he had survived the journey, he had been convinced would end in tragedy, he soon sobered to reality. Caleb was still held captive and all that he was assured of was temporary survival. There were no guarantees of anything else.

"Sit," he heard someone, whose voice sounded different from the two in the boat, say. Caleb struggled to do so, but was in the end pushed backward and plunked down heavily on the stump of a tree.

"For goodness' sake, untie his hands. This is ridiculous!"

"Sir?"

"Just do it!"

Caleb felt the cold of the steel blade on his wrist, as the man slid it between the rope and his hands. Feeling the bonds around his hands loosen, Caleb stretched his hands as the rope fell away.

"Now, no sudden movements," the voice that had commanded he be untied said, "Fold your hands in your lap.

There, where we can see them."

Caleb did as instructed. He was still gagged and blindfolded. There were at least three different voices around him and at least one of the men was of formidable size, since he had both the strength to lift Caleb from the boat and the force to cause him to sit. No, it would be too dangerous to try to outmaneuver these men, without benefit of his eyes.

Caleb's ribs and back ached from the rough treatment, but he pushed aside the pain, relieved to be alive. And whoever his captors were, he had presumably been given the courtesy of a face-to-face meeting with their leader.

From the treetops, birds twittered happily. Their songs spun a connective thread across the branches over their heads and Caleb wondered what events would weave his own story.

"What is your name?" The deep voice of the man in charge said. Caleb said nothing, still unable to speak because of the gag. Realizing the reason for his silence, the man said,

"Let him speak."

As the gag fell away, Caleb's lungs heaved at the rush of fresh air. He hesitated for a moment in answering. His identity had already caused a ruckus with the man who'd sprung him from jail. Being caught in a lie seemed the more dangerous option, though, and so he spoke the truth.

"Caleb Haroldson."

"Hmm—Caleb Haroldson," the man repeated, "Do I not know your name from somewhere?" A wave of dread washed over Caleb, burying his comfort with his decision for the truth. With a snap of his fingers the man said,

"Oh yes, you are that cabinet maker, are you not?"

Cabinet maker? That is why you know me?

"Yes, that is right," Caleb said. His words were spoken with the stall of caution.

"Take off his blindfold," the man said.

"Sir?"

"Take it off! Do not question me. I know what I am doing."

Caleb felt the knot loosen in the fabric at the back of his head. His vision was blurred and he blinked back the stream of sunlight, trying to see. As his eyes opened fully, they watered at the brightness. Caleb blinked again to suppress the moisture. Lifting his eyes to the figure before him, his breath caught in his throat.

"You?"

CHAPTER FORTY-ONE

"A spy for the king?" Peter said, in disbelief.

"Yes," the man said.

"How do I know that you— "

Peter's voice trailed off, as he looked at the man before him. If there were one thing that Peter could be confident of it was that thoughts could be cumbersome and fickle, but his ability to tell if someone were telling the truth was always reliable.

He pried his fingers away from the man, feeling that he really ought to have controlled his temper better. One couldn't go around roughing up spies for the king.

"Is Caleb in some kind of trouble?"

"As I said, he associates with a dangerous crowd."

"But, what crowd? He shared a house with me and I never— "

You shared a house with him and you never knew he was in love with Rebecca Turrington, until Molly told you. Oh you might be able to read the truth in someone's face, Peter, but there certainly does seem to be a lot that slips past you unnoticed.

"People are not always as they seem," the spy said. He braced himself for Peter's rough hold. When Peter did not lay a hand on him, he said,

"So, I should have told you I was a spy in the beginning, then. It certainly would have prevented a lot of wrinkles in my clothing. Though you can, of course, understand why it is not practical to disclose such information, even for the sake of an uncreased coat."

Peter's brow furrowed.

"You do not seem to take your work very seriously."

"What do you mean?"

"You have told me that Caleb Haroldson is in dangerous company, but you do not seem to care. I would say you care more about your coat than Caleb."

"Why should I care?"

"What?" Peter said, his face wrinkling far more than the spy's coat had.

"Look, do you care about what happens to each piece of iron you work? 'Tis your labor. I care about my coat, because it is my coat. Caleb Haroldson is only my work. He is my weathervane, so to speak. When I am finished, I no longer care, so why should I care now?"

"Because," Peter said, "he is not a weathervane; he is a person. He is my friend."

"And as I said before, perhaps, you would be better off with some other friends."

Peter shook his head.

"But, it seems that you are determined not to take my advice, so we might as well get on with it."

"On with it?" Peter said.

"You do want to find Caleb Haroldson, do you not?"

Peter nodded. The idea of working with a man who compared Caleb to a piece of iron unsettled his nerves. He had come this far, though, and Peter had vowed to protect Caleb.

"Good. Now, what do you know about Caleb Haroldson?" the spy said. He straightened his coat as he spoke, demonstrating that he really did think of Caleb only as an assignment.

"He is my friend," Peter said.

What am I supposed to say? Do I tell him everything I know or will that put Caleb at risk?

"Yes, that I know, but tell me something useful."

Peter bristled at the comment, unaccustomed to being insulted. Other men, wiser ones, took note of Peter's size and considered their words before speaking.

How did so vexing a man become a spy, anyway?

"Well, some men were looking for him."

"Ah," the spy said, shifting his attention from his coat to Peter, "Now, we are getting somewhere. Who were they?"

"Do you not think I would have found him by now, if I knew that answer?" It was difficult not to be irritated, when the comments raked acrimoniously across him.

The spy pursed his lips and tilted his head to the side, as though to question Peter's statement. Then, thinking better of it, he settled for the more refined answer.

"All right, well, tell me what they looked like."

"Big hats, long coats, a group of them maybe— "

"Three or four?"

"More like five or six."

The spy looked at Peter.

"Why, is that important?" Peter said, noting his reaction.

"It may be. Tell me, have you ever heard Caleb Haroldson speak of Lord Furton?"

CHAPTER FORTY-TWO

Caleb's eyes adjusted into focus on the figure before him. It was Rebecca's eyes that looked at him. It was Richard's mouth that moved in speech.

"I mean, Lord Turrington," Caleb mumbled, to mask the surprise of the more informal "you" that he had first spoken.

"You are familiar with me," Lord Turrington said, nodding to accept the fact and not sounding surprised.

Father to the woman I love. The reason she planned to run away. Oh, I know you, all right.

Somehow, in the middle of the forest, these labels seemed out of place and didn't fit this man. He looked like a king at court perched on a stump, much like the one Caleb sat on now. Despite his mannerisms, Lord Turrington was dressed in the regalia of a hunting party and did not look unmatched to this scene.

"Mr. Haroldson, was it?"

Caleb nodded.

"Yes, that is right."

"Well, Mr. Haroldson, I do apologize for the rough treatment."

You might have taken the trouble to discover 'twas me, before you put my life at risk.

"You had your reasons," Caleb said, doing his best to remember his manners when in the company of a lord. He didn't dare say what he really thought, having already received a foretaste of any obstinate behavior. He had merely been looking for the door that the monk had shown him to try and find—

Richard. Is he protecting Richard? Perhaps, I did stumble onto the secret passageway, after all.

"I am glad that you are so understanding, Mr. Haroldson. Now, I must insist that you tell me what you were doing."

You do not seem very trusting of me. If only you knew

how much Rebecca trusts me. I wonder if that would even matter to you.

"I was searching for a friend," he said.

"In the ground?"

Weighing his options, Caleb drew up his height. With his back straightened, he said,

"I know of the tunnels under this forest."

Lord Turrington's eyes rose.

"Who is it that you were searching for?"

Your daughter. Always, Rebecca. The answer to all that I do is her.

"For the man who showed the entrance to me."

"Please, Mr. Haroldson, you must tell me who this man is."

"I am afraid that I do not know his name, Lord Turrington."

He sat forward, earnest in his expression and the demeanor of nobility falling away.

"Mr. Haroldson, I really must know who he was. It is a matter of most importance."

"He was just a man," Caleb said. A breeze whispered over him, ushering in a shifting feeling. Lord Turrington was speaking to him, nearly begging him, in the middle of the forest. No, all was amiss.

"Mr. Haroldson, if you have ever had anyone you care about, then you will understand why I must know. What do you know of the man?"

If I have ever cared about anyone? I have loved Rebecca, since first I saw her. I have refused to allow anything to stand between me and her— not death, not distance, not even you.

The man before him had lost all threat. Instead, Lord Turrington sat looking lost in thought and alone. As he saw him there, Caleb felt the odd sensation of understanding that look. The bitterness that wrapped itself around his thoughts of Lord

Turrington began to slide away. How could he possibly have anything in common with Lord Turrington? Still, though, it seemed that he did.

In compassion, Caleb said,

"He was a monk and— "

Caleb hesitated for a moment. He had been warned not to mention the name of Turrington. Did the warning apply even when speaking to a man with the same name? Was he really supposed to conceal the son's location from the father? Surely, Lord Turrington already knew of Richard's location or he would not have so violently defended the door to the rooms where Richard lay.

Lord Turrington looked at him with the same pleading eyes that Rebecca had flashed at him so many times before. He had never been able to deny her and he could not do so now. He was powerless against Rebecca's eyes, even if these eyes were not a beautiful part of her but instead belonged to Lord Turrington. To Caleb, they were still hers.

"The monk led me through some passages and he showed me a wounded man. He showed me your son. I spoke with Richard."

Lord Turrington stood from the stump and crossed to Caleb,

"Then you must join him."

"Join whom?"

"Richard. You were looking for him, were you not? You have just said that you were searching for a friend."

Caleb looked at Lord Turrington, confused at the words.

"I did not know that he had made friends with a— I mean, that you are friends, but your loyalty is evident and I cannot fault you for your status because of that loyalty."

Fault me for my status? What are you talking about? I am a cabinet maker, not some scandalous drunk.

"Lord Turrington, I was not looking for Richard."

"You were not?" Lord Turrington said, his brow knitting together.

"No."

"Then, whom were you looking for?"

"The monk."

"The monk? I do not understand. Why should you be interested in the guardian of the Turringtons?"

"The guardian of the Turringtons?"

Caleb had taken that mantle upon himself, but what was Lord Turrington talking about? And why had Rebecca never mentioned this guardian?

"The monk. His family has been loyal to the Turringtons for generations."

"But, he is Irish, 'tis he not?" Caleb said, confused at how someone with so distinctive of an accent could have been a defender of the English for decades.

"That is right, Mr. Haroldson. Why were you searching for the monk?"

Lord Turrington's gaze narrowed on Caleb. He expected an answer.

"I hoped he might help me find someone," he said, simply.

"Oh, I am afraid that will not be possible," Lord Turrington said.

What do you mean 'twon't be possible? I gave you information, but you will not give me any?

" 'T'won't?" Caleb said, his foot shifting and scraping the bark of the tree stump.

"He has departed," Lord Turrington said.

"Departed?" Caleb repeated, feeling foolish that his words had been reduced to those of a parrot.

"There was a sudden rash of funerals he was asked to attend to, most unusual. The bodies kept disappearing, as if they were not there to begin with. It really is an odd predicament, but well—"

Lord Turrington's words evaporated into the cooling breeze around them, but Caleb's mind had become a net, determined to fill its haul with clues.

"People dying that are not really dead," Marion's raspy voice sounded from his memory.

"Then, I must go to him," Caleb said, before making the conscious decision to do so.

"Fine, yes, I will send a man with you to show you where he is and he can be replenished with more supplies."

Traveling with one of Lord Turrington's men was not at all what he had envisioned but surely, it must prove advantageous. Yes, he would set out to find the monk who would clear up the mystery of the not truly dead and then together they would bring Rebecca home. Finding her would be some happy chance, not the planned objective as far as Lord Turrington was concerned. When Rebecca was safely united with her father again, Lord Turrington was sure to oblige her rescuer.

Rebecca's hand in marriage for my reward, if you please.

With his acceptance of their wedded desire, running would no longer be necessary. Rebecca would not be forced to deny all that she deserved.

"When do we set out?" Caleb said, standing in his eagerness to hasten the future.

"Soon enough, but first you must agree to something."

A vow of secrecy about the monk being your defender? Not to mention the Turrington name?

"Yes?" Caleb said, eying the man who still clearly held all the power, despite his earlier pleading presence.

"You must join Richard. He needs all the men he can acquire."

CHAPTER FORTY-THREE

Coarse ropes embedded themselves in Rebecca's back, as she lay on the hammock. The sky stretched endlessly above. Reclining on the English grass, she had marveled at the expansive blue. Compared to this sky, though, it seemed small in her memory. Towns and forests punctuated the skyline of England, anchoring Rebecca to solid life. Here, there were no bookends to contain the clouds. Endless options seemed the exciting normalcy when at sea. No longer did Rebecca dread the churn of the waters. Lulled by the waves, which now felt gentle rather than violent, she began to drift into slumber. A mild breeze swayed the hammock. She felt a brush against her cheek, as someone bent to kiss her.

"Rebecca, you have forgot me," Caleb's faraway voice whispered.

He kissed her again.

"You have been untrue."

"How, Caleb? I would do no such thing."

"You know very well how," he said, his words mixing coarsely with his kisses, as sea salt does in water. Rebecca shook her head and struggled to sit up.

"You are in another man's bed," he said, his lips pressed to hers with hardly enough room to escape.

"No," she said, "No, no, you have misunderstood. John is only my friend. He built this hammock to teach me."

"You are certain, Rebecca? Maybe, he is teaching you how to love another man," he said, taking her hand in his now and kissing it. His lips, dripping with accusation, burned hot against her skin.

"Of course, I am certain! John does not even know who I really am. He thinks that I am a man!"

"You? A man?" Caleb said, pausing to look at her, "you know perfectly well 'tis not true." His hand trailed from her neck over her chest.

"Caleb, no! Do not give my secret away!" Rebecca said.

"Caleb? Who is Caleb? And what secret are you talking about? You have no secret. The whole world knows you are a girl," the woman from the docks said.

"Wait, I thought you were my friend," Rebecca said, shaking her head in disbelief.

"Why, Miss Turrington I was indeed right. You are nothing, but a harlot! You certainly keep company with them," Lord Furton said now, reaching greedily toward her.

"Stop it! Stop it! Stop it!" she shouted. With a kick, Rebecca landed in a thud.

"Ay, are you harmed?" John said, stepping nearer.

Rebecca blinked back the heavy curtains of sleep, which had pulled themselves over her eyes. For a brief moment, she waited for him to offer her his hand to help her return to her feet.

Rebecca, do not be foolish! Do you desire to give yourself away? Men do not help each other up!

She scrambled to her feet, embarrassed at having fallen from the hammock. Discomfort settled against her, like wet wool pressed into the skin.

"Fine, yes, thank you," she said in answer to John's question. Moonlight bathed his face and glimmered at a scar above his eyebrow. It zigzagged over his skin like a bolt of lightning. He looked at her intently and Rebecca felt a clamminess drag itself over her skin. Suppose, her dream had come true and he knew her secret.

"So, you have spotted my scar, Richard," John said.

Her nerves relaxed and the feeling of panic abated. No longer worried that he knew the truth, she was free enough to realize that her staring might have been rude.

"Sorry, I—"

"Do not be apologetic. I am not! I got it in my first battle.

Do not worry chap; that face of yours may soon bear the same badge of honor. I know how it is to be young and wish for such things. But, do not hasten battle. I know the thrill of it can be exciting but when you are in the thick of it, well truth be told, you desire nothing more than to be finished with it."

Rebecca swallowed, not at all sure what to say. It was not envy that she looked at his scar with, but pity. Have one of her own?

Fine lot you have cast for yourself, my girl. 'Tis bad enough that you have to pose for a sailor, but now it seems you will have to be a soldier too.

The heavy appeal of treasure chests laden with gold as a means home and the promise of a swift ship had left her blind to certain realities. In Rebecca's books, pirate treasure was discovered but the pages of a story conveniently skipped where the treasure came from. Those tales of pirates that her grandfather had told her now seemed grimmer, darker. They had hung for a reason; they were criminals. For all the enchantment and democracy she had seen among the crew, the idea of them being scoundrels of the sea had escaped her.

"I told you war is coming and I meant it. There will be plenty of battles. How good it will be to turn the king's men's coats deeper red!"

John's eyes blazed in passion as he spoke. The words had transfixed the man in front of her into a version of himself that seemed contrary to the one that she knew. How could a man care about something as trivial as her bed and yet be so keen to kill another?

"Worry not, Richard. You will kill plenty of lobster backs!"

John's good-natured slap on the back, sent a chill of terror through her. Rebecca wanted to escape England's guards, not kill them.

CHAPTER FORTY-FOUR

Ushered through a hidden door, behind a slab of slate, Caleb followed the back of one of Lord Turrington's men. Glad to be free of the physical constraints these men had bound him with earlier in the day, the tightening bands of obligation wound around him.

This passageway seemed more solidly constructed than the earthen hole Caleb had disappeared inside of with the monk. Wooden beams leaned against the cavernous interior.

Caleb wondered who had built so elaborate a network of tunnels. Obvious signs of age, rusted nails in the beams and mossy foliage clinging to the cracks, were visible from this sector. A heavy drop of water fell from the ceiling and sloshed onto Caleb's brow. He wiped it away with the back of his hand.

The guard lifted his hand and pounded against a door, which seemed to materialize from between the clustered stones and wood. Caleb's body protested at the earlier rough treatment it had received, as he watched the force of the man's fist strike his blows on the door.

Creaking, the door opened. In its frame stood a monk and, for a moment, Caleb thought that Lord Turrington had been mistaken in saying the monk who had first brought him here was absent. Ushering Caleb and the guard inside, the monk bolted the door behind them.

The room they stood in was lined with crates of provisions. Woven baskets abounded with vegetables. Leafy green carrot tops and dirt-covered potatoes tumbled over the edges. Autumnal harvest was present here, though it was still summer.

When Caleb had been here the last time, sparseness had marked the confines. Now, the walls looked as though they would heave under the weight of so many goods. Not only food, tools and weapons were more plentiful, but people as well. The last time he had been here, Richard, "Virgil", and only one or two other monks were present. A group of monks, hoods pulled over their heads, now filled the space. One of them stepped forward. As he pulled back his hood Caleb could see that his skin was rough in texture, like the gnarled bark of a tree.

"Richard," Caleb said, when he realized who stood before him. A guard turned and scowled at the lack of respect Caleb had shown the son of the lord. His familiarity was not boding well among those assembled.

"Mr. Haroldson," Richard said, signaling to Caleb the tone he ought to take. Caleb stiffened. Pretenses and titles had never been to his liking. If Rebecca hadn't tricked him into loving her—But no, that seemed too harsh. Yes, he had not known her identity when first he saw her blazing across the meadow on Dandelion. And yes, it is true that he would have taken more caution when approaching to speak to her, if he would have known that she were Lord Turrington's daughter. Still though, he couldn't be cross with her.

"I only wanted someone to like me for me and not because of what everyone knows about me, or at least thinks they know," she had offered as explanation, when he had pressed to know why she had only introduced herself as Rebecca.

Dear Caleb, do not be cross with me. He heard her voice so clearly that he was certain she had appeared in the room. But no, he realized with a falling heart, that wasn't the case at all.

My mind is only playing tricks on me. It is only because I have spoken to Lord Turrington and now to Richard. My Rebecca is not here.

An ache in his heart demanded that he suppress further thought of her, at least for now. Richard was doing his part to turn Caleb's attention to other things, as well. He had turned his back, retreating from the others. Caleb followed. Richard sat at a simple table that stood at the far end of the room, in almost the identical place that Richard had lain on the pallet the last time that Caleb had seen him.

"What are you doing here?" Richard said, in a near whisper so as not to be overheard.

"Your father's men brought me here," Caleb said, trying not to stare at the disfigurement that streaked itself across the once proud face.

"My father's men?" Richard said, his eyebrows rising in surprise. The shift of facial expression pulled uncomfortably at the contours of his face. He winced at the pain, but swallowed to push it aside.

Dear sweet Rebecca, it would pain you to see him this way now.

"They—bound me in the woods, carried me downstream. Luckily, your father recognized me," Caleb said, speaking in the same low volume that Richard had used.

"My father knows who you are? I thought you and Rebecca were more discreet," Richard said, a hint of scolding in his words.

"We were discreet," Caleb said, offended at Richard's accusation. Seeing how transformed Richard was prevented him from being cross for long, "He only knows me as a cabinet maker."

"I see," Richard said nodding. Whether he had detected the sharpness in Caleb's tone was uncertain as he said, "And what of Rebecca? Have you found her? Why did you return?"

He looked at Caleb with such a mix of mingled hope and despair that Caleb had to look down to prevent from gushing over, as the same duality rose in him.

"I have not yet found her. I returned to speak with the monk who brought me to you. Your father says he will give me a guide to take me to him and that he is some sort of guardian of your family, but first I must help you. Make some sense of it for me, Richard."

Now, away from the others, Richard did not correct

Caleb for calling him by his first name.

"He is a guardian, yes. He took it upon himself, inherited loyalty."

"I do not understand," Caleb said.

"Have you ever heard of the Battle of the Boyne?"

Caleb shook his head no.

"'Twas between the Williamites and the Jacobites in 1691."

"How does that connect—"

"'Twas in Ireland. A Turrington was in the battle and he spared the life of one of the monk's ancestors. In their gratitude, the family has been loyal since then."

"I see," Caleb said, only half-meaning the words.

"But what do you need protecting from?"

"From the people."

"The people?"

"There has been great unrest against the government. Surely, you have heard of the trouble in the colonies?"

"Of course," Caleb said, only having a vague notion of what was really going on.

"Good, then you will help?"

"Help with what?" Caleb said.

"In preserving England for Rebecca. England must be safe for her."

CHAPTER FORTY-FIVE

The later summer winds tugged on the sails of the ship. Long gone were the heat-drenched, humid days of the Caribbean. Rebecca remained on deck as much as possible. Late summer showers, as they raced up the coast of the Atlantic, now drove her below deck on occasion. Nausea, which had plagued her stomach so severely on her first crossing, now only visited her intermittently. Even the well-seasoned sailors, such as Philip and John, looked paler than usual when she felt the rising tide in her stomach.

John continued to teach her. Rebecca's earlier worries about appearing burdensome dwindled, as she found her place among the men. No longer did she remain glued to the mop. Instead, she joined in with the others as much as possible and found herself particularly useful in mending sails and clothes. At least then, the tireless hours she had spent bent over embroidery had proved of some use.

"When will I ever need to embroider heaps of linen?" she had asked Lady Turrington one rainy afternoon when she was nine.

"These things are important, Rebecca," her mother had said. It was a simple answer, but then Lady Turrington's words often were.

In those earliest days away from home, Rebecca had missed only Caleb. It was his voice that she longed to hear. Now, weeks or perhaps months—she had lost all track of time—later, she found her thoughts settling on the faces of her past. They had misunderstood her, even underestimated her, but they had also, Rebecca realized now, prepared her.

Oh these things are important, Mother, but not how you would have dreamed. A smile leaked from her lips at the thought. The look of sheer horror on Lady Turrington's face, upon discovering that she had insisted Rebecca learn a skill useful among pirates, only further pulled at the edges of Rebecca's mouth.

"What are you smiling about?" John said, breaking into her thoughts. He whittled away at a lump of wood, its intended shape as yet indistinguishable. Rebecca had not realized she was being watched and felt an inner blush. Though she masqueraded as a man, her ladylike manners had not been entirely abandoned. A man was staring at her and pressing to know her private thoughts. Of course, John had no idea what he was doing and could not be faulted. Before Rebecca could scramble in supplying some excuse, he answered his own question.

"I bet you are looking forward to going ashore."

Ashore? Were they to land soon?

"Bit of drink, bit of cards. Well, we have those here already, so I suppose 'tis something else you desire. Ah, I know what it is. You are anxious for a girl. Well, so am I. I have not seen a girl in—well, there certainly is not one around for miles. Depressing, no?"

Rebecca swallowed, both congratulating herself on the success of her masquerade and fearing that all John's talk of girls would cause her disguise to melt away.

Seeing Rebecca swallow, John laughed.

"Worry not. Girls are not so scary."

So scary? Was it possible that men fear us, as I feared Lord Furton?

It seemed almost too wild to accept as true.

"I shall find you someone nice, worry not," John said, picking the wood back up and chiseling away at it again.

Something about the caution not to worry often produces exactly the opposite result. Rebecca's heart began to beat more loudly, like the rushing raindrops against a sail in a sudden downpour.

You are not a man. You are a girl. You are not a man. You are a girl.

The words of the woman at the dock replayed through her thoughts.

Just relax. Think about something else.

Rebecca watched, as John's fingers worked over the wood.

"*You have been untrue,*" Caleb's voice, from her dream, cut across. Set on edge by jarring nerves and unhappy prospects, Rebecca struggled to break loose.

Overhead the sky pressed against her, growing gray. How was that possible? It was not yet night, was it?

Seeing Rebecca's face, John said,

"Sorry, Richard. I did not mean to—"

His words trailed away, as heavy drops catapulted onto the deck. In a matter of seconds, the rains fell in sheets, rolling across the ocean and threatening to erase all who stood in its way.

The sails whipped in the wind, sounding as if they had been torn in two. For the moment, they remained whole but, Rebecca didn't trust the strong aerial hand to leave the ship alone.

"Hurry!" Philip shouted, appearing at the helm.

Rebecca stood with her feet planted on the wooden boards of the deck. Around her, sailors hustled to secure the ropes as Philip grabbed the wheel, throwing the full weight of his tall frame into steering.

The clouds above shouted at them with roaring claps of thunder. Waves raged against the ship, pitching it like a toy boat along its careening masses.

How fickle the sea could be! It had lured her into feeling safe. She had admired its turquoise beauty, which shone with crystal brilliance. Now, it foamed white, like a pot boiling over and threw itself over the sides of the boat.

With a thud, Rebecca fell against the floor, holding desperately to the side of the ship. A wave of water, taller than any tree she'd ever seen in a forest, taller than any building she'd ever seen in a city, looking more like a mountain than water, rose behind the ship.

Rebecca turned away. With fingers gripping the rail so tightly that they had turned white, she prayed the only word that she could manage to say in her terror.

"Please."

CHAPTER FORTY-SIX

Peter shook his head.

"No, I have never heard of Lord Furton."

The imposter Caleb Haroldson, who had identified himself as a spy to the king, cradled his chin in the cupped palm of his hand as he paced beside the river.

He stopped to stare at something across the river on the other side of the shore. Peter, well-rehearsed in the exercise of patience when it came to craftsmanship, had little tolerance for the manner in which this man dangled bits of information in front of him.

Peter pressed the heel of his boot into the soft mud beside the river. A man of physical prowess, he struggled to rein in the urge to seize the spy and demand an answer.

"No? Well, that does surprise me."

"Who is he?" Peter said.

"A dangerous man."

Peter balled his hands into a fist and pounded them against his side. In the most leveled tone he could manage, he said,

"And why is he so dangerous?"

"How devoted are you to the king?"

"What?" Peter said, confused at the change in subject.

"How devoted are you to the king?" the spy repeated, separating each word with slowed speech for Peter's benefit. Visibly annoyed at the condescending manner of the spy, Peter's face flashed with a bristle of irritation as he said,

"I am a man of my word. A man of honor. I know what is important."

The spy looked at him, mentally calculating the strength of his words.

"Yes, that is all fine and good, but you have not yet answered my question."

"I thought I had," Peter said, his words cutting crisply through the warm summer air.

The spy shook his head.

Some spy you make! You cannot even recognize when a question has been answered! Why, I ought to—

"I am a devoted and loyal servant to the king," Peter said.

"Are you prepared to stand by those words?" the spy said, as though questioning whether a guilty man had really pleaded innocent.

"As I stand on the soil of England, I stand on my loyalty to the king."

The spy nodded.

"It is refreshing to hear you say so. Let us hope that you do keep your allegiance. Lord Furton did not. He turned his back on the gentry. Well, he was never even really one of them. I suppose you know all about that."

"I do not understand. What do you mean and what does this have to do with Caleb?"

"Are you certain you desire to know?"

"What? Of course, I do!"

"If I tell you, then you will be sworn to secrecy. You will not be able to tell anyone, not even your wife— "

"I have no wife," Peter said, with such haste that it brought an amused look to the spy's face.

"No friend, no one."

"Fine, yes, I understand. I will tell no one. I am a man of few words."

"Good. You are certain that you wish to know?"

"I just told you I did," Peter said.

"If I tell you, there will be no undoing what you know. You will become part of something much larger than either of us. Your very life may be in danger."

"I can take care of myself," Peter said, his chest puffing out involuntarily as the muscles in his arms, toned from the same force that chiseled the iron, glowed in the stream of sunlight.

"Very well. Simply, Caleb Haroldson and Lord Furton have both broken their loyalty to the king. They are a part of a subversive group. Others are sought out to join this band of rebels."

"But, why? What is their purpose?"

"Good questions— ones that I am hoping to find the answers to. Ones that, if you are serious about your loyalty to the king, you will help me find."

"I will help you," Peter said. An unease wrestled at the pit of his stomach. He was loyal to the king, yes. Perhaps, in part though, he had reaffirmed his devotion so that he could learn more about whatever trouble Caleb found himself in. Had he gone too far now? In trying to help his friend, had he just agreed to betray him?

Too many thoughts. Too troublesome. Stick to what you know, Peter. Stick to the metal.

But, it was too late. He had said that he was sure that he wanted to know and now he had locked himself in a cage with bars more fearsome than iron.

"Good. First then, you must know whom we are looking for."

"I am looking for Caleb," Peter said. Wasn't it obvious?

"Caleb Haroldson is just the beginning. He is one of them, yes. Why else would I have taken his name?"

The words grated uncomfortably across Peter's conscience. Using friends as pawns was hardly something he was used to and, frankly, it wasn't something that he wanted to become accustomed to.

"We are looking for dozens, perhaps hundreds. They are elusive but, with your help, I am certain we will find them."

Dozens? Hundreds? Peter's strength felt as though it were draining from his knees.

I am a simple man. I work iron. What do I know of

groups of people?

"They go by the name of the Across the River society and —"

A bullet spiraled through the air. It sliced the spy's words before lodging itself into his back. In a heap, he fell.

Peter stared, transfixed. He too was struck, not by a bullet but, by the strangest thought: *He is going to be terribly disappointed that his coat is ruined.*

CHAPTER FORTY-SEVEN

A steady rush of water poured over Caleb's head. From his spot between the jagged rocks, he lowered himself into the crystal pool of water. Dirt caked thickly on his clothes. Falling off in clumps, it muddied the water, turning it the color of a deep mahogany.

Hmm— So, that is what I should do to the wood to turn a heftier profit—dye it in a vat of mud! Ah, I speak in jest! My days as a carpenter seem long gone.

It was not so much the feel of the wood he missed under his fingertips, as the scent of his companion. Rebecca loved to watch him work.

"It seems like such good honest work," she had said, as he slotted a shelf into place in the cabinet, "you create something useful, something loved. That is not the world I come from."

"Ah, but you have never known the pangs of hunger, my love. That is not the world you come from either," he had thought. Such words would turn her angelic face to sorrow and he couldn't stand for that. Rather than voice his thoughts, he had simply said,

"I am glad my work is pleasing to you."

Ah Rebecca, what about now? Would you love me as a soldier? I suppose you should think the whole thing rather silly. It is so far removed from you. If only I knew where you were—

He pushed the thoughts aside. She was safe, of course. No gentleman would harm her, especially having rescued her. No, he was probably trying to woo her for himself. That had to be it. That had to be why she had not returned. Caleb's stomach protested at the thought of her being in another man's arms.

So long as she is safe, that is all that really matters.

It was far easier to think the thought than to believe it. Plunging himself under the water, he tried to wash away the subterranean grime and the dried blood from his rough treatment. Richard had set him to work, cleaning the tools and preparing for battle, before he had the opportunity to ask hardly any questions at all.

The water gushed cool across his skin, working itself under the dirt and dislodging it. Thoughts and questions could not be so easily removed and swept across him like a plague.

"You must help."

"You must bring them back."

"You must do it for Rebecca."

And then, as clearly as if she were at arm's length in front of him, Rebecca's face appeared to him. Her deep eyes, brimming with the light of conviction and overflowing with her love for him, now shone with a more startling fright than he had ever seen.

"Please," she said.

Caleb felt a strong punch to his stomach, though there was no one else nearby. Chains seemed to tighten around his body, grabbing him by the throat and dashing him against the rocks. Caleb struggled to break the surface of the water. Emerging, he gasped for air. Drinking it in, Caleb was convinced that there was not enough. The source of plenty seemed exhausted.

"What is wrong with you?" a soldier, dressed in monks' clothes, said.

Caleb jumped at the voice, startled by the man's presence.

"Nothing, I am fine," he said.

"Well, if that is how you look when you are fine, I would not want to see you when you are not. You look as though you have seen a ghost!"

"I fear I have," Caleb said, shaken at the watery apparition of Rebecca.

"What does Turrington want with him anyway?" the man muttered as he left Caleb, dripping from the water and searching for an answer.

"Mr. Haroldson, can I speak with you?" Caleb turned to hear Richard's voice. His discarded shirt still lay on the rock beside him.

"Of course," he said, still feeling the strain of so formal a greeting from Richard.

The shirt clung to Caleb's skin, as he pulled his arms through the sleeves. Water-drenched, it got stuck on his back as he yanked the material over his head. He reached backward to bring the shirt down to cover his still wet skin.

Richard's face bore the deep-set creases of worry that alerted Caleb that his mind was busy at work. It was remarkable how alike the two siblings were. Would it have terrified them to know? But no, they each cared for the other; that was evident. Somehow, though, they each seemed to most misunderstand the very quality in the other that they most closely shared.

"You need to blend in more," Richard said, "There is uncertainty everywhere and anything out of the ordinary is going to draw the attention of eyes we do not wish to see us."

He didn't bother to say who was watching them, but he spoke in a warning tone that more than suggested that he shouldn't be ignored.

"Here," he said, drawing out a robe identical to those worn by the men gathered around them.

Caleb took the robe and dutifully slipped the coarse material over his head. With his wet shirt sandwiched between his still wet body and the itchy fabric, he was uncomfortable to say the least.

"Will we not— " Caleb began, but Richard had already turned his back to him and made no indication that he had heard.

"Stick out more dressed as monks in a country that has been less than friendly to the men we are imitating," Caleb finished for his own benefit. Still, in London, the plaque commemorating the Great Fire of last century spoke of the Papist frenzy that had caused it. The Papists were denied the right to rule. None could ever sit on the throne. Of course! That made sense, didn't it? The Turringtons were masquerading as a group that lacked any power to prevent the rebels from turning against them. They would preserve their power through whatever means they could. A sickening swell mounted in Caleb's stomach. In protecting Rebecca, was he guaranteeing the strength of the yoke over men like himself? He swallowed hard.

The robes hung loosely around him, draping him in a foreign life and robbing him of the last remnants of his own identity. First, Rebecca had slipped from his life, then his friends and his profession. Now even his appearance and allegiances were altered. He was to do the bidding of men whom he merely tolerated in ordinary circumstances. The oppressive hold of the laws, mandates and their lack of investment in Caleb as an appropriate suitor for Rebecca had been merely prelude to the dictation of his life they now held in their hands. The crushing weight of their grip was palpable, but it was another man's hand that now drew his attention.

Through a grove of trees, Caleb watched as a familiar back bent over a body. Dressed in the finest clothes, a form lay lifeless.

"Peter," he whispered, the voice catching in his throat.

What have you done? What have you done?

Caleb's belief in all he had known wavered, as he watched his friend transformed into a murderer. Well, perhaps, that wasn't true but they were alone in a secluded part of the forest. Peter had done it. It was the only explanation that made any sense. Horrified at Peter's drastic change, he watched as he reached into the man's coat and pocketed a gold watch.

A murderer and a thief. How could you? How could you?

Caleb turned, pulling the hood of the monk's robe more fully over his face. Yes, it was better to disappear.

CHAPTER FORTY-EIGHT

Rebecca held her breath. The deafening roar of the waves, swirling mercilessly around the ship, dissolved in the intensity of her own thoughts. Though the others rushed around her, ardently trying to throw their weight into some powerful show against the waves, she remained planted. Unable to move from the rail, Rebecca felt the depths of the sea churn up the mire of their bowels and release its grit and brine over her. Her face stung from the abrasive assault. Still, she clung to the ship.

"Richard!" a voice called to her. In her panic, she forgot her disguise and did not recognize that the name was intended for her.

"Richard!" a voice, relentless in his pursuit of her, sounded again.

This time it registered. She willed her eyes open slowly and turned to see John holding a rope,

"Tie this around you!" he yelled. He threw it to her. The wind caught hold of the loose end, whipping it wildly like a crazed snake in the books about the desert she had read when young.

"Let go!" he shouted.

Let go?

"Let go! Of the rail! Grab the rope! Grab the rope!"

The monstrous waves threatened to strike the vessel, pinning it to the floor of the ocean. Everything inside of her screamed not to let go of the rail.

Do not do it! Do not do it!

Rebecca felt her fingers pry loose of the rail. The rope flailed in the wind. Jumping, she caught hold of it and pulled it toward her.

"Tie it around you!" John said again. Her fingers worked the ropes around her, securing the ends with the tautness of a knot that John had taught her. No thought was given to the task as her fingers took over, tying her to safety. Secure, she turned to see John.

He nodded to her to confirm that yes, she was safe. All that could be done was in place.

"Thank—" The wind whipped the words away from her, as a thunderous wave lifted the stern of the ship. Now a part of a reality that was more vivid than any nightmare, Rebecca struggled to keep her balance.

Rolling along the deck, sailors and machinery tumbled toward her. The last in the line of the rope, Rebecca realized that a length of it extended from her own.

"Take hold!" she shouted, to the men farther down the deck.

Gathering the remainder of the rope, she flung it toward the men.

"Grab a hold!" she yelled again. One by one, the men tied themselves to the rope, links on a chain of hope and survival. A surge of bravery and a feeling of having found her purpose emerged, as she turned to look at John. He too was looking at her and, if she were not mistaken, that was most certainly a look of pride on his face.

Overhead, the looming clouds clapped angrily. John might have been proud of his protégée, but the storm had no regard for any of them. Rebecca's eyes blurred, as the rocking boat shook both her resolve as well as her stomach.

Be brave, Rebecca. Be brave.

Still at the helm, Philip hunkered against the wheel. A silver finger of lightning punched through the clouds. Catching the sail, it burst into flames. The rains continued to pound the deck, as the winds fanned the fire.

"Cut it loose! Cut it loose!" Philip shouted to the crew. Before his words had even fully processed for Rebecca, John untied himself and leaped toward the sail. Brandishing a knife in one hand, he sliced through the ropes. Catching the loosened material of the sail, the wind lifted it, carrying it like a small dropped handkerchief.

The winds were not placated by the release of their new toy and wailed against the ship. A mighty wave, seething with insurmountable power and foaming white-hot at the mouth, rushed over the side of the boat.

Rebecca struggled to lift her head above it.

"There!" she shouted, barely believing her eyes.

"Philip! Philip!" she screamed, "I see land!"

CHAPTER FORTY-NINE

"Peter, what is ailing you?" Molly said, as she draped her arm over him. He was seated on the stool at the tavern, as she stood closer to him than was respectable for a lady to stand. She had never been reared as a lady, though, and saw no reason to adapt to foreign ways now. No, ladylike behavior seemed only like a bridle to stifle the truest passions of her wandering spirit. While it was well and good to have a transient spirit, having a man follow suit was only an annoyance. She preferred her men to be predictable, especially when it was someone such as Peter. Molly admired him for his honesty in a town where lies dwelt and she liked his raw masculine strength, when silken stockings were the rage among gentlemen. Rustic and natural were more attractive attributes to her and Peter embodied them so well.

"Just thoughts," he said. Another man would have said nothing, but Peter could not lie.

"Thoughts about what?" she said, bending in to influence him with a kiss.

"Today," he said, accepting the kiss but, not becoming more specific.

"Mol, we should go somewhere," he said. He lifted the tankard, its size dwarfed by his hand, to take the last swig of cider.

Her eyes lit up. Yes, she would help him feel better. Taking him by the arm, she nearly pulled him into the street.

"Over here," he said, leading them to a quiet side street. She turned, looking expectantly for that flirtatious glimmer that transformed his strong demeanor into her playful companion.

"Take me in your arms and kiss me," she said, well aware that a lady would never dare to even think such a thing. That life of duty over love was behind her. Molly had been turned out, abandoned by her brother's sanity, when she had failed to guarantee their social standing in gaining a place as a lady, under

Rebecca Turrington's sheltering care. Truth be told, she hadn't really wanted to be a lady and only asked the maid for an audience with Rebecca. When she'd told her brother that she was unsuccessful, he'd vowed to win Rebecca's hand in marriage to secure their place for himself. That was when the obsession had set in. It had begun innocently enough. He'd asked a question here or there about what might win a lady's heart. By the time that he woke Molly long before dawn each morning to pray for Rebecca to love him and kept her up well into the night, planning how best to ingratiate himself to Rebecca, Molly had left to seek employment at the tavern. When Lord Furton saw her standing in the tavern's door, the wrong idea had jumped to mind and his face had clouded in a crash of anger.

"You are your mother's daughter," he'd said cryptically, before departing in haste.

Peter, less complicated and more dependable, she could count on. Only now, he was shaking his head, as he said,

"Not tonight, Mol."

Putting her hands on her hips, she pouted.

Peter was unwavering in his resolve. Her tactic having no use on him, her hand rose to the shoulder of her garment. She tugged it down on one side, exposing her shoulder in the moonlight.

Peter looked at her. He crossed to her. Ah, now she had his attention. With a sly smile and a look of satisfaction at achieving her goal, she moved her hand to expose the other shoulder.

Peter stood in front of her. She waited in anticipation for his lips to press against her skin, but no. He did no such thing. He put his hand over hers, preventing her from moving her shirt off her shoulders.

Molly looked at him, her eyes slanting into a question.

"Do you not like me anymore, Peter?" she said, confused by the man in front of her.

"I like you, Mol," he said, "but, 'tis not why I wanted to come out here with you."

"'Tis not?" she said, her blue eyes taking on an innocence in the moonlight that he'd not seen there before. If he didn't know better, he would have thought she were the sister of some lord and not merely a tavern worker.

In a world of danger, she held the promise of good in the simplest form. He was tempted to pull her close to him, to breathe her in, to erase the memory of today. His eyes lingered on her creamy complexion.

I should like to kiss you, my Mol. To start at the tip of that small nose and not stop until long after dawn.

"I brought you here to talk to you," he said, in a low voice.

"Peter Black, have you found yourself another girl? I know I do not have a ring on my finger, but I did not think you would let go of me so quick."

He shook his head.

I should like to put a ring on that finger.

His eyes held her hand, as though its smallness was wedged between his own strong hands. Tempted as he was to reach out to her, he knew he could not touch her. If he did, he'd be unable to follow through with what he'd begun.

"I am leaving, Mol."

"You are going away? Where?"

Such dismay overcame her that, he wished he could take back the words. Even if he had, though, his feet still would have completed the journey.

"'Tis not safe for me here, not right now anyway."

"Well, where are you going?"

"I have not decided," he said. He looked away from her now, resisting the urge to abandon his plan.

"Let me come with you!"

"'Tis too dangerous," he said, shaking his head.

"But, what if you get lonely," she said, doing her best to charm him.

He shook his head.

"Peter," she said, her voice growing serious, as she realized that he really was leaving without her.

"You will come back, yes?"

Peter looked at her, savoring the image of Molly, unsure of when he would see her again.

"I hope so," he said, "Be careful, Mol. Do that for me, will you?"

She nodded, wanting to hold onto him, to sear herself into his flesh, to burrow into his heart. As he walked away, his shadow stretching the length of the street, she realized that, perhaps, she already had.

"Why, Peter Black," she whispered, "I do believe you love me."

CHAPTER FIFTY

Caleb lay stretched on his back, under a star-strewn sky. Some nights are marked by the sight of the familiar constellation or a handful of sparsely flung stars. Tonight, though, the blinking diamonds filled the expanse above him, becoming more plentiful the longer he looked, as if he were witness to a celestial pageant of creation.

For all its obvious beauty, the jewels of tonight mystified him and settled over him with a sweep of sadness. Their expanding luminosity only shone as a blinding reminder that he was surrounded in a sea of questions and very few answers.

What am I doing here anyway? Wasting my time, that is what I am doing! I should be out looking for Rebecca. Instead, I am stuck here as a prisoner of my own lack of direction. If only I had not—

But, that chain was too long to find its beginning. If only he hadn't, what? Never come back? Met the monk? Met Marion? Heard those dreaded words of crossing the river? The beginning of his troubles lay in a tangled heap of dead-ends, of unexplained mystery and dire results. Caleb had followed all the wrong leads or, at least, arrived at the wrong destinations.

Aggravated, he turned to his side and pounded his fist into the dirt beside him. A shadow fell over him. He scrambled to his feet, as he realized whom it was.

"Lord Turrington," he greeted him. He had not seen Lord Turrington since a few weeks ago, when he had first been brought to Richard's camp of stockpiling materials. Its only purpose consisted of standing and waiting. At least, that is how it seemed to Caleb.

"Who is winning, Mr. Haroldson?"

"Pardon?"

"You seem to be having a fight with the ground," he said, with the hint of an amused grin.

"Merely trying to get comfortable," Caleb said, unwilling to divulge his frustration.

"I know you must be restless," Lord Turrington said.

Restless. Did it show on Caleb's face? Had he betrayed himself?

"But, I am convinced more than ever that we will soon all be on colonial soil."

"Sir?" he said, not at all understanding.

"The colonies," Lord Turrington said, as if that explained everything.

"But, the monk, I must see him," Caleb protested, resisting the urge to tack on the childish, *"you promised"*.

"Yes, well," Lord Turrington said, stepping back and rubbing his hands together.

Caleb's shoulders prickled at the action. A Turrington rubbing his hands together could not bode well. Rebecca only ever did so when delivering the most disappointing news. She was going to be away for the summer. There was yet another suitor who had joined the competition for her hand.

"That is why I have come to see you," Lord Turrington said.

"I have decided not to keep my promise." It seems about the kind of thing you would say. At least, dear sweet Rebecca seemed to always think that you broke your word to her.

Instead, Lord Turrington's face took on that compassionate fatherly expression that Caleb had not seen for himself since he was very young.

"I am sorry, Mr. Haroldson, but I will not be able to keep my word."

Ah, I was right, after all. Oh you are cunning all right, trying to—

"I am a man of my word and I do not like to break it, especially when I have made an agreement with another man, such as I made with you. It is only that— you will not be able to see the monk."

What do you mean I will not?

Caleb fumed inside, quite convinced that steam must be pouring from his ears.

"The monk is gone, dead I am afraid. Mr. Haroldson, he has crossed the river."

An icy chill washed across Caleb's skin. The image of Peter standing over the body of the stranger in the forest played across his mind. Bursting through his thoughts, Rebecca's face haunted him.

"*Please*," she said in that small, pleading voice.

"Please," Caleb said, voicing aloud the word Rebecca had spoken in his mind, "Tell me his name."

"Mr. Haroldson, you do not even know his name?"

"He only identified himself as Virgil," Caleb said, feeling the blood drain away from his face. Had he made some foolish mistake in admitting he didn't even know the name of the man he sought?

Lord Turrington looked at Caleb. Apparently, he looked trustworthy. At least he had remained here when asked to do so, even if rather persuasive means had been used to get him here.

"Seamus is—was his name," Lord Turrington said, a cloud passing in front of his face.

"Thank you," Caleb said. Lord Turrington nodded and turned to leave,

"One more thing."

"Yes?" Lord Turrington turned, unaccustomed to a commoner speaking so freely.

"What town was he in—Seamus, I mean?"

Lord Turrington's eyes went wide.

"You cannot go there, Caleb," he said, taking on the fatherly tone once again and abandoning all formality. Before Caleb could inquire about what had provoked the reaction, Lord Turrington said,

"As I told you at our last meeting, there was a rash of funerals that he was called to attend to. He must have succumbed to the same sickness. No," he said, shaking his head, "I could not in good conscience send a man there. My own dear daughter is away from us and I would not allow harm to come to another."

He turned away, leaving Caleb without his answers. Or maybe, he hadn't left Caleb without an answer after all. Lord Turrington muttered to himself,

"Imagine, imagine me sending a man to Beckshire."

CHAPTER FIFTY-ONE

Rebecca stretched, arching her back as a cat does in the morning sun. It was precisely those same solar rays that she was after. Since washing ashore days earlier, Rebecca felt unable to soak in enough sun to thoroughly dry her out. The near constant rains since they'd returned to land did little to help.

Her feet had stumbled, uncommitted to the belief in accepting the land under them, when the crew had first washed onto the beach. Tumultuous waves and fierce winds wrapped their arms around the ship, plunging it from the sea onto the land. Dripping, like soaked dogs, they had emerged water-logged from the journey. Rebecca had spent the better part of a day wringing out the water from her clothes, but she had survived. That was all that really mattered.

Despite the crew coming through, the ship had not fared so well. Sails torn, masts snapped in two like twigs between the wind's fingers and boards suffering badly in need of repair, confined them to the land. No one seemed to much mind. They had docked as intended, not really so far off their determined course. The only thing that had changed for them was the uncertainty of how long they would stay. Ship repairs necessitated a longer layover than simple trade with the colonists would have.

To Rebecca, the happenings did not seem as burdensome as they did to Philip. For him, the destination was far less important than the constancy of his hard-won ship. Never mind that he had stolen someone else's property. He had struggled for his freedom, as she had. That was all she saw now among the men whom she worked beside. The idea of men like these hanging beside Tower Bridge now seemed ridiculous.

And yet, to Rebecca, the means of getting home meant little, so long as she did get there. Rebecca's eyes traveled over her fellow shipwrecked sailors. Huddled around a deck of cards, she heard the excited cheers of onlookers as a winning hand was presented for all to see. The seed of a smile slipped from her lips. John played a game of dice with a wooden board and coins with another man. He caught her eye and nodded to her. Well, maybe she did care about the ship after all, or at least about the crew. If she had to journey home by ship, she might as well do it with an amiable crew. At least, that is what made sense. Rebecca tried to convince herself of the logic, but a persistent pull at her feelings told her maybe those weren't the only reasons.

"Ah, you are a cheat!" Pete exclaimed, overturning the wooden game board that he had been playing with John. Pete stood up, leaving John behind with the scattered pieces.

John righted the board, picking up the pieces from the ground. Rebecca stood and crossed to help him.

"I hear you are a cheat," she said, with a wry grin.

"I will have you know that I most certainly do not cheat! Everyone knows that Pete is a terrible loser."

As though proving John's point, another man's voice rose above their conversation,

"Not now, Pete. You always throw the pieces down when I win."

John looked at her as though to say,

"See?"

Instead though, he presented her with another question.

"So, what do you think of my home?"

"Pardon?" she said, suddenly confused. They had been camped on the edge of a town, well away from the nervous eyes of the townsfolk. The crooked streets of a sailor's haunts in the Caribbean were constructed for men such as themselves. Here though, in the colonies, families dwelt and the mention of pirates made them nervous.

"I was born not far from here," he said. The flash of a fish skewered on the edge of his knife, as he likened it to King George, appeared in front of her.

"I did not realize that," she said, feeling her interest piqued at his exotic origin. Or maybe, now standing on colonial soil no longer made it such a foreign place. Rebecca tried to push away the thrill that crawled across her skin.

"We all come from someplace," he said, with a shrug.

"What do you say, beautiful day, shall we go for a swim?" one of the younger men said to the others. Beautiful days and pirates didn't seem to go together. Perhaps, he'd not been around them long enough to learn what right words to use. But, then neither did the cut-throat imagery of her books present an accurate depiction of these men. No, none of them seemed to much match the label they wore.

"I could go for a swim," John said, pulling off his shirt. His tanned body glowed in the sunlight. Yes, it made sense that he was from this side of the water, where freedom, or at least a yearning for it, seemed kindled, more alive in the thoughts and actions of men.

Why, Rebecca Turrington, I do believe that was a treacherous thought!

The shock of it thrilled her, fanning the embers of her own freedom fire. What was so wrong with men wanting to decide for themselves, anyway? She certainly had wanted to be able to do that.

"Come on, Richard," John said, turning back long enough to address her, as he dashed toward the river that they were camped beside.

Me? Swim?

Rebecca's chest tightened.

Sensing her hesitation, John called to her,

"Come on, Richard. I will teach you, if you do not know how."

That was not the problem. Oh, she could swim all right. What she couldn't do was reveal herself. Despite identifying with these men's yearning for freedom, Rebecca had to accept that she was far less free than they were.

Confined by the female form of her body, she shook her head,

"I think I will stay out here. I am only now finally dry."

John gave her a sympathetic look, which seemed to suggest he believed the storm had caused some paralysis of fear in her.

"You are certain?"

She nodded, though really she was not sure at all.

Turning, John ran toward the water and, with a whoop, plunged into the river.

If only I could join you.

"Rebecca," Caleb's voice traveled to her, striking her with an icy chill far more palpable than the torrential rains had heaped on her, "have you forgot me so soon? Do you care more for this place than for England, than for your home?"

Rebecca shut her eyes, to shake herself free of the words. In the beauty of the late summer day, Rebecca had been stung, not by the buzzing bees that encircled the flowers near her, but by the confrontation of past with present.

CHAPTER FIFTY-TWO

"Why did such a thing happen to me?" Peter muttered, trudging through the streets of London. When he had set out days earlier, his intended destination had been as much of a mystery to him as it was to Molly. Now, the buzz of the city engulfed him, sweeping him into a foreign world. Could this place also be England? It was so unlike the farmland and wooden-beamed buildings he was accustomed to. Titans of power, of business and of government ruled the happenings, not only of the country but, of an expanding empire from within this city. Gray buildings, fashioned in the style of the classical architecture of Greece and Rome, rose from the planned streets in Georgian splendor.

"Watch it!" someone shouted roughly, as Peter dodged an oncoming horse carriage. At home, no one would have spoken to him like that. No one dared cross Peter Black. Here, though, no respect was paid for his muscles. No one seemed to care where he came from or who he was, only that he was in their way and they wanted him out of it. Well, perhaps, that was better. He had left, feeling too much of a target. Being a marked man was not to his liking, especially when his only crime had been to befriend one man and talk to another. Maybe, he shouldn't have left Molly behind. It would be nice to have someone to talk to, someone who did care that he was Peter Black.

If I had known 'twas going to be like this, I could have brought you along.

But, he hadn't known. What he did know was that there were more urgent needs that required his attention. Growling, his stomach urged him not to forget it in his dealings. When had he eaten last, anyway? Was it last night? No, he had pushed on, thinking he was nearer London than he had been. Well, perhaps, it was yesterday afternoon then. No, that wasn't right either.

He had left quickly, before his customers had paid their

debts. Entering London without jangling coins left him few options. His pockets were not entirely empty, though. Caleb Haroldson's watch, the real Caleb, filled the fold of fabric in his jacket. Drawing it out, the sun glinted against the glass of the face. The broken clasp, which had convinced him it was Caleb's, was no longer the only defect. Its near pristine condition had been ruined when the spy had fallen, causing a crack in the glass.

Just how had the spy come across the watch anyway? And what had he meant about looking for dozens or even hundreds? Peter felt sorry for the miserable end that had come to the man but, with his earthly departure, he had severed whatever bonds Peter had to these people. Yes, the only thing he was looking for was a sizable profit to exchange the watch for.

Sorry, Caleb, but you understand. At least, I hope you do.

He had no way of knowing if the real Caleb Haroldson would come back to claim the watch or even if he were still alive. There was no place for sentimentality though; there was only ample room for practicality. Men were disappearing around him. If he had anything to say about it, he would not be next.

Freshly baked bread was in his vicinity. Its tantalizing aroma wafted toward him. Peter's already ravenous stomach leaped at the smell, begging him to pay attention to it. Following his nose, he rounded the corner. Dodging puddles, horse carts and people, he came to a stop in front of the bakery. The price in the window informed him that the little in the way of money that did fill his pockets wouldn't be enough. The watch weighed heavily against his pocket, persistently urging him to consider its worth.

As though summoned to him in his stomach's urgent appeal for food, a shop caught his eye. Wedged between two larger buildings, a sign hung crooked in its window.

London Jeweler.

Well, that seemed simple enough. Peter crossed to it. Catching sight of his reflection in the glass window pane, he stopped abruptly. London gentry rushed past him, dressed in finery. Peter Black stood in contrast, looking very much like the country blacksmith that he was. Smoothing his windblown hair with the back of his hand, he straightened his shirt with the other. There. Was it any better? He stepped forward and backward, trying to focus more clearly on the image in the waving glass.

Giggles from two young girls sounded in his ears like twittering birds. Realizing that he was the subject of their amusement painted his face in a most unbecoming shade of red. Thrusting his hands into his pocket, he marched into the shop.

"Good day, sir and what... can... I... do for you?" The shop attendant's nose had been buried in a ledger as Peter entered. Now that he had looked up and seen that it was no gentleman that had entered his shop, his words had slowed in an unnatural halting rhythm.

Thin wire-rimmed glasses perched on his nose and the gray coif of hair suggested that he might have been in this shop long enough for the dust to settle on both his shelves as well as his head. A nervous expression gripped his face, as he looked from Peter to the grandest of items and back again at Peter.

Not realizing at first what was happening, Peter stiffened as the full force of the insult hit him.

He thinks I am here to rob him!

Wanting to put the man at ease, but wanting even more to get on with his business, Peter reached into his pocket. With a tense expression, the attendant continued to survey the finery of the shop that he undoubtedly believed would disappear from under his thin pinched nose. When he saw that it was a watch that Peter had pulled from his pocket, a relieved sigh settled over him.

"I would like to sell this watch," Peter said, holding it out for the man to examine. He looked at the small marred piece in Peter's hand and said,

"I am sorry, but we do not buy pieces. We only sell them."

"But, I must have money," Peter said. It seemed logical enough. He was in a jewelry shop. He had a piece to sell. The man ought to buy it.

Looking nervously over the merchandise again, the attendant decided that it would be better to pay Peter than to have his merchandise stolen to finance Peter's need.

"Your name?" he said to Peter.

"Peter Black," he said, not sure why his name was needed for the transaction.

"Well, Mr. Black, let me see what I can offer you for it."

He picked up the watch, then turned it over, examining it in detail.

"CH?" he said, reading a tiny inscription that Peter had not seen.

"What does CH stand for?"

"Caleb Haroldson," Peter said, unable to say anything but the truth.

"But, your name is Peter Black?"

"Yes," he said, a pinch of uneasiness coming over him.

"Then who is Caleb Haroldson?"

"My friend," Peter said. The man raised a questioning eyebrow.

"You are selling it for him?"

For having such a nervous disposition, he did ask a lot of questions!

"He is dead," Peter said. Whether his friend Caleb Haroldson was alive or not, he couldn't know but the man who had last had this watch and identified himself as Caleb Haroldson certainly was.

"I see," the man said. Peter's answer infused him with an urgency that resulted in a quick end to the transaction. Paying Peter more than the watch was worth, to discourage him from returning, the attendant sent him on his way. Reemerging onto the London street, Peter felt the reassuring jangle of coins in his pocket, the seeds of his new life. Caleb Haroldson was dead, but Peter Black was fully alive.

CHAPTER FIFTY-THREE

Gathering wood to fuel the fire, Caleb bent his back toward the ground. The bruises from his rough treatment, which had served as his introduction into his present circumstances, had long since healed. His frustration at being held captive in the quicksand of the present had only become more aggravated.

The numbers of the men accumulated, spreading their tents over the wooded terrain. Amassed supplies now filled the underground tunnels, filling the space where the first few men had once lived.

"What do you know of Beckshire?" The question rose in him, as one of the hooded men came closer to Caleb as he gathered additional fuel for the fire.

"Good evening," Caleb said, instead, to breach the silence. Turning away without answering, the man moved away from Caleb.

"Not feeling very polite, are we?" Caleb grumbled to himself. The wood that he gathered fit easily into his hands. His touch lingered on it.

A memory, far more delicious than the smell of the cooking fish stew, washed over him. A piece of wood, about the size of the stick he held now, had been in his hand. Whittling away notches of wood, a chair leg had slowly begun to emerge. Looking up from time to time, he was rewarded by Rebecca's sweet smile.

I should like to go back to such a time.

A loud pop from the fire drew his attention. He looked from the wood in his hand to the flames. Tossing it into the fire, Caleb couldn't help but feel as if that's what was happening to his entire existence. The potential of the wood, alive and ready to be shaped into something both beautiful and useful, was consumed by the ravenous dragon's breath of the fire. Transfixed, Caleb stood, watching the remains of the wood disappear. Only a steady stream of black smoke remained. Choking on it, Caleb turned away.

'Tis about the sum of it.

⋆

It had been days since Caleb had seen Richard. Lord Turrington had also not returned.

"In preserving England for Rebecca. England must be safe for her." Richard's words hounded him, wherever he was tempted to leave the camp. His conscience and his duty to her were the only things keeping him from going. The man's ignoring him earlier had happened time and again. Although assuredly not real monks in their stockpiling of weapons and combative nature, these men seemed to have taken a vow of silence. Of all the attributes they might have taken on from the robes they wore, it was the most unfortunate for Caleb. Feeling increasingly isolated, his thoughts raked over the mounting pain of being without Rebecca for so long. As days became weeks and now stretched to months, the hope of finding her seemed like little more than a desperate attempt.

"Faith as small as a mustard seed," Rebecca's voice whispered to him.

"How do you know, my love, that we will be together?" he had said to her, as she laid her head on his chest in the late spring air. It was a night much like the one that he had last seen her on. His heart sank, like a pebble cast into a pond, at the thought of it.

"Because, only faith the size of a mustard seed is required for assurance and Caleb Haroldson," she had paused, to momentarily press her lips against his, before continuing, *"I do love you so much more than a mustard seed."*

"And the length of her legs, I should say—" the voice of one of the men drifted across the fire, landing in Caleb's ears.

You will talk to each other, just not me. Why should you

treat me like some outsider? I am more loyal to the Turrington name than all of the rest of you put together! Why I ...

"Ah, I wish she had never left. I could certainly be happy marrying her," the man continued.

Well, whoever she is, 'tis a good thing for her sake that she did leave. Poor woman to have to marry you. I bet you—

"What do you mean left? She died in the fire."

Caleb's heart quickened.

"N'ah, that was only a story. She is as alive as we are."

"Then why?"

"No doubt, so she could run off and marry whomever she pleased. My sister was a maid for them and she said that there were plenty of occasions where Rebecca Turrington spoke out about marrying whom she pleased."

She did not. Rebecca is far smarter than to do such a thing.

"Wish I was the lucky man she ran off with."

Caleb's stomach churned.

"Right now I would have those lovely legs curled around me." Caleb felt the ire rise from the pit of his stomach.

"Ha! Rebecca Turrington would never go for you," the other man said.

Well, that certainly is true.

Caleb swallowed, trying to dissolve his anger.

Come on, Caleb. Breathe. It will only get you into trouble.

"She would. A woman like that just has not been handled right. I would think for her, teach her what to do. Be her master."

With his thoughts blocked by his anger, Caleb stood, marched to the man and said,

"Let this be your master!"

With a hard wallop, fiercer than the blow he'd landed on Peter, Caleb punched the man straight in the jaw.

"Hey, watch it!" the man roared, punctuating his point with a strong swing of the arm. Caleb ducked.

"Oh, you want a fight, do you?" Caleb said, abandoning all wisdom. He swung his arm to deliver another punch, but the other man struck him first. The wind flew from Caleb's chest, as the man's fist landed in his stomach.

Caleb hit him for the vulgarity of the statement and then he continued, unable to stop for Rebecca's honor, for her reputation, out of duty, out of love, out of hatred for their separation, out of fear and the sickening swell in his stomach that he'd been left behind and that she'd moved on. Then came the guilt for accusing her of such a thing and then there was the quiet dissolving of the pain and the anger, as he accepted that perhaps Rebecca had no choice and was forced into marriage. Then came the fear that he would never see her again.

Still his hands pummeled the air, flailing in the torrent of thought, failing to deliver the wallop that a man, a better man, someone like Peter could have delivered. Perhaps, Caleb wasn't man enough, strong enough to protect her. Maybe he'd never even deserved her. Blinded by the inferiority and wildly-thrown punches, he heard the crowd gathering around him and didn't care. Dust flew at him as sweat stung his eyes, the salt of his anger and exertion mingling with his agony.

"What is going on here?" a voice cut through. A crowd was gathering around them. Unwilling to give in to the other man, Caleb swung again, landing a blow on the man's nose.

"Caleb Haroldson!" the voice said, catching his arm. Horrified, Caleb's eyes focused. It was not the man who had made such disparaging remarks about Rebecca whom he'd hit, but Richard Turrington!

"Richard I— I am sorry. I thought—"

"No, Caleb, you did not think," he said, speaking lowly, "There is no room for any of this here."

"But, you do not understand! I was only defending Rebecca."

A flash of warning came across Richard's face.

"I am glad that she is gone. Your temper is far too dangerous for her to be around."

The words only stoked the flames. Struggling to control his anger and prove Richard wrong, Caleb appealed to his logic.

"But, what about what you told me? About finding her."

"Mr. Haroldson, 'tis clear now that the only reason you did not yet find her was your anger. Leave. You are not welcome here."

Stunned, Caleb turned to leave. The jeers and taunts behind him fought to turn Caleb's steps back toward the men. No, he would not give Richard the satisfaction of being right.

I am coming, Rebecca.

He stepped forward. There was only one place he was headed. He knew it, without ever deciding.

Beckshire.

CHAPTER FIFTY-FOUR

The days of sun disappeared into a steady stream of autumn rain. Rumors raced that they would be forced to stay until spring at the earliest. The anticipation of wanting to leave, which Rebecca had expected to course through her, was absent.

You are free to leave on any ship at any time.

Philip had told her as much in the beginning. This was a democracy; there were no rules or family obligations to keep her here. There were, however, the chains of loyalty. An uneasy nudge lodged itself in her chest.

Well, perhaps, I cannot join any ship I please. I will have to prove myself all over again.

Even as she thought it though, Rebecca knew that it would not be as difficult of a task this time. She was now practiced and adept at many of the skills of the sailors. No longer would she be confined to taking up a mop to prove herself useful on the first day of sailing.

It was more than her loyalty to the crew that prevented her from immediately jumping aboard another ship. There was a newness, an excitement in the colonies. Having overheard many of the villagers speak of wanting freedom, Rebecca identified with their longing. Well, perhaps, she was overstating it.

The rains and cooling temperatures had driven the pirates from their tents into the taverns of the town. Rebecca sat before the fire. A discarded book on a table drew her attention. How long had it been since her fingers had turned the crisp pages where her friends dressed in the permanence of ink resided? As though looking at some long-absent friend, she cast her eyes lovingly on the cover.

"Go ahead," the tavern owner's wife said, causing Rebecca to jump at the sound of her voice.

"Pardon?" she said, turning.

"Go ahead and read the book. Someone left it here last

week and never came back to collect it."

Rebecca stared at the book, her heart stirred at her first love. Long before she had ever seen Caleb Haroldson, books had cast a spell over her.

"You are able to read?" the woman said, sensing Rebecca's hesitation.

"I can read," she said, hastily. The woman smiled, as though to once again say that Rebecca ought to read it. Turning, she left Rebecca alone with the book.

Picking up the worn volume, Rebecca's heart leaped as she saw the title.

Romeo and Juliet.

Opening the pages, her eyes traveled over the words and she was swept away into that secret place that Rebecca had been convinced was banished from her new life. Many of the others were gathered around a hand of cards downstairs and so, left alone with the book, Rebecca sank deeper into the story. She was so engrossed that she did not hear the footsteps on the stairs.

"Ah, there you are." Rebecca jumped at the words.

"Oh, hello," she said, seeing John. Then, remembering that she was reading *Romeo and Juliet*, she shut it quickly and set it down on the table behind her.

"You can read?" John said, pulling up a chair and sitting backward on it.

Rebecca nodded.

Please, do not let that have given me away!

"Always wished I could."

"You do not?" Rebecca said, unable to mask the surprise in her voice. She knew, of course, that many people could not read, but John's knowledge had seemed limitless to her.

"Never learned," he said, with more than a hint of regret.

"I could teach you," she said, with perhaps more of a flush of pleasure than she really ought to have had.

"Now, that could be a worthwhile activity while we are

here," he said, thumping the table for emphasis, "I do not much suppose that anything of interest will happen this winter. It does not seem to me like a fight would be able to start."

He was looking at her, waiting for an answer. Still unaccustomed to anyone caring much for her opinion, especially on politics, she said,

"Yes, it does not seem like a very worthwhile usage of supplies to go about things in the winter. Surely, it would be difficult to transport so many men at such a time." Though she had said little and wished she had more to supply to the conversation, John said,

"You are entirely right, Richard."

I am? A swell of pride rose in her. She was valued.

She reached for something else of value to add, but her limited knowledge on the subject supplied her with nothing to say. It didn't matter, though. John had turned the topic back to reading.

"So, what were you reading?"

Should she tell him? It hardly seemed the manly material that a pirate would read. Still, it had been written by a man. That had to count for something. Besides, if Rebecca were going to teach him to read, this was the only book she had to use.

"*Romeo and Juliet,*" she said, waiting for him to answer. He said nothing. Maybe, he hadn't heard of it. Maybe, there had been no reason to worry at all.

John looked to the ceiling, snapped his fingers and said,

"*Romeo and Juliet,* is not that something about love?"

If someone had told Rebecca a year earlier that she would be reading *Romeo and Juliet* on a rainy afternoon today, she would have readily believed him. If, however, he had said that she would be dressed as a man, in the American colonies and that a pirate had just asked her if Shakespeare's classic tale were about love, she would have dismissed him as crazy. Nonetheless, it had happened and she found the conversation flowing easily as she said,

"Yes, but really 'tis about something more than that. It goes with what we were talking about."

John's face wrinkled in thought,

"'Tis about King George?"

A note of laughter dripped from Rebecca's lips and she swallowed to suppress it. Her voice could pass for a young man, who had not vocally changed, but her laughter was decidedly feminine. Luckily, his curiosity had not seemed to alert him to her slip-up.

"No," she said, "but, 'tis about freedom."

John's eyes lit up, convincing her to continue in her explanation.

"At the beginning, there are two young people who are in love, but their families do not wish them to be together."

Caleb's face danced before her, as she spoke the words. She had never fancied herself as Juliet. Juliet's love story was tragic, not Rebecca's. Only, a chill went through her, maybe Rebecca's story was to be tragic after all. Pressing on, she said,

"So, in youth, they struggle for freedom from their families' wishes. But by the end, they have struggled for freedom against death. They would not allow anything to keep them from each other. Youthful freedom from family turned to ultimate freedom from death."

But, you have turned away from me, Rebecca. You have your freedom from your family and left me behind. The words, spoken in Caleb's voice were far harsher than any he would have truly delivered. Still, she could not help but feel as though the air had gone out of her and she'd been punched in the stomach.

"I think I will get some air. The fire is rather hot," she said, standing.

"Aye, well, come join us in cards if you want when you return."

"Yes, I might," she said.

Leaving the tavern, a wash of cool air flowed over her. Breathing it in, as sails inflate in the wind, she began to feel better.

It was not a large town that they were in, just a collection of shops and houses really. There were no grand palatial homes like Turrington Manor. There was, however, a welcoming river. Rebecca allowed herself to follow it. Not wanting to become lost in the American wilderness that pressed in around her in the form of high pine trees as the town gave way to forest, she followed the sparkling strand of silver. It was the first time that she had been truly alone for more than a minute or two. As she looked around, there was no one in sight. Rebecca's steps slowed. The river opened into a secluded pool of water. Birds called to each other from the trees above her head.

"Go on," they seemed to say. Her skin, unwashed save from the buckets of rain that had poured down on it, begged to feel the cool, calm, clean water on it.

Dare I? Maybe, just if I wade for a minute or two.

The thought had barely formed, as she reached down to take her shoes off her feet.

They are all inside playing cards. No one is around. Go on.

The clothes fell away as layer after layer of masculinity dropped behind her. Stepping over the smooth stones, the waters welcomed her as she stepped in first to her knees, then to her waist. A shock of cold ran through her and she moved to keep warm, stepping tentatively from side to side. Serenading her, the birds sang from their branches. Throwing back her head and embracing her freedom, she laughed her lyrical, wholly feminine laughter.

A rustle in the bushes drew her attention. A bird flew out, joining in her song.

"Well, hello, beautiful," a fully human voice now said.

Rebecca froze.

CHAPTER FIFTY-FIVE

Peter shoveled food into his mouth. The benefit of coins jostling in his pockets had been quickly put to work. The beef felt chewy between his teeth, but the potatoes were hot and he was too hungry to notice the flaws.

"I would like another plate," he said, continuing to wolf down the food.

"Are you speaking to me?" the girl at the counter said. She had been polishing pewter plates. No one else was present in the room with them and so Peter thought the answer to her question was obvious.

"I said, are you speaking to me?" her voice rose.

With a mouthful of potatoes, Peter said,

"Yes, I want more food."

"But, you have not finished that yet, have you?"

He took a coin from his pocket, not allowing the movement to stop his eating, and plunked it on the table. This motivated her to fetch another plate.

"Well, if 'tis food you do want, food I have. Mighty peculiar though, being so hungry and 'tis not even mealtime. Lucky, I was open, you are." Her words became muffled, as she disappeared into the back to heap more food onto his plate.

When she returned, his plate was empty and he set to work immediately on the newly arrived food. He didn't bother to look up, as two men burst through the front door.

"What can I do for you gentlemen?" she said. Peter wondered why the same courtesy had not been extended to him. Glancing up out of the corner of his eye, he took in their appearance. Ah, that was why. With white powdered wigs and silk stockings, it was clear that they were gentlemen of standing. The serving girl was used to men such as Peter frequenting this place, but their presence was something out of the ordinary.

"We are looking for someone."

Someone to exchange clothes with, no doubt! You look ridiculous.

The potatoes she had brought for him were cold. Ignoring this, Peter continued to eat.

Hmm, dry too.

Shoveling in another bite, one would have been surprised that he had any adequate time to form an observation about his meal.

"Who are you looking for?" the girl said.

"A man by the name of Caleb Haroldson, ever seen him?"

The potatoes that Peter had been eating turned to lead in his mouth. Sputtering them out, he tried to breathe and not choke. Too absorbed in their own search, neither turned toward him. The girl thought for a moment.

"No, I have not seen a man by that name. Not that I can say that they all give me their names. The man there, for instance, he just came in asking for food. They do not bother to introduce themselves. For all I know, he could be Caleb Haroldson!"

Peter felt the uneasy crawl of his skin. He raised his hand to swat away the invisible spider.

"Are you?" the man said, turning to Peter.

"Am I what?" he said, pretending he had not heard.

"Caleb Haroldson."

"No," he said, shaking his head. Thank goodness they hadn't asked if he knew Caleb Haroldson; he was such a poor liar.

"Caleb Haroldson, friend of mine."

His own voice flashed through his mind now. He was still near the London jeweler shop and if these men were questioning each shop holder, they might very soon be asking him just what he did know of Caleb Haroldson. The prospect of landing in the Tower and rotting there or else meeting his demise, because he had admitted Caleb Haroldson was dead, were not welcomed vision.

No, he could not allow that to happen. As the men left, he stood from the table. A half-uneaten plate of food remained behind.

"I thought it would be too much for you," she said.

Not bothering to correct her, he nodded and made his escape out the door. The men were not in sight, as he walked down the street. The gusting autumn breeze rippled through his hair and quickened his step. They had asked for Caleb Haroldson, but which Caleb had they meant? Perhaps, it was not the real Caleb at all, but rather the spy. He had spoken of London. He had—

"There he is!" the voice of the jeweler cut through. Looking over his shoulder, he saw the two men from the tavern. Only now, they were not on foot; they were on horseback and headed straight toward him.

CHAPTER FIFTY-SIX

Startled by the voice, Rebecca remained where she stood. The breeze danced over her skin, making her feel all the more exposed.

"Come, will you let me see your face?"

Rebecca's back was to the man. Her eyes went wide, as she heard his voice in the steady stream of words.

You? Oh, what am I going to do? What am I—

"I will not hurt you. I just have a weakness for beauty," he said.

Run.

She had to escape. She believed him when he said he would not hurt her, but she couldn't let him see her. It would ruin everything. Darting through the water, Rebecca's foot slipped on a rock. Down she fell, landing in a heap. Standing, she shut her eyes as she realized that she was facing the wrong direction.

"You?" his voice said.

Realizing that she was exposed, she opened her eyes. John stared at her.

"You—you are—but how—I guess you are not—who is Richard Haroldson?" he said finally.

"Please John, hand me my clothes."

In his surprise, he had overlooked her nakedness. Now, realizing that she was not some stranger he wished to pay an admiring compliment to, but the man—no, the woman— whom he had worked alongside of, he picked up her clothes, tossing them to her. Turning with an embarrassed look on his face, he said,

"Rich—I guess I cannot call you Richard. Anyway, I am sorry. I only—you do know— how—well— " Tangling himself in knots in his words, he sat down, his back to her as she dressed.

When she had recovered herself in her masculine layers,

she crossed to sit in front of him.

He stared at her face.

"How could I not have seen it? You are really rather beautiful," he said. His gaze dipped over her body, as he said it. Then, realizing what he had done, he refocused his attention on her face.

"You are not sixteen," he said. It was an odd place to begin, but they had to start somewhere.

"No," she said.

"Well, how old are you?"

"Does it matter?"

"Well, I do not know what I am supposed to ask my fellow sailor who turned out to be a woman," he said, stumbling over the words as he said them.

"All right then, I am twenty-four," she said.

"But, I am twenty-four," he said, as if it precluded her from sharing his age. He took off his hat, balled it in his fist and then straightened it and put it back on his head.

"Who is Richard Haroldson?"

"I am," she said.

"Ah, stop fooling me. I know you are not a man! Who is really Richard Haroldson?"

"There is no such person. They are simply the names of two men."

"Who?"

"My brother and my fiancé, at least the man that I plan to marry."

John's eyebrows went up, as a look of discomfort crossed his face. He seemed none too keen about the idea of Rebecca becoming a wife.

"Marriage would be wasted on you," he mumbled.

"What?"

"Being a wife would not suit you."

"How do you know?" she said, offended.

"Because, you are better than that."

The words struck her, knocking her thoughts off balance.

Better than that? Do you mean that I am valued and so—

"Why did you run off anyway, if you were betrothed?"

"I did not run off," she said, "I was kidnapped.

She hadn't intended to say so much, but a sense of liberation at being able to reveal the truth spurred on her words. Besides, it wasn't just anyone that she was speaking to; it was John. He had quite possibly saved her life. Guilt brushed against her cheeks at the thought of sharing her secret with him, a secret that even Caleb did not know.

'Tis simply because he accepted you. He cared about your opinion; that is all.

"But, you got away?"

She nodded.

"I disguised myself. Philip found me. I secured passage home."

"So, you were using us!" John said, his temper flashing as he beat the ground with his fist.

"What? No, 'tis not like that," she said, shaking her head.

"Well, then, perhaps you would like to tell me what it is like—R— "

"Rebecca," she said.

His eyes softened at hearing her name, but only momentarily.

"From where I stand, it seems as though you have broken our code of loyalty, Rebecca."

Rebecca. Ah, you have said my name!

It sounded delightful to hear it in his American accent.

You are just glad to hear your own name again. That is all.

"Break the code? But, Philip told me from the beginning that I was free to go as I wanted."

"Of course, he did," John said, "If you find the conditions of the ship disagreeable or the treatment of the crew unfair, then you may leave. Purposefully intending to sail in only one direction, 'tis not part of the bargain. You know us now. You could betray us. We do not all wear disguises, you know."

Rebecca shook her head. Reaching out to lay her hand on his arm, she said,

"Please, John, I would not do that. You know me."

"I knew Richard Haroldson and you have told me there is no such person. I do not know you."

CHAPTER FIFTY-SEVEN

Peter's muscular legs propelled him forward, as he ran. Escaping the men on horseback would be no easy task.

I wish I had never heard the cursed name of Caleb Haroldson!

Hoofs, heavy on the street, were gaining on him.

"Peter Black, you were the last man with Caleb Haroldson before he disappeared. Peter Black, you were the last man with the spy known as Caleb Haroldson before he was killed. You are hereby sentenced to a slow and torturous death for knowing these men." The sentence rang like a death knell in his head. Not running from the men never occurred to him. The act of running causing him to look guilty didn't register in his mind either. Instead, he ran. Logic had long since abandoned the events of Peter's life. When in doubt escape, was the ruling order.

The hooves thundered in Peter's ears. His heart pounded unrelentingly, forcing the blood through his veins. Winded from the weight of his muscles, his breath caught in labored gasps in his chest.

Peter Black, you are finished. Give up.

The muscles of his legs screamed out, begging him to give into his reasoning mind. A loud whinnying from the horse convinced him that he would soon be caught.

"Stop! By order of his Majesty's guard, stop!"

Caleb Haroldson, the spy. Surely, he was the reason they sought him.

"You will come back, will you not?" Sorry Mol, I do not think I will be able to keep my word. I do—

A sliver of hope pierced his thoughts. The cobbled lane gave way to a slip of a path between two buildings. Was it a dead-end? There was no way to tell. The narrow alley curved, preventing Peter from seeing down it. A horse would be unable to squeeze through so slender a space. In that moment, it was all that mattered.

Peter ducked inside the passageway, not bothering to look over his shoulder at the others.

"Stop him! Stop him!" the guard shouted. They scrambled to dismount, but Peter now held the advantage. Racing down the alley, he stumbled over a pile of garbage. He fell hard against the wall, but braced himself from falling to his knees. Peter's hands scraped the wall, leaving them raw. Recovering from the stumble, he hurried on his way. The alley narrowed more. Peter felt the hands of panic grip his body. Trapped between his two pursuers and the prospect of coming face-to-face with a wall, Peter did something that he had not done for longer than he could remember.

I know I have not always been the best man, but if you could help me now, God, I shall try to do better. I shall even make an honest woman out of Mol, if you will give me the chance.

Peter drew to an abrupt stop. A wall blocked his path. He had received his answer and been given a no.

You are not good enough to be rescued, Peter Black.

Emerging from the bleakness of his thoughts came the flutter of a bird.

"Where did you come from?"

"Stop! Stop!" the man's voice hounded him.

Frightened by Peter's voice, the bird rose, fluttering away. There was a bend in the path! The alley widened and gave way to a bustling street. Dodging the oncoming horses and pedestrians, Peter rushed across the road. Continuing to run, enlivened by a second chance, he spotted a forest of sails on the horizon. Without fully comprehending what he was doing, Peter moved swiftly toward the docks.

The crowds of people obscured the guards' view of Peter. With a considerable advantage ahead of them, the path under Peter's feet gave way to the wooden boards of the dock. Waves leaped at the posts, as barnacles clung to them. No such desperation to stay on the land coursed through Peter's blood, as he pulled to a halt in front of an upturned barrel. A sailor leaned against it.

"Where do I go to join up?"

"What?"

"I would like to join the navy."

"You would what?"

"I want to be a sailor."

"Yes, I heard you all right. I just cannot rightly say that I am used to anyone coming here willingly. Well, come on then."

CHAPTER FIFTY-EIGHT

Entering Beckshire, an eeriness whispered to Caleb. Although still light, the shutters were closed. No one walked along the streets. Even the persistent chirping of birds, which had accompanied Caleb for much of his journey, was strangely missing. Silence enrobed him in a cloak of ill-fitting stillness. Everything was amiss. The town should have been teeming with the daily noise of its inhabitants.

Caleb's eyes lifted to the rooftops. No steady streams of smoke rose from the tightly-packed stone chimneys. The characteristic huffing and puffing rising above the village, testifying to the preparation of the evening meal, was nowhere to be seen.

Could it be that the entire town was abandoned? That hardly made sense. It was not so long ago that Lord Turrington had said Seamus, the monk, had been requested to come here.

Caleb swallowed. The dryness of his throat irritated him. From the corner of his eyes, he spotted a well. Crossing to it, he searched for any sign of life. Shouldn't there be some hungry dog, some twittering bird, some woodland squirrel? Looking up and not watching the ground he was walking on, Caleb stumbled. He caught his balance without falling, but his eyes were forced down.

On the ground, smeared into the dirt, half-caked with mud was a silver pendant. Crouching down to further examine it, Caleb flicked the dirt away. Arms outstretched, it was undeniably a crucifix. Turning it over, Caleb caught sight of a tiny inscription.

Seamus.

Lord Turrington had said that he had died, he was gone, but finding the crucifix in the dirt, rather than serving as confirmation to this, only churned up more questions for Caleb. If Seamus had succumbed to sickness as Lord Turrington had intimated, would he have lost his crucifix? It seemed more like the happenstance of one driven away in haste.

Pocketing it, Caleb trained his eyes on the ground. Footprints were sparse and, where present, the rain had marred their visibility. Blurred and crushed back into the earth, they offered little information.

He had begun to feel as if he were reading a book that was full of blank pages. Only a scattering of oddly placed words were present in the vastness.

"Into the bowels of the earth, I shall be your Virgil," Seamus's words leaped at him, from the haziness of memory.

"Of course!" Caleb said, breaking the stillness of the scene.

The well rose invitingly from the moist ground. A bucket stood beside it, still attached to the thick rope. His parched throat no longer on his mind, he lowered the bucket over the side. A ruckus of the metal bucket slamming against the stones on its descent rose from the well. The rod that held the rope had fallen to a slant and made for a route that was far from direct. With a loud thump, the bucket hit the ground of the well. There had been no slosh of water when it landed.

Just as I thought.

Feeling a shiver of excitement at the turn in his luck, a plan fell into place. Grabbing hold of the rope, Caleb reeled it back in and untied the bucket that had served as an anchor. Discarding it to the side, Caleb yanked on the rope. It held.

He tied a knot and pulled on the ends to test its strength. The first knot slipped.

You are going too fast. Slow down.

For a second time, he tied the knot. Testing it again, this time it held. Secured by the knot, a loop of rope awaited him. He stepped into it, pulling it up around his waist and fastened it taut.

Perfect.

Caleb perched on the side of the well. It was narrow, but

surely that would serve to his advantage. At about ten feet deep, if he were to fall it wouldn't be entirely disastrous. Unless of course, he bashed his head against the wall.

No, no, do not think like that.

Pushing his doubts aside, he straddled the well.

Well, here goes.

Hoisting his other leg over the well, he wedged himself against its walls. With his back pressed into one side, he used his feet to push off from the other as he rappelled deeper into the jaws of the earth. Overhead, a bird cried its evening song.

Yes, I am not as alone as I thought.

Pleased by the discovery, he descended farther. His foot hit a loose stone and he lost his foothold. Sliding the last couple of feet, he landed unharmed at the bottom. Only his hands had suffered, rubbed raw from the rope burn. Ignoring this, Caleb was spurred on by the imminence of his success. Not knowing where he was searching for, he had arrived.

In front of me should be a door, if I turn around.

He turned, but no door met him. Tapping on the walls, no stones budged.

But, that is not possible. I know 'tis here.

Pressing his weight against the walls, they stood unrelentingly. Unwilling to give up, he dropped to his knees. Scratching in the dirt and moving piles of it aside, he searched for a hidden panel.

Yes, that was it. That had to be it. He simply had not dug deep enough. He had to—

From the grounds above, he heard the unmistakable sound of horse hoofs. Caleb froze.

Who was coming? Had someone from the town returned?

The sound of a rider dismounting came to him now. Maybe, they wouldn't notice him.

"There— "

Discovered, Caleb said nothing.

"Where are the rest of them? We told you we would come for them. Running away does nothing, but break the law!"

CHAPTER FIFTY-NINE

Stunned, Rebecca had watched as John walked away. Now wearing Philip's old clothes once again, she no longer felt the security they had once offered. Though dressed, she was fully exposed. Her secret, which she had struggled to maintain for over two months, was out. Worse, perhaps, was John's treatment. He had thrown away their friendship all because of something she couldn't help: her gender.

But no, that wasn't it at all. He had felt betrayed and lied to. The worst part was, Rebecca had been unable to deny his parting words. It was true; he knew Richard Haroldson and not her. It would be uncomfortable sailing with John now cross with her, but she would just have to make do. They wouldn't be sailing for months, anyway. Besides, she was well-regarded among the other men.

Whether known to be female or disguised as a man, Rebecca had always been well-liked. Sizing a person up by his character, rather than his status, was a practice that found her running counter to her family. A nuisance to her mother, who couldn't understand why Rebecca wouldn't simply enjoy her privileged position, the practice had served her well. There were many she had called friend, beginning with the maid's children, that if she had observed the social views of her mother she would not have. Then, of course, there was Caleb. Dear, sweet Caleb. The chiseled features of his face now blurred in front of her, as though looking at a distorted image in a pool of water.

She reached out, shutting her eyes to see him more clearly. Her hand brushed against his cheek. Then, the lines of his face blurred and the memory burst. No, she could not reach out to touch him. She was here in the colonies, not in England. Her own situation, and not only that of her home, lay questionably, uncertain before her.

Sympathies for the colonies flowed freely, when

embodied in the words of freedom spoken by the crew. John turning away from her had changed that, though, or at least had planted a hindering seed of doubt. Perhaps, America was not so unlike England. Her true identity still confined her and still produced thoughts about her, often unwarranted, from others.

Rebecca Turrington, you are quite simply going to have to press on.

A whipper-will answered her with a muted song.

"Yes, you are right," she said, "I am not yet Rebecca Turrington again. For now, I must remain Richard Haroldson."

Her stomach tangled into a pile of knots, as she followed the river back to the town. She would have to rely on John's decency to preserve her. Waiting through the winter months on land, without ample opportunity to prove herself at sea, seemed a hindrance. As the town came into view, some of the crew were hammering beams into place. Maybe, she would not have to wait so long to prove herself after all. Not wanting to draw undo attention to herself, in case John had reneged on thinking being disloyal was the worst thing one could do, she slipped in beside the others.

If I continue to help rebuild the ship, then I have every right to sail on her! My goodness Rebecca, these men have changed you more than you realized. Your logic sounds like theirs.

She took delight in the realization. Although always unhappy with the disregard that people had previously paid her, now she felt the ability to stand up to others for herself. Running was not the only option in having one's own way or in living for one's self.

A pile of tools lay on a sheet of canvas in the grass. Rebecca knelt down to pick up a hammer and nail. The rhythm of fastening the massive wooden beams together whirled her into its easy flow.

At this rate, we will be sailing well before spring!

Rather than invigorate her, the thought slowed her hand. Sailing again surely meant returning to England. Freedom slipped away with each blow to the nails. Her life as a pirate, bucking society's rules, would come to an end all too quickly. If she had become embroiled in the savage piratical acts of the stories she had read and heard, certainly she would have run from them now that she was on land. But, Rebecca did not know these men to be murderers, raiders or cohorts of violence. They were sailors, who practiced a harmless bit of smuggling.

"Harmless, Rebecca? They seem to have stolen your heart, or at the very least, your ambitions," Caleb's accusatory voice cut into her thoughts.

Caleb, that is not fair!

"You seem so eager to put yourself before me."

She shut her eyes. These were not the words of the real Caleb Haroldson, not her Caleb. He would have put her happiness first. There was no question about that.

Then, why do I feel so guilty? Because, you know 'tis true.

Rebecca pounded the nail into the beam, to quiet her conscience.

No longer comfortable with your own morality, you are a pirate.

Bang!

The metal drove into the wood, spewing sawdust.

Caleb would not even want you anymore. John does not know Rebecca Turrington, but neither does Caleb Haroldson, not anymore.

Bang!

The nail went sideways. Wedging the hammer under it, she pulled on it. Everything had to be set straight, beginning with this solitary slanted piece of metal.

"Richard, you are truly dedicated to the ship. Shame to see you leave," Pete, the cheat, said. Rebecca had righted the nail.

Leave? What do you mean, leave?

She lifted her head but Pete had already moved farther down. Several men were between them and remaining inconspicuous dictated that she not yell across the others. Her stash of nails had been exhausted. Bending back down, another replenished her supply of nails.

"Here you are, Richard. I wish we would have known each other better."

"What?"

"I understand, of course. Cannot say I do not envy you some, ah but the sea is where I belong."

She nodded, not understanding what he meant. The man returned to his work, working a saw over a long plank. Looking down the line of men, Rebecca saw the massive amount of work that still needed to be completed on the ship. Her uneasiness at the ship sailing sooner than she thought, had been misplaced. An abundance of questions now filled the space. From above the heads of the men, Rebecca spotted a statuesque figure crowned with a long wispy feather extending from an upturned hat.

Philip.

Before she had even begun to walk toward him, she realized he was approaching her.

"Richard, I understand you will be leaving us. Well, you have been a fine crew member. I must admit that I was not certain how you would fare when I found you in that cave. You did look a bit scrawny, if you do not mind me saying. Anyway, you proved your weight. I wish I could convince you to stay, but I understand that we must seize upon opportunity."

Opportunity?

"I—"

Out of the corner of her eye, a lank figure stood. His arms crossed over his chest, as he leaned against a tree.

John.

Rebecca swallowed.

"I want to thank you for the time on your ship."

Philip raised his hand to brush aside her comments.

"Our ship, young master Haroldson."

She swallowed again, to suppress the rising tide inside of her. She was respected, a part of something and now it was slipping through her fingers.

CHAPTER SIXTY

Running away?

Stuck at the bottom of the well, the cogs of Caleb's mind started moving before his body. The people of this town were deceased, not missing.

Rebecca.

She too had been declared dead near Turrington Manor and was now simply gone. Or, at least she had been.

"*You have to find them, Adam,*" Marion's raspy voice crackled to him from the stones of the well. None too pleased at the thought of once again being bound, gagged, and taken away by a group of men, he hesitated to move.

"Tell us where they are."

Caleb said nothing. He didn't know the answer, but his silence was a choice more than a result of his lack of information.

"I said, tell us where they are," the voice said, rising both in volume as well as gruffness.

"I do not—"

The muzzle of a musket, hoisted over the side of the well, alerted Caleb to their commitment.

"Climb up!" the man with the musket barked.

"Ungrateful bunch, the lot of you," another said.

With no other choice, Caleb secured the rope around his waist once again. Looking up at the men, his eyes scanned the stones of the well's walls searching for footholds or handholds. So sure had he been that the well would lead to an underground tunnel, like the ones beside Turrington Manor, that he had not bothered with how he would logically climb back out. Caleb had assumed there would be an easier exit, as there were many doors to the tunnels in the forest at home. He had chosen to descend into the well to avoid the time that would be required to root out another entrance.

"Make haste!" Musket Mouth shouted.

Annoyed, Caleb stepped into a crack between two stones. One step and one reach at a time, he hoisted himself to the top. Suspended by the rope, he was reduced once again to a puppet controlled by someone else pulling all the strings.

"What is your name?" Musket Mouth said, when Caleb was nearly to the top.

Concentrating on maintaining his balance, he didn't answer.

"Answer me!"

You do not want me to fall, do you? No, no, you would not much care what happens.

Before he could reply, the man turned to look at something behind him. Besides Musket Mouth, there were at least two other men standing at the top of the well. All of them seemed preoccupied, as he took his final step over the well's edge. A helping hand might have been a welcomed relief for his sore palms. On the other hand, Caleb had his fill of rough manhandling from Lord Turrington's men. Standing on his own feet was at least some improvement.

Scrambling the last steps over the well, Caleb saw that it was a woman that had drawn the attention of the men. She harbored none of the innocence and joy of youth and was not well dressed in the beauty or elegance of women like Rebecca who often drew an appreciative eye. Instead, she was small in form, haggard in appearance and spoke with a—

Marion.

As the man in front of him stepped aside, her face was as clear to him as his own reflection.

"His name is Adam," she said. He shot her an inquisitive look, but she paid him no heed.

"You know this man?" Musket Mouth said, casting both his glance and his pointing finger in Caleb's direction.

"We have had tea," she said, as though it were a perfectly normal reason. And, it's true, it would have been, if not for

Marion's unorthodox approach to tea and to life.

"Speaking of tea, perhaps, you gentlemen would like some?"

The two nodded their agreement, though Musket Mouth muttered something about already being late.

"Ah come on, if we cannot even have tea, we might as well be in Boston. Would you like that?"

Musket Mouth shrugged.

"I suppose you might like it," the other said, shaking his head. They waited for Marion to disappear inside of one of the nearby houses to prepare the tea. Only Caleb seemed unsurprised when she did not move.

Ah, at least I know she does not think I am the only fool.

"Here you are," she said, drawing a cup from the air and pouring the invisible brew.

"What, are you daft?" one of them said, lacking the tact that Caleb had exercised on the hostess of invisible tea. Looking offended, she turned to Caleb.

"Well, I can count on you to have some tea with me, can I not Adam?"

Caleb looked from her to the men.

"Ah, they are both batty—climbing into wells and drinking nonexistent tea!"

"'Tis real," she insisted, "you do not have to see something for it to be true."

"Come on," Musket Mouth said, putting a hand on Caleb's arm to lead him away.

"Wait," Marion said.

Ah, at least I have someone who cares, who will appeal for me.

"What about my money? I told you I would show you where they were. I kept my word, did I not?"

Money? Do you not even care that I am being taken away?

"There is only one man here. You did not keep your word at all," Musket Mouth said.

"I told you I would show you where they were. This is where they were. How am I supposed to know where they are?"

"Fine, pay her the money."

The other took a pouch from his pocket, pulled out a coin from it and tossed it to the ground. It landed at Marion's feet. As Caleb was pulled away, he saw her fall to her knees, searching for it as a dog does for scraps.

"Buy yourself some tea," Musket Mouth said, laughing.

CHAPTER SIXTY-ONE

"When will you be leaving us?" Philip said, as they stood beside the ship that Rebecca would assuredly never sail on again. John stood, resolute at the corner of her vision. She looked up at him and his face was painted in deeper tones of somberness than was usual for him.

Ah, when she would leave he had not determined for her. He must have said that she would be leaving. Some great opportunity awaited her, whatever that was. The warning in his eyes testified that she would be wise to go as soon as possible. His look was clear. He had done her a favor; she shouldn't take advantage of it.

"Unfortunately, right away."

A tinge of sadness—were pirates sad? Well, they really were just people, this crew anyway—pulled at Philip's dark wide-set eyes.

"Such is our life, Master Haroldson. We are carried on the wind."

How I wish 'twere not so changeable!

The frost of late autumn was still perhaps a month away, but John's stance bore an iciness more extreme than the harshest winter.

Rebecca gathered what few belongings she had from her room in the tavern. There were a couple of fish hooks that John had taught her how to carve and one or two additional pieces of clothing. *Romeo and Juliet* sat waiting on the bedside table for her to lift it up and carry it with her. She crossed to it, the floorboards creaking under her, picked it up, then thought better of it and put it back.

No time for sentimentality, Rebecca.

Walking with the setting sun to her left, she pushed north. For much of the night, she continued to walk. If she were close to Philip and the crew, she would be tempted to return to them. But, of course, she could not and so she put as much distance between herself and them as possible.

Following the coast, the waves lapped against the shore on her right. Moonlight glinted off the water, illuminating silver patches to guide her. The sea was calm tonight. Its saltiness settled pleasantly into her nose. Having slept on the deck for so many nights, she had not realized how much she missed the nocturnal sea these past few weeks on shore. When had the storm been? Was it two weeks ago now or three? It nagged at her that she could not remember.

"Well, I do not suppose it much matters, anyway."

Tempted as she was by the charms of this side of the world, with each step Rebecca began to realize more that it was time to go home.

"I shall find a ship. I shall return to England," she said. Months ago, in the humid summer days in the Caribbean, she had formulated such a plan. Philip and his crew had merely been a distraction, a pleasant one, but nonetheless a distraction. John too.

She swallowed and her foot missed her step.

You are just tired. You have been walking all night. Of course, you would stumble.

But, even as she thought the words, she began to wonder why she felt the need to justify any of it. Rebecca continued to walk, pushing aside any thought that hindered her resolve. As the first blush of the day's sunlight settled over the water, she felt the assurance that her time aboard the ship had not only been a distraction but had served some useful purpose. Taking a fishing hook and bit of rope from her pocket, she cast it into the water. Rebecca Turrington of England, though clever and firm in her wits, was not proficient in these skills that were secondhand to

Richard Haroldson.

The rays of light bloomed into the rosy pinks of flowers in a garden, as they spread their lazy fingers over the horizon and toward her. With the benefit of daylight, Rebecca built a fire and roasted her fish breakfast. Able to see farther ahead of her than she had all night, a town appeared in the distance.

If I keep walking, I should be there in a few hours.

A yawn burst through her thought. Lulled by the friendly waves, Rebecca began to doze. Jumping awake, she shook the sleepiness away. Its hold, stronger than irons clapped onto prisoners, exerted itself. The muscles in her legs grew heavy.

Maybe, just for a minute.

Leaning against her belongings as a pillow, Rebecca fell asleep as her new life dawned around her.

CHAPTER SIXTY-TWO

Journeying with Musket Mouth and his companions drew a steady crowd. No longer was Caleb their sole captive. Instead, many joined their ranks. Always male and always close in age to Caleb, a growing suspicion rose in him.

When they had walked, gathering others from towns and farmland, for more than a week, someone said,

"I know where they are taking us."

"Where?" Caleb said.

"London."

"Why would they take us there?" he said, answers no longer making much sense and only leading to more questions.

"To fight their wars for 'em, of course."

The colonies? Seriously? Have I escaped the fate of joining Richard's men in America only to be shipped there, far away from dear Rebecca?

Feeling as though his mission had been hung decisively and for a final time from the gallows, Caleb struggled to maintain his breathing.

"Not keen on war, eh?" the other said, taking note of his paling face, "Cannot say I am looking forward to it either." Armed with only glum answers, he continued,

"But eh, 'tis the way of it. They send us poor to do their fighting, to keep our poor American cousins in the chains of poverty through taxes."

He shrugged, showing his indifference to the situation,

"But, 'tis the way of it."

'Tis the way of it! 'Tis not the way of it! We are not condemned to live the life of another man's bidding!

They had been sitting under the trees, allowed to rest in their long march to London.

No doubt, they only care about themselves.

Caleb's bitterness served little purpose, except further inciting his anger.

Imagine me, Caleb Haroldson, in a press-gang! Do they not know who I am? Do they not know that Rebecca Turrington is to be my wife?

But, of course, they could not know.

"All right, come on," Musket Mouth said. As the number of men grew, so too did the number of guards. Musket Mouth had remained as the one in charge.

A steady autumn drizzle began to fall, as they continued to walk. Puddles soon pooled under Caleb's feet. As he trudged through the mud, his spirits were further pulled into the mire. Caleb's steps fell into a slower pace. The late hour of the day and the continually darkening clouds cloaked them in a shield of dimness. With his walk slowed, shoulders passed in front of Caleb. The ranks passing him by, he sank farther back and was absorbed as a shadow into the darkness.

Dare I? Can I? I must.

Musket Mouth was now far ahead, busy talking to another man from on top of his horse. Caleb's muscles stretched, as he walked in longer strides. Preparing to make certain that he was not kept from Rebecca and England any longer, he took in a deep breath. The faces of the men around him were indistinguishable in the fading light.

"All right, stop. We camp here," Musket Mouth's command filed down the ranks. The rain continued to fall, its pattering a metronome for their steps. The men slowed to a stop.

Now! Do it now!

Caleb turned away from the others.

You will not take me to America! I will not fight your blasted war!

His heart quickened, keeping time with the tempo of the rain.

"Stop him! He is escaping!"

Caleb's heart seized. His air caught in his chest in jagged

bursts. His escape had been discovered! Not bothering to look over his shoulder, he ran. Momentarily, hundreds of hands would be around him. The odds that he would be faster than all of the other men were too great to overcome.

On he ran. No gaining footsteps could be heard. Greater distance was put between him and where he'd left the others. Still, no one caught up to him. How could that be? Glancing over his shoulder, he saw the enlarging chasm between him and the others. The men stood, unyielding to Musket Mouth's command. They had been unable to fight their own pressing into service, but they would not help in capturing Caleb. They would gain nothing by pursuing him. Instead, they held their ground.

Spurred on by their show of will for him to escape, or at least their lack of commitment to capturing him, he focused ahead. A tree emerged in front of him. He turned, narrowly missing running straight into it.

"Stop him! I said stop him!"

The clicking of muskets into place ripped through the night. With a bang, the first went off. Jumping to avoid the first bullet, Caleb watched as it landed a couple of feet in front of him. Mud spewed from the impact, sloshing against his legs.

Whizzing toward him came the second bullet. Caleb ducked, as it scraped the air where his head had been seconds before.

"Let me live! Let me live!" every cell screamed, as they pushed his body forward. A third bullet fired, zooming toward him. Slicing through the air, closer it came. He was certain that this time he would be unable to dodge it.

With a hard yank, a hand reached out and pulled Caleb behind a tree. The bullet slammed into the pine, splintering chunks of wood around him.

"Make haste!" a voice said, in a loud whisper.

Caleb felt himself pushed onto a moving lump. Whoever had pulled him behind the tree jumped on behind him as the lump rose. Hearing a neigh, Caleb realized that it was a horse that he had been pushed onto. A click of the reins set the righted animal galloping into the night.

CHAPTER SIXTY-THREE

Wetness washing over her foot woke Rebecca.

Why am I having a bath at this hour?

The thought made little sense, but those encountered upon first waking seldom do. Tiredness pulled at her eyes and she quickly fell back asleep.

"Stop licking me, Samson!" she said.

Samson? Samson, the cook's dog, is not here.

Opening her eyes, Rebecca saw the approaching tide wash over her feet.

"Oh!" she said, scrambling up a bit too quickly. A rush of dizziness flooded her senses. Seeing that the tide was progressing much slower than she had feared, she wobbled to the side trying to regain her balance. It was only the distorting hands of sleep that had convinced her that she was in more danger than she was.

She stretched, arching her back in the sunlight. A golden ball, suspended in a tranquil sky, it warmed her from its seat high above. Alerted that it must be well into the afternoon, she ignored the gnawing in her stomach and gathered up her belongings to continue on her way.

The town beckoned to her from a distance. She was in no hurry to get to it, if all it meant were another place where she was not a part of and somewhere else she had to hide.

"Caleb," she said aloud to the rocks, "with all that has changed, can I count on you to remain constant?"

An arching maple dripped with resplendent colored leaves. As they fell to the ground, she said,

"No, I suppose you are right. Everything must change."

As the woodlands and coast transformed to the architecture of the town, Rebecca was swept into the sentiments of alteration. Farther south in Georgia, where she had first been shipwrecked with the crew, there was a muted enthusiasm for colonial rights. Dismissed by its northern neighbors as a penal colony, it had not been included in the present gathering of colonies. In Philadelphia, right this moment, there were men gathered in what they referred to as a Continental Congress. It was their ambition to send a powerful message to England. Rumors streamed through the streets, as comets race across a night sky in a meteor shower. Much as Rebecca's identity and her loyalties to Caleb and her home and to her freedom in this new land were divided, so too were the ideas of those both at the Congress and surrounding her now.

Some supported John Galloway's, the Pennsylvanian delegate's, call for union with Britain. Reconciliation with their transatlantic cousins seemed logical enough. For Rebecca, there was appeal in thoughts of her homeland accepting her for the new ideas she had grown into. There had already been enough bloodshed against France; why should they now turn on each other? But, there were also those who, like John, spoke of freedom. If England would not respect their right to rule, then why should they continue to pay taxes?

Last year in Boston, crates of tea had been dumped into the river. Now, there arose a movement to dispose of all British imports. If all went according to plan, as of December first, barely over a month away, there would be no British imports in the colonies. Furthermore, the tropical islands to the south—where Rebecca had first been wooed by the exotic colors, people and climate of this hemisphere—would be cut off from trade with the colonies if they did not cut ties with Britain. Small and powerless as they may have seemed, this collection of colonies was prepared to deliver a wallop to their British overseers. The thought of actually fighting against Britain seemed laughable. With no army and no navy, it was ludicrous to challenge any country that was armed, especially when that country happened to have the best of both in the world.

Economically, though, a mighty punch could be delivered. Without a growing American market for British goods and with the possible threat of cutting off American supplies of raw materials, there were more than a few reasons to become nervous of the uncertain future.

"There is another protest being organized," someone on the street near Rebecca said.

"Yes, so what is different about that?" his companion asked.

Yes, what is different?

Intrigued by the men's talk, Rebecca followed the two into the merchant's shop they had disappeared inside of. The shelves teemed with goods.

"No tea?" a woman asked the merchant.

"Not selling anymore here," came the reply.

Rebecca stayed close to the men she had followed into the shop, without trying to appear as though she were doing so, in hopes of hearing more of their conversation.

"Women are organizing it."

"Women?"

Women?

Rebecca held her breath. Was it some joke?

"'Tis true. Well, I suppose we can use all the help we can get."

"I suppose. Now, where is that—"

Their conversation passed into other topics and Rebecca turned away.

"Can I help you?" the merchant behind the counter said. Realizing he was speaking to her, Rebecca said,

"Oh, no, thank you. I have what I need."

Leaving the shop, the man's words replayed in her head.

Women are organizing it.

Was it possible? Could she peel off the layers she had worn as disguise these past months and have some power?

The thought seemed too tantalizing to be true.

Could I be free to be Rebecca Turrington again?

Floating for a moment on the thin veil of dreams, reality descended heavily over her from the voice of a stranger.

"Closing Boston harbor was a mighty fierce mistake."

The harbor, yes, of course.

No, she realized sadly; Rebecca Turrington could not yet surge to life again.

Perhaps, American women were at liberty to organize a protest, but the thought of openly sailing as a woman was too far-fetched. Getting home required sailing. Sailing required either money or being a sailor. Money was not something that she had, but being a sailor was something that she could take pride in saying that she now was.

Best press on.

There was no harbor in the town. No harbor meant no ships and thus no way home. The buildings fell behind her. As she looked back over her shoulder, they blurred into the muted gray haziness of twilight coupled with distance. Pushing farther north, Rebecca willed herself forward. The air around her this evening was chilly. November would soon arrive. Wandering without benefit of shelter and dressed only in Philip's discarded clothes would be an unsuitable way to pass the winter. Freezing would little serve her purpose and—

Rebecca's feet stopped, as a small house appeared in front of her. Hidden among the trees, she was sure that it would have gone entirely unnoticed had she not seen the rising smoke of its chimney. In front of the house, a line of clothes hung drying from the day's wash. Dresses were the sole garment flapping in the wind.

Drawn to them, Rebecca reached tentatively to them as a child extends his hand toward flames when knowing better. Heat raced to her fingertips, as the fabric brushed against them. Dressed in the clothes of a man, she had forgot how soft feminine clothes could be.

Try it on!

The thought startled her. How could she think such a thing? It was far too dangerous a notion to entertain. She had stolen Philip's clothes to acquiesce to life as a pirate; dare she steal back her own identity, even for a moment?

"Who is there?"

The door crashed open. Dropping the fabric from her grasp, Rebecca fled.

CHAPTER SIXTY-FOUR

Holding tightly to the reins of the horse, Caleb rode in the dark. The man, who had jumped on the horse behind him, guided the animal without benefit of voice until the sounds of Musket Mouth died down behind them.

Who are you?

Before he could speak the words aloud, the rider spoke to him,

"It is good to see you again, Caleb Haroldson."

"Seamus?" he said, with such surprise as he tried to turn to look at the man that he nearly fell off of the horse.

"You have been asking about me," Seamus said. Perhaps, it was a question, but Caleb wanted answers of his own.

"How did you know I was here?"

"I did not know," Seamus said.

"What? I do not understand."

"There will be time for questions later, Caleb Haroldson. For now, we must wait until there are not so many around us that would wish us harm."

With that, they rode in silence. Trees flanked them, threatening to conceal these never-do-wells that Seamus had alluded to in his warning. As the first light broke over them, the white painting of frost's fingers revealed itself to the world.

Dear sweet Rebecca, I hope that you are warmer than I.

He blinked, taking in his surroundings as he reemerged into consciousness from the dozing of the night. A scattering of buildings, looking much like the ghost town that he had been captured in, beckoned to them. As they drew closer, Caleb tilted from one side to the other.

"Is something wrong, Caleb Haroldson?"

"Why have you brought me here?"

"Where?"

"To Beckshire," he said, opening his eyes wider to look for any remaining members of the king's guard.

"We are not in Beckshire," he said. Caleb continued to look at the approaching town. It was too similar to be another place entirely. But then, Seamus was supposedly dead and he had rescued him, but not realized that it was Caleb that he was rescuing.

Ah, do not try to figure it out! Nothing makes sense any longer.

"I suppose," Seamus said after a moment, "It does look similar, but that makes sense since it is the same people."

The same people?

"Do you mean—"

"Yes, Caleb Haroldson, the people of Beckshire are here."

"Then they are not—"

"No, not dead, merely across the river."

The words struck Caleb. The horse pulled to a stop and Seamus jumped from its back. Caleb stared at Seamus.

"What do you mean?"

"There will be plenty of time for questions, Caleb Haroldson."

Nudging Caleb, the horse demanded attention. He turned to look at it fully for the first time.

"Dandelion," he said in surprise.

"Do you know this horse?"

"He knows the horse," another voice said. Bent over a grave, leaning against a shovel, stood the old man that he had last seen Dandelion with.

"You," Caleb said, none too pleased to see him. Turning to Seamus, he said,

"I thought you said they are living."

"Truthfully, they are, Caleb Haroldson."

"Then, why is he digging a grave?"

"Because, we will need it," the man said. Turning his back to Seamus, Caleb marched to the man and said,

"What? Do you plan to bury me? Having me arrested

'twas not enough?"

"You do misunderstand," the man said, "I was protecting you."

"Protecting me? From what?"

"From those who turned against us."

Caleb's brow furrowed, as he struggled to make sense of the words.

"Besides, why are you cross? I left you a means of escape, did I not?"

"You sent the man to free me?"

"'Tis time to cross the river."

The words flashed through his mind. Weight, accumulating from the heavy knowledge that none of these strange events had been random, pressed against Caleb's chest.

"Rebecca!" he said, a ray of light bursting through the claustrophobic clouds of uncertainty.

Seamus and the other man exchanged glances.

"You told me Rebecca crossed the river. Everything I have heard about crossing the river is now connected to this place. Take me to her!"

Seamus looked at the older man.

"Whom does Caleb Haroldson speak of?"

"Rebecca Turrington," the older man said.

"Seamus, take me to her," Caleb said. So close to her now, he would soon hold those hands in his own! She was here! She had to be!

"Caleb Haroldson, Rebecca Turrington is not here. She never has been."

CHAPTER SIXTY-FIVE

When Rebecca was certain that she had put enough distance between herself and the house at the edge of the forest, she hunkered down in a bed of leaves and pine needles to pass the rest of the night sleeping. After a breakfast of berries and fish, she set out again.

The land was flat here and lacked the sheer cliffs that she had seen long ago at the beginning of her journey. Beaches, with sand so white it nearly shone, mingled with easy swaying hills and thick coniferous forests. Mid-morning, another town rose to greet her. This one had a harbor. As she approached, she soon realized that this was no ordinary town; it was a sprawling metropolis. Having been to London on a few occasions, Rebecca observed that this was the closest thing she had seen resembling it.

Could I be in Boston?

But no, that didn't make sense. Boston's harbor had been shut after the so-called tea party.

Well, then perhaps it is Philadelphia?

The thought of mingling with the colonial delegates at their Convention seemed too tempting to avoid. But no, she hadn't walked that far yet. At least, she didn't think so.

Having merely seen glimpses of accurate maps over Richard's shoulder hindered her knowledge of American geography. No one at home had seen any point in young Miss Turrington poring over maps of far-flung lands. The maps in her books were intended for plotting adventure, not for planning calculable distances between places that truly existed.

On the shoreline, palm trees fanned their fronds as she had first seen in the Caribbean. Buildings painted in vivid colors, like those of the tropical birds, appeared on either side of her.

"Pardon me," she said, to a man walking with a limp. He hoisted a barrel over his shoulder and made no attempt to answer Rebecca.

"Pardon me," she tried again, this time on a man who looked most decidedly to be a sailor.

"Yes?" he said, not stopping but at least turning toward her this time.

"Can you tell me where we are please?"

"Where we are?" he repeated, as though she were daft.

Rebecca nodded, not minding the peculiar looks so long as she received her answer. For a moment, she thought that he would walk away, dismissing her as the first man had.

Instead, he said,

"Why this here is Charles's Town. Some say 'tis the finest city in these colonies. I say 'tis the finest in the world and I have seen much of the world."

With that, he left.

"Thank you," she called after him.

Charles's Town. Was that North or South Carolina?

She shut her eyes to visualize the map Richard had studied.

"Watch it!" someone on a horse said, disapproving of Rebecca stopping in the middle of the road. Yes, perhaps, it did not matter so much if she were in North or South Carolina but that she was in the middle of a bustling city. The miles spent walking with the birds as her only companions were far behind her.

Rebecca's stomach rumbled loudly. In her pockets were a few coins that Philip had slipped her in the way of a good luck token at her parting. A shop beckoned to her. Its doors, flung wide, provided ample room for the many that passed.

As Rebecca entered, a flurry of activity pressed around her.

"I need plenty of flour," one woman said, leaving Rebecca wondering how one could determine such a measurement.

"And I will say it again, we ought to have

representation!" a man said, speaking as a lion growls when on a hunt.

"Do you purchase or only sell?" another man asked, this time addressing the attendant behind the counter.

Rebecca's eyes ran the length of the shelves, trying to determine what food was easy enough to prepare while being ample enough to fill her appetite and pleasing to her few coins' longevity.

"I purchase, if the item is of worth."

"How about a gold watch?"

Hmm, perhaps, I should buy—

"What are these initials here? CH is it? Hmm—clasp seems broken too."

Rebecca's hair on the back of her neck stood up. As though someone had laid his icy fingers on her, a chill raced through her body. Caleb's laughter, absent for so many months from her ears, now echoed in her mind.

"You hear my watch—" The vibrant green grasses of the English countryside pressed into her hands, into her mind. She shivered against the chill of the night, against the haunting words. They'd been so innocent last summer. She'd spoken those very words to Richard, hadn't she?

"Promise me, Brother, you will not speak of our innocent secret," she'd pleaded. Caleb's watch was here in America; there could be nothing innocent about that. She pushed it from her mind, trying to rid her thoughts of the awful seed they'd planted there. Already, she felt the unease clawing at her stomach.

"Say anything and Caleb Haroldson—" No, she couldn't finish the thought. Lord Furton's words were too vicious, too unwelcome, too impossible. Weren't they?

"'Tis in good order," the man continued, "'Tis working, there is age to it, 'tis gold. Whose was it? Yours?"

"I bought it from someone who got it from someone else."

From Caleb? Why would you have sold your watch?
She demanded the answer, in desperation, but she knew there was no good reason. He could have done so through no deliberate choice, through no decision lightly taken.

Rebecca pressed toward the counter to hear more clearly.

"And furthermore, if England—" The man who spoke as the lion was drawing closer. Skirting her way past two women, Rebecca stood as close to the men as she could. She picked up a carved spoon, turning it over in her hand.

"From this CH?"

"No, CH died the chap said. It was—"

Rebecca's air flushed from her lungs, leaving her unable to breathe.

No, no, 'tis not possible. That cannot be right! I would know! I would know!
The dread had been building in her, from the moment she'd heard them speak of his watch. Time no longer beat in its gold-plated precision. It hung lifelessly before her.

Without Caleb—

She felt a strong punch to her stomach, from deep within her, unable to make sense of the thought. If Caleb were not alive, days could not continue effortlessly, with trading and bartering and the buying of tea and the selling of other men's watches, wonderful men, her man, her Caleb, her life, her time, all time—

Struggling not to collapse, she turned to face the man who had said the terrible words. She had to speak to him, to know what had happened.

"Well, I might offer—"

He said some figure that Rebecca could not hear.

"Ah, 'tis worth far more than that," the man said angrily, snatching the watch from the attendant's hand. As he turned toward Rebecca, her heart went cold.

Lord Furton's man.

CHAPTER SIXTY-SIX

"What do you mean she is not here? You said she crossed the river," Caleb said, in defiance to the old man's answers.

"I did," he said, making no apologies, but also offering no explanation for having done so.

"But, she is not here," Caleb said, spreading his arms wide. "Why did you lie to me?"

He stood in front of the man, dwarfing him in comparison and shook a threatening fist. Previously never a man swayed by his temper, he had been inclined to oblige the surge of power that now surrounded him when his words were backed up by the more persuasive power of his fists.

"Caleb Haroldson," Seamus said. A glow of sunlight descended around him, reminding Caleb that he was in the presence of clergy, "If he told you that Rebecca Turrington crossed the river, then she did."

Caleb's head swirled. Like a mighty tidal wave, their words only churned up more questions.

"Would someone tell me what is going on?" he said, struggling to maintain his slipping perception of reality.

"Rebecca Turrington and you were both rescued by a group," the old man said. Seamus shot him a look that seemed to ask whether he thought it wise to divulge such information to the distressed Caleb. The old man shrugged. Having seen much in his numerous years, he was unfazed by the headstrong youth in love.

"You said my rescue was not planned. And, you rescued me on horseback. A rider took Rebecca. Was that also you? But no, you did not know about her. Unless, that was a lie."

Seamus shook his head, looking disappointed.

"Caleb Haroldson," he said, "I promise you that I do not lie. Everything I have ever told you is the truth."

But, you speak in circles and tell very little truth.

"To answer your first question, no, I did not know that 'twas you that I was rescuing. All I knew was that 'twas someone who did not wish to fight for the king. Such men fit in well among us."

More riddles! More questions. If I ask you what you do mean, you will only tell me more that leaves me wondering.

"What about Rebecca?"

"Oh yes, she was rescued on purpose. She had been on our list for a long while," the old man said.

"List?"

"Of suitable candidates."

Caleb dared not ask for what, lest he should only encounter more questions. Instead, he said,

"Then you know where she is."

Seamus shifted.

"Not entirely."

"What do you mean not entirely?"

Caleb said, his already thin patience shredding.

"There were complications."

Complications? Why can you never answer my questions?

"We are not entirely certain what happened to her," the old man said.

"You are not certain what happened to her?" Caleb felt the steam rising under his collar.

"She is not some teacup that you have misplaced!" Caleb said, balling his hand into a fist and striking it in the air.

"We think," Seamus began. Caleb turned toward him and, seeing the impatience painted on his face, Seamus wasted no time in continuing, "that she may be in the colonies."

"The colonies? What colonies?"

"In America or, perhaps, the Caribbean."

America? Rebecca may be in America and I have fought against, turned and run twice from two different groups who would have landed me there? I have run from my best chance of

finding her!

Dizzy at the discovery, Caleb's face paled. His stomach tensed at the reality of his chance of finding her slipping from his hands, but also at the thought of her being so far.

Some fool I am! I had planned to search all of England for her. Ah, if only I had known at the beginning. So much time has been wasted!

"Why did you not tell me this before?" Caleb said, turning to face Seamus.

"Because, I did not know."

"And you, you might have said something," he said to the old man.

"I told you," the man said, "I was protecting you. The king's men were after you."

"The king's men?" Caleb said, shaking his head, "Why should they be in pursuit of me?"

"Because of Lord Furton."

"Lord Furton?" Caleb tried to make sense of the situation. Had Lord Furton discovered their love and employed the king's troops to silence the man who loved the lady he planned to marry?

"Lord Furton turned against us. I am sorry that we did not know before, when he was sent for Rebecca."

Caleb's head swarmed with questions, louder than any hive of bees.

"I could not risk you exposing yourself, making that mistake, when you were in danger. At least in the jail, you were away from their detection."

"Truthfully? What mistake?"

"You would have gone after her."

"You are right. I would have," Caleb said, "You stopped me before. You will not stop me again. This time I know where to find her."

The words spoken and the decision made, Caleb waited

for no more answers, no more questions and no more riddles. A cloud of dust rose from the steady beating of his feet against the ground, as he turned to leave. Dandelion neighed her own quiet goodbye, as Seamus called after him

"God bless you, Caleb Haroldson, God bless you."

"He shall certainly need that," the old man said.

CHAPTER SIXTY-SEVEN

Rebecca tore from the shop, following close behind the man. The streets of Charles's Town, bolstering with promise and opportunity moments before she had entered the shop, now stretched cold before her. Her chest burned from not enough air surging through her lungs. Caleb wasn't gone. He couldn't be. But, she had seen Lord Furton's man. Rebecca's stomach churned, revolted at the memory of his words. He had threatened Caleb on so many occasions, if she did not do what he asked of her. When she'd left him in the Caribbean and then found Philip's crew, his power over her had diminished. No longer did it hold the same menacing threat that it had. With Lord Furton out of her sight, she had assumed that he no longer would bother with someone he obviously thought of as inconsequential.

But, with a stabbing pain in her heart, Rebecca now realized that he had.

Ah Caleb, how could—I am so sorry—I—ah, 'tis all my fault.

Scarcely able to form a sentence, she did not allow the man to escape from her sight.

Rebecca stopped.

There in front of her, not twenty paces away, stood Lord Furton. His cape, which had sent shivers of dread through her as it had brushed her arm in the Caribbean, hung smugly from his shoulders.

Before, she had been fearful of his hold over her. Now, with benefit of her experience behind her and with too great of a sorrow stifling any fear, she marched to Lord Furton and prepared to face him for what he had done.

"Lord Furton," she said, loudly. One or two people stopped to look, but soon continued on their way again. A sailor speaking to another was hardly something to cause excitement in a seafaring city of this size.

He turned. His body emanated with a palpable repugnance.

I wish you had never picked me up on that horse! I would have found my own way out!

Even as she thought the words, the memories of weeks at sea flooded over her. But no, Lord Furton had brought her nothing good. She would have run away to sea by her own accord and had Caleb beside her. It was too painful to go on.

At hearing his name, Lord Furton turned. His eyes played over Rebecca still dressed in Philip's clothes.

"If you wish to sail with my crew, you will have to come tomorrow like everyone else," he said. With a dismissive wave of his hand, he turned to leave. His power had grown in the colonies. He now referred to a ship as his own and must have found some other means, than Rebecca's intended bride price, to fund his endeavor. Rebecca held her ground.

"I do not wish to sail with your crew."

Lord Furton paused and turned to face her.

"Then, what is it that you desire? I do not have time to be bothered."

"But, you have time to murder."

The words ripped from her mouth, before she could sieve them through a net of caution. His eyes flared, looking like a stallion who is ready to buck his rider. Lord Furton stepped nearer.

"What gives you the right to make such a claim?"

"Because, 'tis true," she spat back. All reason and caution abandoned, Rebecca stood on the dangerous precipice of accusation. She watched the words hurdle toward Lord Furton, like a whirling snowstorm, with all of its weight and none of its beauty or softness.

"Do I know you?" Lord Furton said, the malice in his eyes now flaring from his nostrils as well. He stepped closer and stared so intently, that she was certain he had scorched her soul.

A spark of recognition lighted his eye. He knew it was her. She had gone too far.

Run.

Rebecca turned to leave, but her escape attempt was blocked by the man who had been in the shop. A quick whistle alerted a gang of his henchmen. Surrounded, Rebecca felt smaller than she had ever felt. No bigger than a child, she was encircled by strong-armed men. Stepping closer, she was reduced to the size of a dog but lacked any of its agility to escape through their legs.

"So nice to see you again, Miss Turrington," Lord Furton spewed, as he snatched the hat off her head. Shrinking again, she was no larger than a mouse.

"'Twas intolerably rude of you to run out on us before. But, worry not. We shall forgive you and let you join us again." His hatred mixed with sarcasm and an eerie pleasure in his own accomplishment.

"Really, Miss Turrington, you ought to take better care of yourself. Your appearance is frightful. But I shall make certain that this time you do everything according to my liking."

Ground under his feet, Rebecca now existed only as a spot of dust.

CHAPTER SIXTY-EIGHT

Caleb, angry and confused, channeled his feelings into his legs. Stopping only when absolutely necessary, he walked faster and crossed a greater distance of land in a shorter amount of time than ever before.

"Caleb Haroldson," a voice called out to him from behind a thicket of trees.

Unmistakably, it was Seamus's voice.

"What do you want with me?" Caleb said, turning to face him. Seamus sat high on a horse riding bareback and looking slightly out of place, though he was obviously an adept horseman.

So, that is how you caught up to me.

"I must tell you of a vision, Caleb Haroldson."

"A what?" he said.

"A vision," Seamus repeated, his answer delivered in an arch as he dismounted.

What do I want with a vision?

Caleb turned to Seamus,

"Too much time has already been wasted."

"Please, Caleb Haroldson, if you depart now in haste and in anger, more than just time will have been wasted."

Ah! Why do you have to drop such tempting morsels in front of me?

Hooked, he turned to Seamus.

"Let us sit down, Caleb Haroldson," he said, gesturing to a log beside the stream. Water babbled happily, gurgling against the rocks in pleasant accompaniment. Stiffly, more from resistance of mind than of muscle, Caleb allowed his legs to fold. Seated beside Seamus, Caleb turned to him. The way the sun hit his face highlighted hints of crow's feet beside his deep, searching eyes. Compared to the old man who had been with Dandelion, Seamus had seemed young. Now, seated beside the water, Caleb observed that Seamus had not only accumulated questions for Caleb, but also years for himself.

"You had a vision?" Caleb said, prompting the first answer. Seamus shook his head.

"But, you said..."

Seamus looked at Caleb, as though to say patience was necessary when arriving at the answer.

"A friend had this vision."

"What friend?"

"Her name is Marion and— "

Caleb shook his head in disbelief. All the threads had been tied too neatly to even begin to entertain the notion that there might be some other Marion.

"I am not interested in hearing the vision of a woman who drinks invisible tea."

Seamus raised his eyebrow. Plucking a blade of grass and running it through his fingers he said,

"Then, you have met her?"

"The last time I saw Marion, the king's men were paying her for showing them where the men of Beckshire were. Are you certain you trust her?"

"Caleb Haroldson, were the men of Beckshire present?" Seamus asked, with a tone that conveyed he was illustrating a point rather than asking a question.

"Well, no, but— " Caleb's voice faded, as he realized there was no true argument to make.

"If the men were not there, then how could Marion have betrayed them?"

"Fine," Caleb conceded, pressing his palms firmly against the ground, "Maybe, she did not betray them, but still she is crazy!"

"On what grounds do you make your accusation, Caleb Haroldson?" Seamus said, in that same calm and measured tone he spoke all his words in.

"She sees things that are not there."

"Does she?" Seamus said, looking up from the twirling grass to Caleb.

"You know about her invisible tea!" Caleb said, feeling the lunacy had spread beyond only Marion.

"Caleb Haroldson, granted Marion is not the most conventional person," Seamus said, realizing that if he did not start providing answers soon Caleb might very well leave, "But, by the measure of logic you have used to judge her as crazy, others might judge me as well. I cannot see our Lord, but I know He is there."

"But, that is different. Everyone else knows there is no tea."

"Marion sees things differently. 'Tis real to her. Just because she has certain—" Seamus paused, searching for the right words, "unique attributes, does not discredit all about her. Did it ever occur to you, Caleb Haroldson, that those who are not understood are often underestimated?"

No, the thought had not occurred to him. The waning sun in the sky added extra hope that Seamus's sermon on empathy would not be long-winded. Going on a quest to bring back Rebecca, as well as seeking information about the others who had been declared missing, surely counted toward curtailing its length. Rather than the expected sermon, though, Seamus said,

"Sometimes, being underestimated means escaping detection from the authorities."

Caleb stared. Was he hearing him right? Was Seamus talking about treason?

"But, what about your loyalty to the Turringtons?"

"I served them well," Seamus said, shifting from one side to the other. It was the first time that he had borne even the faintest sign of discomfort. He looked to be a man wrestling with his conscience.

"'Tis all? You have left them?" Caleb said, scarcely believing his ears. A priest had bonds of loyalty, didn't he? Didn't they also extend to monks?

"Caleb Haroldson, this may be hard to understand, but we are not so different. Not really. We both are committed to defending what we believe in."

"Yet, I am willing to fight for the Turringtons and you do not seem to be. They think you are dead. You are going to do nothing to correct it?" Caleb said, shaking his head.

"Caleb Haroldson, if I did that, our secret would be out. Are you so convinced that you are willing to fight for them, perhaps even to die for them, to defend their right to rule?"

"What is that?" Caleb said, looking around.

"What is what?

A thumping resonated in the ground. Growing louder, it thundered as the riders approached. Pulling Caleb by the collar, Seamus dove behind the split log as an army of cavalry ripped over the land.

CHAPTER SIXTY-NINE

Tossed into a cellar, like a sack of potatoes, Rebecca landed on the stone floor. Her side ached, but even this pain was mitigated by the agonizing emptiness that had begun to gnaw away at her.

I should have married Lord Furton long ago and been done with it. At least then Caleb would be alive. And I would not know the freedom that I will never taste of again.

"Too much rebellion, too much," Lord Furton mumbled now. His voice carried through the slats in the floor.

Unable to do anything else, Rebecca drew up her knees as she sat against the wall.

Sleep.

At least if she were not awake, then time could pass more quickly again. At least, it would take the sting of the terrible day away from her.

Caleb ought to be mourned.

The thought replayed itself, as she dozed. But no, Rebecca had done this. It was her fault. Tears were a luxury she did not deserve. Other women who lost the men they loved had earned that right; they had not caused their downfall.

Rebecca Turrington, you are worse than a pirate. You are a murderer.

In her pit of despair, Rebecca coughed hard, feeling the wretched hands of nausea pull at her stomach. Her head pounded, as though a stake had been driven through it. The physical pain only served to further incite her doomed thoughts.

Finally succeeding in willing herself to be captive by slumber, she fell into a deep sleep. It was a dreamless night; all her dreams had died with Caleb. She awoke once with a violent shake. Realizing that it was only a product of sleep, slumber soon reclaimed her.

It cannot be true. It just cannot.

Sinking into the deep jaws of night, she remained absent from the world of thought and alertness. Rebecca's heart raced as she was jolted awake again, this time by the sound of approaching horses.

A long whinny, as a horse was brought to a stop, traveled through the slats. Muffled voices mixed with the horses' pounding hoofs.

"—come to get... we left like you."

Rebecca stood, her legs groaning under her. Her foot had fallen asleep, after being scrunched against her so long. She pressed her weight against it to get the blood flowing again. A surge of prickles rushed into her foot, as the sensation began to return.

"Turrington—" Rebecca stopped shaking her foot to fully concentrate on their words.

"Across the—England—"

So, I am to make it home. But, now it is too late.

In the beginning, when first kidnapped, Rebecca had firmly decided that she would return to England. It not only held Caleb, but also her identity. When she had spoken of running away with Caleb, she had assumed it would be to some hamlet tucked among the hills. Instead, she had journeyed across the depths of blue and forged a new life. Caleb had become the sole reason why she even entertained the idea of returning. But now, if Caleb were gone—she swallowed, suppressing the rising lump in her throat—there was no reason to go back.

What if—

No, it seemed too optimistic to even begin to contemplate. Still, the thought proved persistent. Even as she tried to forget it, it grew and developed wings of its own to take flight.

What if she could escape and live among this American wilderness? Carrying the name of Haroldson, she could pay tribute to Caleb. Living as Richard Haroldson seemed the only thing that made any sort of sense. If Caleb Haroldson were gone, then she could no longer be Rebecca Turrington. She didn't make sense without him. But, fate had gripped him away from her with its gnarled cruel fingers. She was to go on living, but only as Richard Haroldson.

Just like Romeo and Juliet.

The thought hit her with such force at the realization that even the tragedy of their story had come to pass, that she shook her head to clear it of the mounting horrors.

Rebecca's thoughts were not all that were being dismounted. The heaviness of boots thumping against the ground, as a rider dropped from the horse, signaled that it was soon time to make her move.

Trying to formulate a plan was proving impossible. She had no way of defending herself, save her own fists to punch with and feet to kick with. Although a fine runner, outpacing a horse would not be an option. The rattle of chains on the cellar door, as someone fumbled with turning the key, ignited her resolve.

Make haste! Plan!

Thinking harder induced panic and rendered her unable to decide on a course of action.

Just hope for the best. Please, help me.

The words of prayer presented, she watched as the door swung open. Lord Furton himself stood in front of her.

"Come along, Miss Turrington."

The frost on his words set in the chill of early winter. Leaving behind the dungeon cellar, she prepared to wriggle free from her chains for one last time.

"Turrington?" one of the others said.

Rather than answer, she looked for who had spoken, barely turning her head so as not to alert the others that she was planning her escape. Someone had noticed, though. Behind Lord Furton, the statuesque presence of the ebony man that she had first seen in the Caribbean, rose as a beacon of hope. Weakened by the devastating news she had received, she gained strength from the proud determined look in his eyes. He looked at her and blinked. Yes, he recognized her too. The bond had been forged, but would it be enough to base an alliance on? In the dim light, his eyes moved over her head and rested on something in the distance.

Lord Furton, oblivious to all, continued to talk to the rider on the horse. Rebecca watched, as the man nodded at whatever lay behind her. A flurry of activity, quicker than she could process, surrounded Rebecca. The man's arms were around Lord Furton. The horse the rider was on spooked and reared, the rider falling in a heap.

"Let go of me! I demand you unhand me!" Lord Furton shouted.

Taking the opportunity she'd been given, Rebecca began to run. She felt her legs extend as they had never done before. Like the wind, she was carried through the night. It was not her legs alone, though, propelling her forward. Flanked on both sides, men ran alongside of her.

"Turrington, we have been waiting for you."

CHAPTER SEVENTY

"Let me go, Seamus," Caleb said, breaking free of the monk's hold.

"Please, Caleb Haroldson. It is dangerous."

"Danger seems to follow me, ever since I became involved with all of you," Caleb said.

"But, you do not yet know everything," Seamus said, in one last appeal to get him to stay.

"Seamus, I highly doubt that you will tell me everything. Besides, I know what is most important. I know where Rebecca is."

Horses continued in long streams past their secluded spot behind the log. Pine needles poked Caleb's arm and filled his nose, as he stood.

"Please, Caleb Haroldson," Seamus said once again. Such fear filled his eyes that they might as well have been the horsemen of the apocalypse.

"Goodbye, Seamus," Caleb said, not looking down at the man. He would spare him that; he would not give away his hiding spot.

As he stepped from behind the log, he heard Seamus say,

"Goodbye, Caleb Haroldson." The tie severed, he stood beside the path as the horses blazed past.

"I want— " he began, shouting to gain their attention.

Jumping out of the way to avoid being trampled, he scolded himself for his reckless attempt to get their attention. Standing farther back and waving his arms, he managed to flag down one of the riders.

"I want to join the navy!" Caleb shouted up to him, his voice competing to be heard in the midst of galloping horses.

The man started laughing. He looked from Caleb to the trees as though to say,

"You do realize we are in a forest, do you not?"

"I mean it," Caleb said.
The man sobered at Caleb's words.
"Well, come on then."

⟡

Late into the night, Caleb and the men on horseback he'd been traveling with pulled to a stop.

"There!" the man said, who had first agreed for him to come along.

We are not in London.

He had assumed that they would ride to London. If one were going to join the navy, he needed to go to the capital. Didn't that make sense?

Misinterpreting Caleb's hesitation, he said,

"Have you changed your mind? Well, if you have, escape while you can. They are bound to catch up to you soon, anyway. I would press you into service myself, only 'tis not in today's orders."

"I have not changed my mind," Caleb said.

"Well, what are you waiting for? We have business to attend to."

Behind the man, a whisper of a ship's form emerged between tall wispy pines. Seeing the flag displayed proudly on the mast, stirred something in his chest. It was not that he had heard his country's rally call and rushed to defend it. Rather, his world had previously consisted only of England. Seeing the flag reminded him that there was a world beyond these shores, a world that Rebecca was in—somewhere.

"Nothing," he said, stepping confidently toward the future.

⟡

A blur of events transported Caleb from the edge of the forest to the stern of the ship. Despite his unorthodox approach, he was not turned away. Below deck, having changed into his issued uniform, he set to work moving the equipment.

Here I am again, doing the king's bidding. When will all the stumbling blocks finally be removed so I can be with you dear, sweet Rebecca?

The men around him were of few words. They bore the grim expressions of those who have had that divine right of freewill snatched from their grasping hands. Sleep deprivation seemed to have plagued these men, contorting their faces as barnacles do to a hull. A sailor farther down the ship whistled a low tune.

"Terrible, just terrible, being taken from them, it is," another said.

"You have a family, have you?" another, looking at least five years younger than Caleb, said.

The first sailor nodded.

"We all have families. But, do they care? Of course not!"

The younger sailor looked at the despondent man, his eyebrows raising in alarm. He was none too keen to have a burden of oppression yoked to his back by his superiors, for having unfortunate judgment in choosing whom to speak to.

"What, sir? No, I did not speak to the man. I am happy to serve the king," his body stated loudly, as he turned away. Ducking, his thin mouse tail was almost visible—almost, but he could be excused for his youth.

"I do not blame him. I would not speak to a bitter old salt like me either," the sailor said, shrugging toward Caleb.

"You are a sailor?" Caleb said. Perhaps, befriending the man would make the miles between him and Rebecca pass more quickly. Of course, once he got there he hadn't yet figured out how he'd free himself from his commitment—or how he'd find her. But, none of that mattered now. What mattered was getting to Rebecca and if there were even the slightest chance that she was in the colonies, then he had to seize it.

What if she is not there though? What if—

"Yes, I have been a sailor all my days. Mostly I fish. You?"

The sailor's words sliced through Caleb's demoralizing thinking. Before he could answer, a voice from behind him said,

"Well, I never thought I would see the day! Proud Caleb Haroldson bending his back to do the king's work."

Caleb turned at the sound of the voice that rang so familiar in his ears. His bulky frame looking colossal in the confines of the ship, Peter stood before him. A flash of Peter bent over the man in the forest appeared in Caleb's mind. The voice may have been familiar, but the man in front of him was now a stranger.

"'Tis not the king I am doing this for."

"No? Then, why would you go against your principles?"

"Because, she needs me."

The sailor's bitterness had subsided, as he became an onlooker to the drama. Caleb turned to leave.

"Who?" the sailor said.

"Rebecca Turrington," Peter answered.

Hearing her name on the lips of a murderer and on the lips of the man who had sent another woman to his bed, Caleb spun.

"Do not utter her name. I will not hear it on your lips again!"

CHAPTER SEVENTY-ONE

Waiting for me?

Who could possibly even know that Rebecca Turrington was in the colonies, aside from Lord Furton? The pieces were shady, but hadn't he just been left behind by the men around her? Rushed to the side of a river, a man turned to her and said,

"Are you ready to cross the river?"

Am I ready?

With no idea what he meant but assuming that he was a friend rather than a foe, or at least an enemy of Lord Furton and surely that must make him Rebecca's ally, she stumbled over her answer.

"Uhm, yes," she said. The murkiness of the river appeared clear, compared to the events around her. The only absolute certainty that she had to cling to was the overwhelming smell of blackberries. Her hand struck the prickly brambles, as she searched for a boat on the shoreline. The water seemed too wide not to need one, if their intention were to cross it. Rebecca drew back her hand at the thorns. Moonlight shone against the wetness on her hand. At first she thought it was blood, but in the light she could tell that it was not crimson but rather had been stained a deep purple.

"Good," the man said. He was dressed as a woodsman, clothed in the skin of a deer. Rather than lead her to a concealed boat, though, he struck terror in her as he said,

"Have you died yet?"

"Have I—" she swallowed hard. The leather clothing he wore taunted her. She was to be the next prey.

"Surely, you must know that to cross the river you must have died. We all have."

Her forehead wrinkled, as her stomach dropped.

"But, you are alive," she said. Even in the moonlight his face looked far from pale, not that Rebecca entertained the notion of ghostly visitors anyway.

He looked at her, studying her hard. Exchanging looks with another over her head, he turned away from her and began talking to someone else. The water raised its silver hands, beckoning to Rebecca. Dare she escape among the waiting reeds? There were many around her. They had been smart enough to outwit Lord Furton; she mustn't underestimate them. Cautiously, she stepped forward. The smooth river-washed pebbles lay temptingly before her. In a couple more steps, her feet would move from the dirt to the rocky riverbed. She stepped forward again.

The man turned back to her. She froze. If there had been a chance of escaping, it had passed.

"You are Turrington?" he said, bending in to examine her closer.

Was it safer to admit to it or not? Sensing her hesitation, he signaled for one of his associates to come nearer. They were closing in on her. Rebecca had the uneasy feeling of a rope tightening around her. Once again, she found herself surrounded. With each step closer, the invisible noose tightened. Having exposed themselves to her, they wouldn't let her escape; that much was certain.

"Is there a problem?" she said, unsure of why the men who had rescued her were shifting in their treatment of her. Although not physically hostile, their faces had sobered. What had been flesh and blood features, animated and visibly alive despite what they had said, now read as stone. It was as though they had put on their death masks.

Rebecca's legs wobbled under her. Oh how she wanted to run and be done with them!

I would rather be in that cellar. At least, then I would be alive.

Feeling once again like Juliet, she looked at the men around her; were they to be the dagger that would be her final undoing in the wake of Caleb's death? A wooziness washed over her.

"There is a problem all right, if you are not whom we thought you were."

"Oh, but I am Turrington!" she said, not stopping to consider if it were wise to admit to the name or not. For deciding earlier that Rebecca Turrington no longer existed, they were hounding her with that identity. It was proving impossible to put that life to rest.

"All right," the man in the skins said.

All right? Was that it? Have I convinced them?

Before she could breathe any sigh of relief, he asked her a question that sent Juliet's dagger through her heart.

"What do you know of Caleb Haroldson?"

CHAPTER SEVENTY-TWO

Peter swallowed his anger.

What do you have to be mad about? So, I sent Molly to your bed. Well, I am sorry for it, more so for me and for her than for you. I aim to make her my wife, I do, so I will not be doing that again. No thanks to you, I almost got killed—twice. And now, I have had to leave my Mol, as soon as I realized I love her. If anyone should be mad, 'tis me!

It was difficult not to scowl, when unable to lie. Why, oh why did Caleb have to be here? His presence taunted him, reminding Peter that this man who had once been his friend was the sole reason he'd jumped ship, quite literally.

"Stupid fire," he muttered, under his breath.

"What did you say?" Caleb said.

"You seem intent on telling me not to talk to you, not to help you and then wanting to know what I have said."

That is what you get for helping a friend, Peter. When Caleb told you not to help him, you should have listened.

Molly had never spoken such words to him, but he heard her melodic voice say now, *Ah, but you are a man of honor, Peter Black, you are.*

Even if she had never spoken such words, he certainly would have liked her to. Whether he was a man of honor or not, he didn't much know. It seemed there was enough evidence stacked up on both sides of that argument. The scales would have balanced, he was quite sure. But, perhaps, defending a friend had somehow assuaged the wanton ways of youth. Yes, Peter realized now that more than for himself, more even than for Caleb, he had done it all for Molly. He had to become a man he thought she deserved. He hadn't put off marrying her, because there was anything wrong with her or because of a lack of affection. He had been with others, but there was only ever any meaning with her. When he lay beside her, it wasn't just a nice woman's body sharing the bed, there was a whole person there with a heart and soul and a mind. Somehow, that made all of her all the more pleasing. His hand raised to his temple and he scratched it.

Too many thoughts.

A rush of understanding had fallen on him, as a waterfall tumbles over the rocks, upon seeing Caleb. Maybe, he shouldn't be so cross with him after all. He did have plenty of questions for Caleb, ones that could not be answered if Caleb were not speaking to him. It would have been simpler to turn away and not care, but he had been unable to do so those long months ago when the strangers had ridden into town asking for Caleb Haroldson and he was unable to do so now. A man of honor would pursue the truth. Whether Peter had yet earned the right to wear that title was debatable, but he knew that he wanted it. Yes, he realized now that the only reason he'd not yet married Molly was because he didn't stack up as a big enough man in his own eyes. Under the stature and muscles, he wanted her to be proud of his character. Caleb might be cross with him, but Peter was willing to set things straight.

Peter shifted from one foot to the other. Caleb had busied himself moving crates, while the older sailor had moved farther down. Most of the men were now above deck. Where they were was quiet, with only the gentle sway of the steady waves of a calm sea.

Peter swallowed at the thought of what he had to do. Apologizing was something that he had not made a habit of in his life. Frankly, he couldn't remember when he'd ever spoken those words aloud. Sometimes, getting metal to bend required putting it on heat. Sometimes, it meant adding pressure. But, it also meant knowing when to stop. Caleb had been through a fire of his own. He had subsequently had pressure applied to him. His very presence here was testament of that to Peter. Now, perhaps, it was time for Peter to help him cool.

"Caleb." The word had come out too quietly and Caleb did not turn to face him. Peter cleared his throat and tried again.

"Caleb."

Just say it. Caleb, I apologize. There. 'Tis easy enough, is it not?

This time Caleb turned.

"I best listen to you, eh? So you do not do away with me, like that other man."

The words flew from Caleb's mouth and even he looked slightly surprised that he had not practiced more restraint.

"What are you talking about?" Peter said, sitting on a crate pushed against the hull.

"I saw you, Peter Black," Caleb said through barred teeth, his voice low, "I saw you in the forest after you killed that man."

"What man?" Peter said, confused.

"Oh! So, there were others, were there? I am shocked. How could I ever have opened my home to you? And did you also have Rebecca kidnapped? Well, did you? Tried to pawn off one of your tramps onto me, I will—"

Peter pushed himself up from the crate, crossing to stand in front of Caleb and towering over him. Every part of him wanted to return the wallop that Caleb had given him.

"How dare you," he said, his hand balling into a fist, "talk about," Peter pulled back his arm, ready to unleash his fury, "Molly."

Speaking her name broke the desire for revenge in him. His fist crashed through the air, purposefully missing Caleb and dissolving into nothing.

"I will not have you sully her good name or spread false witness against me," Peter said, as evenly as he could. Caleb, who had ducked as Peter's arm had gone up, stared at the man in front of him.

"I saw what I saw," Caleb said.

Peter shook his head.

"He did not die because of me. He died because of you," Peter said.

This Caleb had not expected. He looked as though the punch that had landed in the air had been delivered, as Peter said,

"That man's name was Caleb Haroldson and he was a spy."

Caleb shook his head in disbelief. If anyone else had told him such a thing, he would have dismissed them. But, Caleb was well aware that Peter could not lie.

"He spoke of you being a traitor, of having dangerous friends."

Caleb stared at him as Peter continued,

"Of hundreds gone—of a group called across—"

Caleb's face turned paler than the china teacups in Turrington Manor.

"Across the river," he finished for Peter.

CHAPTER SEVENTY-THREE

Caleb Haroldson? How do you know of him?

Fear gripped Rebecca.

Had they been responsible for what had happened? Had they—

Rebecca struggled for control. She had to know what had happened to him and if these men had caused it.

What do I know about Caleb Haroldson? I know that I love him with the constancy of passing days. I know that he was forged for me in true love's flame. I know that he was taken from me and,

"I know he is dead." Giving voice to the words ripped her heart from her ribcage and shredded it on the rusted blade of cruel fate.

The man in the skins and Rebecca stood eye-to-eye, judging each other's expressions for more information.

He nodded.

"Come this way then," the man said.

Had she passed? There was no explanation of what had happened, but also no one had stepped menacingly closer to threaten what little remaining security she had.

He didn't say where they were headed. Without the benefit of options, Rebecca followed close behind him. The path, which she expected to lead toward a boat, meandered away from the shoreline and into thicker underbrush. The branches, which no one bothered to hold back for her, snapped against her skin. Water droplets from a recent rain and the occasional thorn pelted her skin, as the leaves and sticks pressed into her arms. At least she had trousers on and not the billowing fabric of troublesome skirts.

Do they know that I am a girl?

Lord Furton certainly knew that she was no man, but these men who surrounded her now gave no indication that they believed her to be one gender or the other. It was only the most recent question in a list of mounting uncertainty.

Rebecca searched for the silver ribbon of the river to return, but it was nowhere to be seen.

I thought we were going to cross the river.

She didn't dare speak the words aloud. Dirt crumbled under her feet, as the terrain changed. The glimmers of moonlight were absent here with no water to reflect off of and a heavy canopy of arching pines above. For awhile, no one spoke to her. There was only the sound of leaves crunching under her feet and the ax that the woodsman carried thumping against his thigh as he walked.

Where are we headed?

But, that question she didn't dare ask either. She had, presumably, convinced them of who she was. Perhaps, that meant she already was assumed to know where they were going and what was happening. Rebecca wondered at how they could tell where they were going, when she couldn't see anything. When they had walked for quite some time, the woodsman came to a stop. Rebecca almost ran into him, but was able to prevent herself from doing so.

"Here," he said. She followed the direction of his voice and a flicker of light came into view. Around it, a steady glow emanated and log dwellings could be seen. The smell of a hearty stew wafted through the night toward her, as she realized now that the flicker was a campfire.

"This is where they will live," the man continued.

They will?

Now, she was certain that she had passed their test. Although relieved to be safe, or at least relatively so, she wasn't so sure what she thought of taking up residence among the men who were possibly connected to Caleb's—

"Is your sister arrived yet, Turrington?" the woodsman said, breaking into Rebecca's racing thoughts.

My sister? Good heavens! They think I am Richard! But
—

Thoughts waged war against her mind, pounding her senses like the battling rams that had once been used on the castles of her ancestors. Richard had not been to the colonies. He had no dealings with them—none that she knew of anyway. And, surely, Richard wouldn't have had something terrible happen to Caleb, would he? Far from approving of the match, he still would not succumb to such wickedness. Richard loved her too much, didn't he? With so many questions of her own, she hadn't yet answered the one posed to her by the woodsman. Thinking she had not heard him, he repeated,

"Has your sister arrived?"

Was it another test? Or, was he honestly inquiring? Stuck on what to answer, the deliberations were lifted from her hands.

"She is not yet arrived, unfortunately."

The voice startled Rebecca, but the surprise of words spoken in the dark paled in comparison to the shock that raced through her as she saw who had spoken them. Bathed in the glow of the settlement's fire, which they were drawing nearer to, stood John. Seeing him, Rebecca's eyes went wide. John nodded toward her.

"Hello, Richard. 'Tis good to see you again."

"Ah, you know each other, good. Pity you were not back there sooner, John. We questioned his identity for a moment, but that is all behind us now. Right, Turrington?" The woodsman, who had walked in the somber coat of silence now burst free of the confines and gave Rebecca a playful slap on the back.

I thought you believed I was Richard Turrington! Why are you slapping me?

Didn't he know that a Turrington was to be respected? A blush of shame crept across her cheeks. It was well and good for Rebecca to fall in love with a cabinet maker and to set sail with common sailors. But, if she still expected these simple men to pay reverence to Richard, then she had learned nothing. Her brush with true democracy aboard Philip's ship had been for naught.

The others rushed forward at the sight of the settlement. Rebecca's shame mingled with confusion and sorrow and prevented her from joining them. She shut her eyes against the black of night, where everything spun and nothing made sense. Opening them, she hoped for clarity in her solitude. But, she was not alone; John stood looking at her.

"So, you are Rebecca Turrington?"

She nodded. That much was true. That much made sense.

"I did not know you were a Turrington," he said the name as though spitting out hot coals.

"You are one of them," he continued.

"Them? I do not even know who they are. They said they were expecting me. You seem to know them," she said.

John shook his head.

"You do not know them?"

"No, I meant, I was not talking about them."

"Oh," she said. It was such a small word, but filled the void when she was uncertain of what to say or to ask.

"I meant," he said, "that you are part of everyone I aim to fight against."

"Then we are enemies now?" she said. His face twisted in the firelight. He was struggling with a tangled knot of dichotomy too.

"No, I would not have watched over you, if we were."

"You—watched over me?" she said, her voice softening.

"I could not have you wandering through the wilderness by yourself."

"Then, why did you not tell me?"

"Because—you had to know that you could do it. You needed that. I could tell."

"You allowed me my freedom," she said, realizing what

he meant.

"But, I do not understand. Why did you make me leave the ship?"

"I did not— "

"But, you told Philip," Rebecca said.

"I did not betray you. I told him you had another opportunity and you did. That ship was not big enough for you, Rebecca. When you catch hold of freedom, it does something to you. It grows in you. Ah, 'tis hard to explain."

"No," she said, "I do understand. Truthfully." And she did. With all the uncertainty around her, that she did know.

"But, Lord Furton caught me," she said, remembering now that John had said he was watching her and having trouble reconciling the two.

"Look, I am sorry about that," he said frustrated, "But, I got you out, did I not?"

"You—arranged all of that?"

He nodded.

"I made certain they knew someone named Richard from England needed rescuing. I guess they figured 'twas Richard Turrington—er, your brother, on their own. Well, you are free now, anyway. You can do what you want, unless you do marry that fellow. But I already told you my thoughts on that."

"I cannot," Rebecca said.

"Cannot what?" he dragged his heel through the dirt, as he spoke.

"I cannot marry him."

He stopped moving his foot.

"Why is that?"

"Because— he is dead. You heard me tell them, did you not?" she spat the words out, angry at having to repeat them. John shook his head.

"No, I did not know. Sometimes, I had to follow at a distance. I apologize, Rebecca. But, now you are truly free."

Something about the way he brushed the sadness away of Caleb with the tantalizing promise of looming freedom was too unsettling. It was too close to her own conscience and reminded her painfully of those dreams, where Caleb had confronted her about choosing her own happiness over him.

"You are forgetting something," she said, pushing aside the heaviness of guilt. Pointing toward the settlement, Rebecca said, "I am far from free."

John looked at her, his forehead collapsing into a wrinkle.

"You are not captive."

"John, they spoke of death. They said they were expecting me. 'Tis like this. I take my chances in escaping through lands unknown or I take my chances with them. Though, perhaps, their wish to kill me has subsided now that they think I am Richard. But, why that should matter I cannot begin to imagine."

The words had flowed freely. Secrets, hidden desires or insecurities, are spoken much quicker in a conversation in the dark. There is too little light to illuminate the shame, guilt or vulnerability evoked by such words that would be so painfully visible in the light of day. Sunlight could speed a man's steps, but it slowed his words; that was the way of it.

"Rebecca," John said, "you have it all wrong. This place is not what you think it is. Will you trust me? We were friends once."

"We are friends," she corrected.

He nodded.

"Then, will you trust me? Will you cross the river?"

CHAPTER SEVENTY-FOUR

Caleb's iciness toward Peter thawed, as the frozen fingers of winter gripped their crossing. He was no murderer; that much was certain. Peter had even apologized for the incident with the woman. He said that Molly had explained to him that Caleb was in love with Rebecca. He said he hadn't known and that he never would have sent Molly to him if he had.

Forgiveness had come slowly, but tumultuous waves, rats racing through the hull and an endless supply of little other than hardtack to eat had made a friend welcomed and salved the wounds between them. Far from being healed of his own torments, though, the knowledge that others were after him, that a man had been killed with his name and that others knew of his love for Rebecca poured salt into his raw being. If they knew of his connection to her and if he were not safe, then neither was she. Thank goodness, she was no longer in England. At least that cursed group couldn't lay their hands on her there.

No, the across the river group might be absent across the sea, but the embers of revolution and the unspeakable dangers of the wilderness and its people were there. Even scoundrels of the sea, pirates, raked their filthy hands across the Atlantic seaboard. He shuddered to think of Rebecca crossing paths with them.

"Did you think of anything else?" Caleb said to Peter now. His hunger to piece together whatever information he could about all that had happened gnawed away at him.

Peter looked up from the bayonet he was polishing. It was almost like old times again, seeing him hold the gleaming metal in his hands and rotating it, as the cloth was drawn across it. Peter shook his head.

Almost, but not quite.

"I know you are worried about Rebecca." Caleb looked at Peter. Some things had changed. The Peter Black who had shared his house in England observed only metalwork, not people. Caleb nodded.

"But—" Peter said, "they were not asking for her. 'Twas your name that kept coming up, not hers. She is probably fine, sitting beside some fire now, smiling and drawing the attention of an admirer."

Peter had meant the words as solace, but they fell across Caleb harshly.

What if Rebecca were sitting beside the fire now and smiling in—her own home? What if she had married another? He swallowed, the thought almost as difficult to bear as when he had thought another fire, tragic and destructive rather than warm and inviting, had claimed her.

"You! Make haste!" a commander barked. The conversation dissolved, as Caleb and Peter set about their work.

Days passed into weeks, as the ship traveled through the parting waves. When at last they arrived, his desperation had not parted and he was far from delivered. As Caleb stepped ashore, his feet settled uneasily onto American soil. In England, talk of revolution had seemed far removed, some unpleasant possibility, but certainly nothing as real or as pressing as the daily work or the mysterious capers Caleb had embarked on. Here, though the people looked much as they had at home, they eyed him with suspicion.

"Why do you not go home?" a boy, who must have been no older than five or six, hurled at Caleb in his first foray into town. Peter looked at him and said,

"Not very friendly, are they?"

Caleb shrugged,

"Welcome to Boston."

He didn't much care about the frosty reception from this city, where four years earlier on another winter's day, the king's soldiers had opened fire and provoked the wrath of the young

American colonists. What did bother him, though, frankly it concerned him a great deal, was just how big this city seemed. He looked expectantly at the faces of the women who passed him by, searching for Rebecca's face as he had in the long days of the English summer.

Snow crunched under his feet, as he rubbed his hands together to keep warm. How was he ever supposed to find Rebecca in a land where a single city was so heavily populated?

I will find you.

This time the promise rang feeble at best. Was such an endeavor even possible?

Swept from his own thoughts by superior orders, they were marched somewhere else. In the pit of his stomach an urge rose.

The only way I will ever find her is to break free.

The plan had seemed simple enough when he had stood in the forest leaving Seamus behind.

Join the navy, go to the colonies, find Rebecca.

Well, the first two had been accomplished.

"Peter," he said, under his breath. Puffs of smoke billowed from his mouth, like a stone chimney as he spoke. Peter tilted his head toward him.

"I am going to try to escape."

Peter's eyes bulged,

"What? Are you daft?" he said. The decibel of his voice rose louder than Caleb had spoken and Caleb glared at him in warning. Lowering his voice, Peter shook his head,

"You cannot. 'Tis too dangerous."

Caleb, feeling the claustrophobia of the ranks and the regimented life he had locked himself inside of, which was preventing him from continuing his own mission, said,

"I can do it— if you will help me."

A wry grin passed over Peter's lips.

"You told me once never to help you."

"I told you a lot of foolhardy things," Caleb said, as means of apology.

"I will help you," Peter said.

"We need a plan," Caleb said, pressing his thoughts to induce action. Peter shook his head.

"I have one. I took a punch for you once."

Caleb frowned.

"You want me to punch you?"

"No need," Peter said. With a wink, he fell to his knees.

"Ah! My leg!" he said, as loudly as he could. The ranks behind them were forced to a halt, as they struggled not to stumble over Peter.

"What is wrong? Get up! Get up!"

"My leg, I have hurt it!" Peter said again, the agony in his voice making Caleb almost pity his injury.

Well, imagine that. Peter Black, you are a very good liar, indeed.

Slipping backward, as he had in the forest moments before Seamus had appeared on horseback, Caleb broke from the ranks. By the time he heard someone yell, "After him, he is getting away!" he was down a side street. Dodging women with baskets and horses in the streets, he moved quickly from one street to another. It didn't much matter if he were lost, so long as in getting lost he found Rebecca.

A man stepped from the doorway of a building on the street he had turned down.

"Well, now, what do we have here?"

"I will just be on my way," Caleb said, to show the man that he wanted no trouble.

"He will just be on his way, he will just be on his way! Ha! We do not take kindly to an Englishman now, do we?"

Caleb, exposed in his uniform, made his move to escape. Before he could, the man reached out and took hold of him.

"Oh no, no escaping. We have some questions for you.

You would not want to turn down our hospitality, now would you?"

The man in front of him was shorter than he was. He could have a chance if—Winding up his arm, Caleb swung, punching the man in the jaw.

Thank you, Peter.

The inspiration had come to him at the memory of Peter's most recent words to him. Before he could turn to leave though, another man, tanned, taller and of muscles that were a closer match to Peter's than his own, stepped from the shadows of the doorway and delivered a swift punch. The man's fist drove into Caleb's stomach, knocking him backward. He crashed against the brick wall and the snow under him was soiled by his red blood as it began to fall. Seeing it, Caleb put his hand to his head. No, he was not injured there. It was his arm, which had received the brunt of his fall against the bricks, that was bloodied and dotted with mud and dirt.

"I do not think you understand. You are coming with us," the man said.

CHAPTER SEVENTY-FIVE

"Are you ready to cross the river?" The words that had once brought such terror to Rebecca now slipped from her own lips. The eager face of the boy nodded toward her.

"I am."

"Then, let us go."

Since she had first agreed to trust John months earlier, Rebecca had spoken those words to many. It seemed like someone else had lived the life that she had before that night that she had first crossed the river. They had pushed north, gathering others along the way. Rebecca still wore the clothes of Richard Haroldson, though it was Richard Turrington that they believed her to be. Only John knew the secret of her true identity.

Tonight, the wind howled fiercely as fresh snow fell like great lumps of sugar. There was no quality of a confectioner's sweet dream this night. There was only the urge that the river must be crossed, before it was too late.

Rebecca paused and put her finger to her lips, to signal to the boy that he should be quiet. Concealed behind the trees she watched as men, dressed in the familiar red woolen coats of the king's troops, patrolled. Looking like cardinals strutting in the new snow, it was easy to forget that they were a threat. The procession of soldiers passed before them, swallowed by the streets of the town that stretched beyond.

Pride surged in Rebecca. In a world awaiting the eruption of rebellion, everyone seemed to sense it was coming, she had found a way to deliver life and not death. In crossing the river, they died to one world and were born free to another.

"Rebecca," John had said to her, when she agreed to trust him, "the people here are far from dead. You do not need to worry that they will kill you. They are pursuing life and freedom. I knew that with their help, you would be able to also. That is why I made certain they would help you escape—what is his name—Lord Furton"

She had shaken her head,

"I do not understand."

"These people slip from society. Others think that they are dead, but if they were to dig up their graves, they would find that they are empty."

She had tried to understand.

"You did this as well?"

"No," John had said, "There was no reason for me to. I had no family, no friends."

"But, what about Philip and the ship?"

"I found them long after I had crossed the river."

"You have left this—society—group—these people?" she had said, searching for the right word and trying to make sense of it all.

"No, there is freedom fully. You are not held in any one place. If they insisted on that, I know you would not have been right among them. You are free to move as you desire. It is only now, because of the trouble with England, that more are drawn in."

"But, why did they say they were expecting me?"

"I do not know," John had said.

"And what about Caleb? You are certain that they did not —"

He had shaken his head.

"I am certain but, unfortunately, I cannot tell you why. I do not have all the answers."

She had acquiesced quickly to their way of life. It was not so unlike sailing with Philip and his crew. There was the constant movement and always work to be done. She still did not know all of the answers to her questions, but she had not yet trusted them with her identity either. In that way, it was like Philip's ship as well; she still masqueraded in his clothes. Although John had insisted that the people of the across the river group would not kill anyone, the thought of her safety being in jeopardy should they discover that she were not whom they presumed her to be was something that seemed plausible to her. There were rumors, whispered around a dwindling fire on the coldest nights, of a spy who had infiltrated their ranks. His identity was a mystery to them and already she had received more than one questioning look. To admit that she had been dishonest would be her undoing.

So, she had settled into life, burying herself fully in her work with the pain of Caleb lying in his grave too unbearable. Rebecca was comforted in knowing that the men whom she helped escape, such as young Thomas Frampton tonight, could not be torn cruelly from the arms of their loved ones. Death on the battlefield would not be their undoing. Like the ancient Greek ferrymen of Hades, she transported them to greater life beyond. Or, as Rebecca liked to think of it, it was as if they had all awoken one morning with benefit of Juliet's potion and without any of the tragic after effects; they had defied death.

Early the next morning, Rebecca woke to the gusting winds. They were camped on the edge of the town and a stream bordered the grounds that lay between. Rebecca's boots sank into the snow, leaving canyons for the chirping birds to hop into in her wake. Carrying her bucket with her, she bent to dip it into the stream.

Solid.

She picked up a rock and chipped away at the ice. A crack splintered the frozen water and a splash of liquid trickled through the mass.

"Do not leave me ever."

The words startled her. She had thought that she was alone, but caught sight now of a couple. Feeling as though she were watching some faded shadow of herself and Caleb, some younger version that had roared to life, she stopped to stare. They were across the stream from her, laughing, moving as though the world belonged only to them. Rebecca was concealed behind bushes and felt only the slightest guilt in watching them. But, they knew nothing of the woman who had been dressed as a man for so long that she had forgot what it felt like to be looked at as the younger version of Caleb looked at the younger version of herself now. Well, John had looked at her like that, but it had resulted in her discovery. She watched, as he took her in his arms and kissed her.

"I promise," he said.

You used to make such promises to me, Caleb. Did you not mean your words? Did your words hold no importance?

A tear glistened at the corner of her eye and rolled down across her red wind-blown cheek, stinging it.

"Kiss me," the girl said, "Kiss me as though 'twere the last time."

Do not! Do not say such terrible words.

Hearing the girl speak the words that she had spoken, when it really had been the last time, was too much. Pushing aside her hurt at their separation and her anger at Caleb being taken, she dipped her bucket into the stream. This, not the kisses of youth, was to sustain her.

"There will be two more tomorrow and one is as a favor," John said to her, over the campfire later that night.

"Hmm? Oh, fine yes," she said. The two beside the stream had occupied much of her thoughts today. To make matters worse, everywhere she had looked today there had been reminders that life was not meant to be lived alone. Even the chattering squirrels and birds had a companion to pass the long days of winter with.

"Something on your mind?"

"Not really," she said.

Well, it wasn't. Not really. It was, however, lying heavily

on her heart.

What good is freedom, if it means that you are away from everyone and everything you love? What good is freedom, if you are alone?

"Are you happy here?" John said. She looked at him over the crackling fire.

"I am glad to help," she said.

"But, you do not truly feel at home here," he ventured.

Hesitantly, she nodded.

"I think that our journey lies not only in helping others get away, but in something more. There are those among us who want to take an active part in the revolution."

She looked at him and waited for him to go on.

"I think that you could—that— ah heck. I am no Shakespeare, Rebecca, but I admire you. There has been something about you, since I first met you on the ship. You were different somehow and proved yourself a good friend. When I discovered—" He paused, blushing slightly, before continuing,

"Now, that I know who you really are, I just cannot forget."

"Oh," she said, "you think I am not suited to work here?"

He shook his head.

"I think you deserve more. Rebecca, you should be happy. I know that if I were to—" he swallowed— "marry you, I would do my best to make that happen."

Rebecca blinked. Surely, she had not properly heard him.

"You— told me once that marriage was not for me," she said, not at all sure of what to say.

"Regular, ordinary marriage would not be," John said, "But, ours would not be like that. We would be partners, Rebecca. We would be free to see the world, to defend what we want, to never let anyone part us. You know it, Rebecca. I will not let you down. I followed you. I freed you. For so long, even before I knew it or truly knew you, I have loved you."

Rebecca felt as though in a dream. She was not the one that he was speaking to. Surely, there was someone else. He was saying all the right words, but he wasn't Caleb. That was perhaps his only fault, but it was impossible to overlook. But Caleb, dear, sweet, beloved Caleb was gone. She could have everything she had ever dreamed of— not with him, but with John.

He was looking at her intently, his face bathed in the soft glow of the firelight. It flickered over his face, as he searched for the answer in her eyes.

"Do you love me, Rebecca?"

She swallowed as a tide of memories washed over her. John had been the one who had taken her in, showed her the literal ropes, helped her find her place, saved her life in the storm, freed her from Lord Furton, protected her secret, and still the list went on.

"Yes," she said, nodding. They were alone and the threat of onlookers was removed. He reached for her hand, intertwining her fingers with his own. She let him take it.

"Then, will you marry me?"

With a thousand beautiful possibilities before her, there really was only one answer.

"No."

He swallowed, hurt filling his eyes.

"May I be so bold as to ask why not?"

"Because, I love him too much and you too little, for it to be fair to you. No matter how much I love you, and my heart assures me it is true, my love for him remains unchanged. I am sorry, John, I cannot marry you."

He let his fingers untangle from hers and patted her hand. Then, he said those words that made it all the more difficult.

"'Tis all right, Rebecca. I understand."

CHAPTER SEVENTY-SIX

Hustled roughly down the street toward the docks, Caleb was prodded along. His arm continued to drip onto the fresh fallen snow.

"Put that around your arm," a man said, tossing a strip of cloth toward Caleb. He doubted the concern of the man for him when he saw the dirt streaks across the cloth. To hammer his point into place he said,

"Stop dripping! You are leaving a terrible trail."

One of the men beside him must have decided that Caleb looked as though he had more strength than he did after the punch to the stomach and less sense than he ought to have been credited with. Just to make sure that this unwelcome sailor of the king didn't try to escape and make himself even more unwelcome, Caleb felt a rope slide over his wrists.

"You must not escape when the street widens. I swear, 'tis more work to capture you than— "

The man's words muffled, as a sack went over Caleb's head. Unable to see and with his hands once again bound, he was reduced to the stumbling man in the forest who had been sent up river. Having fashioned cabinetry for several years, he was used to securing things into their proper place, not to being the one shut out from the world.

Do not kill me. Not now. If you were going to do it, then it should have happened in England. Not here. Not when I am finally close to Rebecca. Not when we are on the same soil.

Whether they were or not and whether, in this massive land, Rebecca was close he had no idea. But, a man who had been through as much as Caleb had, had to hold onto whatever shred of hope there was. Even if it were only a slip of reasoning he could find and no matter how flimsy it was, he had to believe.

Prodded along, the snow crunched underfoot giving way to stone in patches. Ice slicked over in exposed spots left navigating his path, while hooded, all the more difficult. Unlike the blindfold in the forest, the sack that they had thrown over Caleb's head was threadbare in places, letting in light. It wasn't enough to distinguish form, but it was something at least. Being cast into total darkness had an unnerving effect on him and he was in no hurry to repeat it.

Questions paraded through his mind, taunting him in the form of the diverse characters that had torn him from the fibers of normalcy.

"*You ask too many questions,*" Rebecca said, in that sweet voice that betrayed her ability to sound cross with him.

"*And, you make it truly difficult to concern myself with the answers,*" he heard himself say, in the memory of the last time that he had seen her. He ached, much more than from the punch to the stomach, at his separation from her. That night, the stars had twinkled as bright sparks of luminosity in a field of black. If ever a man needed illumination, now was the time. She had made him willing to forget his concern for the answers, but now he needed them to pave his path to her. Questions had resulted only in the stumbling route of a man separated from the truest answer.

Why am I doing this?

Rebecca.

Why am I here?

Rebecca.

"Rebecca," the muted winds howled in his ears, stretching out her name as though dangling her in front of him.

"Make haste!" one of his guards barked, jabbing his already tender torso with his elbow. Caleb teetered forward. A flash of something appeared in front of his eye.

What was that?

He writhed to make the object reappear. There was a hole

in the sack! Squinting, he blinked back the excess sunlight as he struggled to balance the fabric on his nose so the tiny hole would stay in place. The mast of a ship appeared. On top of it, the blue, red and white of the Union Jack fluttered in the breeze. He had run from his naval ranks, but the sight of the flag had never looked so appealing. If they were taking him back, then he would suffer a flogging but he would still be alive! If he were alive, then he still had a chance of getting to Rebecca.

He had assumed that the accents, altogether different from what he was accustomed to and presumably American, meant that he would be faced with a formidable downfall. But, perhaps, these men were not the enemy! The navy might have paid them, as the guards had paid Marion, to return runaways. But then, why had they said they wanted the English gone?

Just because someone is paid by another, it does not mean that he is happy that he is there.

The thought of being shipped home, before he had been able to find Rebecca, hardly seemed like a threat. England was bolstering her troops. Why would they go through the trouble of sending him back, when tensions were mounting and war was brewing? If they wanted to dispose of him, wouldn't it be easier to do so on the battlefield? At least then he could, perhaps, kill a handful of rebels for them and serve some useful purpose.

The ship stood proudly in the harbor, a curious mix of old and new wood. He had never seen a ship with such a marriage of craftsmanship. The men on deck were too small to make out, especially through Caleb's sliver of a vantage point. He would not have noticed the construction of the ship, were it not for the glaring coming off of the beams that were obviously newer. A bright streak, looking rather like a feather, flashed in front of his eyes. Caleb's foot hit a patch of ice, causing him to slip. A rough hand reached out, steadying him on his feet. Though he had not fallen, the hood had and the ice cost him his viewing hole.

Around him he heard the creak of the gangplank and the

sound of barrels rolling along it, their contents jostling nosily. Pushed along, Caleb felt his feet step onto the deck of the ship and then rushed down a ladder. Tossed into a corner, Caleb's body flopped onto the floor of the ship and the sound of the men's feet softened as they left him alone.

They are just humiliating me.

Soon someone, armed with a cat o' nine tails, would arrive. His punishment would be delivered and he would be one step closer to Rebecca. Expectantly, he waited for the steps of the man to approach. Still bound and hooded, he was unable to move or to see. What little light he had benefit of in the open was absent below deck, too dim to filter through the sack. Alone, he waited.

Any moment. The quicker this is over with, the quicker I can resume my search for Rebecca.

Still, he waited.

Long after he'd been left alone, the footsteps that he had expected to hear echoed through the galley. Caleb raised his head.

I see you are here for me. Do not say it, Caleb. Just be quiet. You have complicated matters enough. Just do not make them mad and then you can be rid of them.

"What do you know about the British plans?" a voice, lacking any hint of a British accent said.

What?

This was not at all what he had expected.

"Tell me your plan," he repeated. Still, Caleb said nothing.

"What do you know?" the man repeated.

"I do not know anything about it," Caleb said.

Was it a test to determine his loyalty?

"You are in the navy, are you not?"

"I am."

"And how long have you been in Boston?"

The man paced as he spoke, his heels clicking on the deck.

"I only arrived."

"And what is your name?"

Caleb swallowed.

My name.

Seamus had warned him not to speak the name of Turrington. No one had warned him against using his own name, but it had seemed to carry a curse with it wherever he traveled.

"Your name," the man repeated.

He swallowed once again.

"Caleb Haroldson."

The man's pacing stopped.

"Caleb Haroldson?" he repeated.

"Yes, I am Caleb Haroldson."

"But, Caleb Haroldson is dead," the man said.

Peter had said that the man in the forest said his name was Caleb Haroldson. Spurred to tell the truth, because deception had landed him nowhere, he said,

"No, it was a mistake. He was a spy who took my name."

"Why?"

"He was investigating some group."

The man crossed to Caleb and slipped a knife against his wrists.

You spoke too much! The truth has undone you as well!

"Speak of this to no one," the man said in a low voice, as the blade slid between the ropes and fell loose. He lifted the hood from Caleb's eyes.

The man in front of him was not dressed in a uniform, but instead in the clothes of a civilian. His body was tanned, contrasting sharply with the frigid winter.

"Soon it will be dark. I will help you return."

Caleb's eyes went wide.

"I do not understand. Why would you do this?"

"'Twas a mistake."

What was a mistake?

He didn't understand, but he didn't dare question the man who seemed to be orchestrating his release.

"Here, put this on," he said, handing his jacket to Caleb. Caleb obeyed and the man said,

"Do not say a word. Let me talk for us. Understand?"

Caleb nodded. Not speaking wasn't too much of a challenge. Surprise at this man's help accompanied Caleb, as he walked off the ship with the other. They moved quickly, emerging into the shadows of the night. Turning down an alley, British voices in the distance sounded in Caleb's ears. The man drew a length of rope from his pocket. Had he changed his mind?

"Let me see your hands." Seeing Caleb's reluctance, he explained,

"You have to go back. They have to think you were kidnapped. All right?"

Well, I was kidnapped.

That much was true. Caleb slipped from the man's coat and then held out his hands for the man to tie, hardly believing what he was doing.

"Wait," the man said. From his pocket, he drew out a book.

"Can you read?"

"Yes, you want me to read something to you?" Caleb said, thinking a dark alley with danger surrounding them was hardly the place for an evening of literature.

"No," the man said, tearing a blank page from the back.

Romeo and Juliet, Caleb saw on the spine.

The man picked up a stick from a fire pit on the side of the alley. Its end was covered in soot.

"Write *Go away English*," he said.

Caleb's brow wrinkled.

"To deceive them," the man said. As Caleb wrote, the man ripped a strip of cloth from his shirt. When the note was finished, the man tied the strip of cloth over Caleb's mouth and tucked the note into the rope of his bound hands.

"Go," he said.

Without ability to speak with the gag in place, Caleb had no way to thank him. He didn't dare dally any longer. As he left his accomplice, he heard him mutter,

"You better love her as much as I do."

CHAPTER SEVENTY-SEVEN

Camped outside of Boston, Rebecca watched the first buds of spring appear. Winter's frost had thawed, filling the rivers with a surplus of water. Rebecca's sadness began to melt as well and her thoughts turned to how her own life would bloom. The days were lonely, with no one else really to talk to. Secrecy prevailed, as the dominant force in the people who surrounded her. Shortly after John had proposed, he'd left to rejoin Philip and the crew. The label of pirate no longer seemed menacing to the people of the colonies when it was attached to any ship of American sailors, running interference and trying to break the blockade. Another woman might have thought that John's disappearance had coincided with her rejection, but Rebecca knew better than that. Besides, if he had been bitter he wouldn't have invited her to come back.

"I will not try to keep you away from Philip and the ship, if that is what you desire. I still think that you have greater freedom here," John had told her.

She had agreed and chosen to stay behind, ferrying those across who wanted nothing to do with the impending trumpet call to war. As winter had slipped to spring, though, revolution had come, not between the colonies and England but within the across the river group itself. Just as the colonists had divided themselves, a ripple of dissension pulsed within the group. Some began to side with John, though John had spoken his own convictions aloud to no one save Rebecca, and thought that escaping from the impositions of society to idly sit was the wrong direction to go in.

"This society has existed for decades, offering an alternative life to those unhappy in their own," one of the men had said succinctly, around a recent campfire.

"But, what good is that, if we are no longer free? We split from our brothers in England, because the king was able to press us back into our old way of life. Now, is the time to rise up and fight him!"

"We should push west," another said.

"Push west? And then what? He will push us until there is no land left!"

Rebecca was stirred by the sentiments. After escaping her own planned future, the possibilities now stretched provocatively in front of her. She was undecided on if she would take up arms to fight alongside the colonists. Perhaps, she would rejoin Philip's ship. She had belonged there. But, that was in a time when she had been Richard Haroldson to all and Rebecca Turrington to no one. Now, she was Rebecca Turrington to John. She couldn't work beside him on a ship, masquerading as Richard, knowing that she loved him enough to make her feel guilty. Maybe it was wrong to live as a widow, when she had never even been married to Caleb. Her heart didn't know that no marriage ceremony had taken place, though. It knew only that she was never supposed to be separated from him. People weren't supposed to be torn from their loved ones. For that reason, though undecided on her future endeavors, she was committed to helping others cross the river. Let them be the masters of their own destinies. Let fate be decided by their own will. Man was set apart from the animals by that divine gift of freewill. For a man to take that from another was unpardonable. Lord Furton had done that to her. He had ripped her away from her chosen life. Rebecca fumed at the thought of him, her hatred seething over.

No one should suffer as I did. No one.

It was the guiding thought that had carried her through winter and through talk of revolution: both within the group, as well as in the colonies at large.

Rebecca bent down, gathering wood for fuel. It had rained this afternoon and much of the wood was wet, making finding suitable pieces all the more difficult. The air was crisp, biting at her ears from under her woolen cap she wore. Philip's clothes, which had served her well in the Caribbean, lacked the insulation needed for the dampness of the early spring evening. The smell of rain and wood smoke wafting toward her from the fire mingled in her nose, making her sneeze. She muffled it against her sleeve. Rebecca had no way to disguise her fully feminine sneeze.

"He is English, definitely English," one of the men was saying. Rebecca was concealed behind a bush and felt as though she were eavesdropping on the conversation.

"He is somewhere in the area, pretending to be one of us, that much I know—"

They turned away from her. Though she could no longer hear their conversation, she knew what they were speaking about. The identity of the alleged infiltrator had been on everyone's minds for months now. If they were betrayed, the integrity of everything they stood for would be at risk. No one would be able to slip away, free to live the life of his or her choosing, again. Existing beyond society would prove impossible, if society knew of their existence. It was the reason that they had splintered from their English roots, as the man at the campfire had spoken of. Many in England had lapsed into a community of descendants of those who had crossed the river, but they were living none of the freedoms that were intended for such a life.

"Please, 'tis my son, I am afraid the soldiers will take him. You must take him with you, protect him," a mother pleaded. Her voice cut through both the air and Rebecca's thoughts and any doubt she had of her place was instantly quelled. Yes, another life would be preserved.

Late that night, Rebecca stood at the edge of the stream. The woman's son was supposed to meet her there.

Are you ready to cross the river?

The question repeated in her mind but if she were to ask it aloud, only the birds would have heard to reply. The man in the furs, who had been there the night she escaped from Lord Furton, appeared at her side now.

"Not here yet?" His voice was low and a deep wood smoke lingered on him. She often wondered if he had ever lived anywhere other than among the trees and woodland animals. He seemed so much a part of them.

Rebecca shook her head. The man motioned and another joined him.

"Where are you going?" Rebecca said, her voice dropping into the night as a pebble does into a pond.

"To get him."

She nodded. This course of action was unfamiliar to her. Never had someone not met her when preparing to cross. She had no recollection of anyone being collected—well, except for her. Perhaps, they'd been too late and the woman's son had been captured by the soldiers.

A chill whispered over Rebecca. They couldn't be too late; they just couldn't! The boy had to be helped, to be saved!

She drew up her knees to her chest and rocked to keep warm, as she sat beside the stream and waited for their return. Rebecca began to doze, catching herself as she jumped awake. The grasses around her were rustling and footsteps approached. She jumped to her feet, pulling the knife from her back pocket in preparation to defend herself if she should need to. There was, she saw now, no reason for such alarm. The two men had returned and had brought with them a third. As they approached, she saw that the other man was bound and gagged.

"Is he an enemy?" she whispered, when they were close enough to hear.

"He is one of us now," the woodsman said.

"One of us—then, why is he bound?"

"He did not want to come."

Rebecca's nerves prickled. This wasn't the way they worked. This wasn't it at all. John had spoken of this place being freedom. To bring someone here against his will was counter to everything they believed. Why, it was breaking the rules!

When Rebecca looked into the face of the bound man, her heart fell.

No, not him. He is not supposed to be here.

CHAPTER SEVENTY-EIGHT

Camped, not far from where they had docked, Caleb spooned a mouthful of the broth through his lips. Peter sat across from him, his form lit by the glow of firelight, as he hastily ate his own soup. Returning to the navy, with the benefit of the kind and mysterious stranger, had not resulted in the harsh punishment he had expected. That he had run away seemed to have been entirely forgot. Gruff words had been spoken, but not at Caleb as he had expected. Instead, the only scorn was for those riotous colonists, up to no good and committed to the unraveling of the king's service. His accomplice's note had served its purpose well.

"Go away, English! Ha! Go away criminals!" the commander had growled upon Caleb's return. Peter had looked at him, surprised and entirely unsure what to think when he saw Caleb. When he found out that Caleb had been kidnapped, he said,

"Do not trouble yourself. There will be another chance."

But, there hadn't been—not yet anyway. The men were grouped close together and kept beyond the reach of the interfering colonists.

"They are unruly children and must learn to be governed! If not, then they will have to die!" Caleb had heard one man remark.

Though he had kept the terms of the man who had freed him and spoken to no one about it, including Peter, the man would not leave his thoughts. Surely, he had risked his safety in freeing Caleb. If these were to be the sort of men that Caleb was asked to turn his ammunition against, then the prospect of remaining in the king's service only grew more unappealing.

Ah Rebecca, where are you?

His eyes searched the trees nestled around them, as though expecting her to dart from behind them like a deer. The thought was, of course, ludicrous. A lady like Rebecca would be in some city or at least a town. His emancipator convinced him that what he had seen of the people, there were gentlemen among these Americans.

Dear, sweet Rebecca, if you have been forced into marriage with no other means, then I only hope that 'twas to a man such as him.

The thought offered a measure of comfort, but it was still too painful to think of her sitting beside the fire with someone else. He swallowed.

Stop thinking, Caleb. Just stop thinking.

The warning offered, he looked over the gathering of men dressed in the same uniform he found his own body clothed in. These men had been gathered from their homes across the English countryside to fight against their American cousins.

Is it really so wrong for them to have a say in Parliament, to be represented? Ah, but what do I know of politics? I know how to fashion a cabinet, not a government.

Cross with himself for entangling his mind once again in a heavy web of thought, Caleb turned to Peter.

"What do you—" Caleb's voice trailed off, as he saw the look on Peter's face. Paler than the winter moon had been those cold months before, he stood staring at someone.

"What is it?" Caleb said. Peter did not answer, but continued to stare as though trying to reconcile something in his mind.

"You look like you have seen a ghost," Caleb said, following the line of Peter's vision, but seeing nothing out of the ordinary. Some soldier had arrived, but surely that would not provoke such a response.

"Caleb," Peter said, his voice lacking its usual strength, "He is a ghost."

"What? I do not understand—"

"Caleb Haroldson."

"I am Caleb Haroldson."

Peter shook his head.

"The man who was the spy, who took your name—"

"The one I thought you killed?" Caleb said, now staring from Peter to the very alive man in the uniform. Peter nodded, his eyes refusing to abandon the other man.

The man Peter had proclaimed to be a ghost turned. Catching sight of Peter, he nodded and walked toward them.

"So, you must have found yourself here as well," he said, as though nothing were out of the ordinary in the slightest.

"You—" Peter stammered, "you died."

"Did I now?" the man said, a look of amusement, which had vexed Peter in those long, puzzling conversations, crossing his face.

"In the forest, near Turrington Manor," Peter repeated, looking very much like he wanted to reach out to see just how real the man in front of him was.

"Caleb Haroldson died on that day in the forest. Not I."

Caleb, having listened to their conversation, now stepped forward.

"I am Caleb Haroldson," he said. Hearing the declaration, the spy turned to look at him,

"Oh you are, are you? Well, it is a pleasure to make your acquaintance, Mr. Haroldson, but really you must not look so surprised. Why 'twas your own trick that I used. You know, appearing dead when not."

"My own—"

"Come now, Caleb, when you crossed the river. Your name was the newest on the list. Why else would I have taken it?"

Caleb looked from the spy to Peter.

Cross the river?

It had been months since he heard those words. Rather than sheer terror, they now only produced utter confusion.

"I am glad to see you are back on our side, Mr. Haroldson. I warned your friend here," he gestured toward Peter, "that you had dangerous friends. I am glad you came to your senses. They were none too pleased when they heard me talking about them in the forest, but I was prepared." He spoke the words with a grin, looking very pleased with himself and tapping his chest. There was a metallic ring to it.

Armor.

"You were not shot," Peter said.

"Oh, I was shot all right," he said.

"But, you were only pretending," Caleb said.

Taking a theatrical bow, the man said,

"I am nothing if not an actor. Good day to you, gentlemen."

He adjusted his coat, as he walked away.

"Never did care about his coat, only cared to conceal his armor. Must be thicker than it looks to stop the sound," Peter muttered.

"What was that?" Caleb said.

"Nothing important. Now, what is this about crossing a river?"

CHAPTER SEVENTY-NINE

Rebecca's stomach turned over uneasily. There must have been some mistake. He could not be here, not bound, not gagged, not taken like this. Even in the faint light of night, she could make out his form and features. This was the boy who had kissed the girl beside the river, whom Rebecca had viewed the memory of Caleb and herself through on that snowy morning. Her work was about liberation, about freeing people to be together. They were not supposed to be separated! She had continued to work with the group, to ensure that others did not suffer as she had and now they were the cause of separation.

Her stomach protested, churning up bile. She coughed to clear her throat.

"I will take him," she heard herself say.

"You can handle him by yourself? You do not require help?" the woodsman asked.

"We will be fine," she said. The others nodded and turned to leave. When they had, the boy struggled against her and it was all she could do to keep control over him. When she was certain that the men would not overhear, she said,

"Stop fighting me. Save your strength. I am trying to help you."

Seeming not to believe her, he continued to writhe.

"I am in earnest" she said again, "I saw you with the girl beside the river."

This got his attention. He stopped struggling long enough for Rebecca to reach for the gag.

"If I untie this, you will be quiet?"

He nodded.

The heaviness of pine in the air settled against her heart. Caleb's workshop had smelled the same on many occasions. It was all she could do to resist kissing the boy's cheek, to establish some connection with the youthful Caleb of her dreams. Already risking her own safety in assisting him, she didn't dare expose that she was not a man.

"Do not let anyone separate you. Move west. Anything. Just do not leave her." She whispered the warning with such conviction, that he could only say,

"No— no, I will not. I will stay with her."

Hearing what she wanted, she cut the ropes loose on his hands.

"Quickly now!"

She waited just long enough to see his shadow disappear, before she turned toward the town. Cutting the boy loose from the ropes had done more than free him; it had severed her ties to those across the river. She could not return without the boy, not when there were such rampant rumors of an infiltrator. Discontent had been stirring within her and a decision had been forming to become more active. A ship that remained docked in harbor could never complete the journeys meant for it. Rebecca had her own sailing to do.

The pull of freedom inflated her sails of purpose, as the spring air infused their breath into them. Until she cut through the ropes, she had not known what shape that journey would take. As the ropes fell away from the boy's wrists, though, she knew where she had to go.

John.

There must be a reason he had continued to appear in her life. Perhaps, someone was trying to tell her something. Whether he was meant to be a friend or something more she couldn't know, but she did know he was meant to be there. Guilt brushed against her at the thought of moving on. Was it more foolish not to, though?

Unable to return for her few possessions, she pushed on. Traveling at night had become such a normalcy to her, that the lonely song of the evening birds no longer set her heart rushing. Rebecca was now proficient in navigating a path, when she had only a lantern's worth of moonlight.

Her purpose renewed and her spirit refreshed at having helped the boy return to his love, she felt a pinch of excitement at the thought of taking a more active role in delivering freedom to this new land. Perhaps, she would even—

Rebecca paused. Cutting through the dark, a familiar voice rose to her.

Could it be?

The voice became louder.

It is! She opened her mouth to speak, but found that her voice had abandoned her. Clearing her throat, she tried to maintain her disbelief that had merged with excitement.

"Richard Turrington?" she said aloud.

"Who is there?"

It is you! Oh dear brother, how good it is to hear you!

He was accompanied by someone she did not recognize, but she was unable to hide herself any longer. Taking off her hat, she said,

"'Tis me! 'Tis Rebecca."

He blinked, staring at her. Then, he crossed to her.

"Rebecca! Oh, it is you!" He pulled her to him and she felt the familiar arms of her closest friend from long ago wrap around her.

"Richard, are you real?" she said, stepping back to see him. She lifted her hand to his cheek, feeling the roughness of his scars.

"What happened?" she said, not having seen them in the dark.

"The fire," he said.

"The one when I was taken?"

He nodded.

"But, how did you end up here? They were only supposed to take you to Beckshire."

"What?" she said, her hand leaving his face as her stomach

turned over uneasily.

"I learned about a group of people who had disappeared. I arranged things with them."

"You did *what*?" she said, the joy of seeing her brother quickly turning to confused anger.

"I wanted to help you escape, but Lord Furton had broken off from them."

Rebecca shook her head. The heaviness of night wrapped around her, concealing her in a world where she had very little power.

"You had Lord Furton kidnap me?" she said. The words left her mouth sounding hollow for all the power they had over her life. How could he have? How could Richard have betrayed her so terribly?

"Yes," he said, "As soon as I knew about you and Caleb, I arranged it. But, 'twas not supposed to be like that. When Caleb came to me—"

"When Caleb came to you?"

"Yes, when he came I had just heard of Lord Furton's turncoat ways, but 'twas too late. So, I sent him after you."

You killed my Caleb.

Though the thought, cloaked in anger and hurt, was directed at Richard, she felt it return to her own heart and stab her there.

You, Rebecca, you killed Caleb. He was searching for you.

"And then, when he returned—"

"When he returned?" she said, "you have seen him twice?"

"Yes, but when I realized we would soon be in the colonies, I sent him away so that he could find you. I was regrettably harsh with him as we were surrounded by many men, but my words would not break him. Only being apart from you would do that to him. I did not know that you were here."

She swallowed. He understood; Richard truly did know,

at least in part, that she was Caleb's lifeblood. And then, upon the horrible realization, Rebecca felt a punch, more powerful than any hand could deliver, drive into her stomach.

"Caleb could have been here," she said, finding it hard to breathe.

"You killed him, you killed him! Did you hate him so much?" she shouted at him, pushing against him.

"What are you speaking of, Sister? He is dead? Rebecca, I promise, I did not know. I only did it so that you could be together. I was only thinking of you. All of it, I did for you. I saw something in you and Caleb that I had never seen in Mother and Father."

She stopped her pounding.

"You did?" she said, looking up at him.

He nodded.

"What was it?"

"Happiness," he said, "They live peacefully enough but theirs is a marriage of family obligation, not of love. I could not allow such a limitation for your life, dear Sister. Rebecca, I would do nothing to hurt you. You do know that, do you not?"

His face was covered in hurt at the pain he had caused her. She looked hard at him. Long ago, in the balmy summer evenings of England almost a year ago now, she had been saddened at the thought that she and Richard were no longer as close as they had once been. Now, standing with him, on the outskirts of Boston and on the eve of war, she realized that she had been wrong. His quiet had merely been concern and his pensiveness had been about a plan for her happiness.

"Yes," she said, "I am sorry."

"Do not apologize, Rebecca. Will you return home with me?"

Home. The word sounded foreign in her ears, but here he was in front of her now.

She considered this tempting offer of a new alternative to

life for a moment. She could have a place again alongside a man who loved her, not as a husband but as a brother. Something pulled at her though and she shook her head.

Richard had been her companion, her truest friend long before she had known dear, beloved Caleb. And he had conspired for her happiness, when she had feared they were no longer as close as they had been. He had earned her loyalty. Despite the opportunity, there was still too much undone. Home was no longer Turrington Manor. It was a state of mind, one that Rebecca feared would leave her, and the thought of its loss made her run cold.

"I cannot. Not yet, anyway."

CHAPTER EIGHTY
April 19, 1775

"The redcoats are coming! The redcoats are coming!" The warning raced across the countryside, as Rebecca walked into the dawn.

"Richard!" she heard someone call on the path behind her. She half-expected it to be the man who had been traveling with her brother, but Richard did not appear at the sound of his name. Instead, it was John who approached.

"Rebecca," he said, as he drew nearer and was certain only she could hear him.

"John, I have to leave. I need to join you and the crew on Philip's ship, at least for now."

"Rebecca, I have to tell you. This was the first chance that I had to get away. Please, understand. I would have had him join you sooner, only an Englishman of his age was in question among the group. It would not have been safe."

"You know my brother? I thank you, truthfully, for helping him. Of course, I understand."

She looked at him with such trust and gratitude, that though it would have been tempting never to tell her, he knew he had to. Loving someone, truly loving someone, meant not only seeking one's own happiness, not when it was at the expense of the happiness of the one he loved.

"Your brother? No, 'tis not what I mean. Rebecca, I freed —"

A bullet shot through the air, piercing John's hat.

"John!" she cried, horrified and pulling him down with her into the field of waving grass.

"Are you hurt?" she said.

He shook his head.

"I do not think so," he whispered back.

Rebecca's blood coursed through her veins, thundering in

her own ears. Through the grasses, John peered.

"Redcoats," he whispered.

Never would Rebecca have thought that England's defenders would fire on Lord Turrington's daughter. But first on Philip's ship and then in this land just beginning to awaken to a new morning in freedom's struggle, all titles and status had been stripped away. Rebecca had been judged only for her merits, only for her own actions and thoughts. It was a position she had coveted and only now fully realized that she had already held: in Caleb's eyes. Through befriending her and then loving her, John had shown her the truth that Caleb had first spoken to her heart. At the realization, a tear slipped down her cheek.

"Are you hurt?" John said, taking notice.

She shook her head.

"No, I— "

Another bullet ripped through the air, above their heads, this time traveling from the opposite direction. Rebecca's eyes went wide.

"We are surrounded?"

From the sack he'd been carrying, John pulled two muskets.

"Here," he said.

"I do not know how to fire."

"Handle the trigger. I will load," he said.

She nodded.

The two sat back-to-back, a musket poised in their hands in each direction.

"Maybe, they will leave. Just stay low. Do not fire, unless they do first," John said.

Rebecca nodded, filled with a fear that she had not known since their ship had been tossed on the tumultuous waves at sea.

"There they are!" Rebecca heard the shout from a man to her left. Horrified, she saw him train his musket on John. Taking aim, she waited.

Just do it, Rebecca. If you wait for him, it will be too late.
Rebecca held her breath.

"John, he is aiming at you," she said, able to breathe only in small gasps. She held her fire. Maybe, by some miraculous chance, they were not the ones who had been spotted. The man fired toward John. Rebecca did something that she thought she would never do; she aimed at an English soldier. She fired. Her bullet missed him but slammed into the tree beside him, splintering bark off from it. John ducked, but turned and started firing. Side-by-side, they struggled in their own private battle against the king's men. And then, it happened. A man stepped from behind the tree. Though dressed in a uniform, his form was undeniable.

Caleb.

Rebecca's heart leaped. He was real! He was alive! The sky brightened and every inch of her surged more fully to life.

And then in a cruel twist, everything changed. A shiver of terror ran through her.

"Miss Turrington, you will not escape me this time," Lord Furton's voice rose from the field behind her.

"I have been watching you, both of you. Would you like to tell Mr. Haroldson that you have been unfaithful or shall I? Wait, I know, we will not tell him at all." Reaching into his pocket, Lord Furton withdrew something golden. The early morning light caught the glint of Caleb's watch.

"Tick tock. Tick Tock. Your time is up, Caleb Haroldson."

In horror, she watched as Lord Furton turned his musket on Caleb.

"No! Caleb!" she screamed, as the bullet hurdled toward him.

"I will finally have you for myself," Lord Furton said, his cackle like the crack of musket fire. He had approached them alone, but did not intend to leave that way. He reached for

Rebecca. His hand closed around her wrist. The bullet spiraled toward Caleb.

"You will never have her," John said, firing. The bullet ripped into Lord Furton. With a stunned expression, he fell heavily, dropping her hand.

"A man is shot! He is down!"

Afraid to raise her eyes and see Caleb's undoing, she forced herself to look. But, he hadn't been hit! He was rushing forward toward them.

Rebecca wanted to stand, to run to him, but she knew better.

He was alive! Well and truly alive! As he approached, she raised to her knees in the grass.

"Caleb! 'Tis me!" Caleb fired. With a groan, John fell behind her.

Seeing her, Caleb dropped beside her in the grass.

"Rebecca? Rebecca!" he said, wanting to believe it was her but finding it hard to do so.

He looked at the man beside her and said,

"You?" His eyes went wide, as he realized he had shot his mysterious accomplice.

"I am fine," John said, "Just my arm. You two, go."

Rebecca shook her head,

"I am not leaving you here."

Seeing the look on her face, John knew better than to try to change her mind.

"All right, play dead," he said, thinking for the three of them. They lay back with Rebecca in the middle. Caleb reached for her hand and gripped it. His cells quickened at her touch and his heart pounded in assurance.

She was real! She was alive! Thank God in heaven! He was with his Rebecca. From the dark depths of uncertainty, which the year had submerged them beneath, they struggled for the surface together. Though they held still, their breathing shallow, life and time moved forward again. Despite all that was wrong in the world around them, all was once again real.

He lay with her in the field and waited. The three said nothing, barely willing to breathe, lest it should make too much noise.

"All right, let us go!" one of the soldiers said at last, when no movements were seen in the grass. Rebecca held her breath, as the sun overhead beat down on them.

When he was certain that the soldiers were gone, John signaled that they could get up. Rebecca threw herself against Caleb and he held her fast.

"Oh Rebecca, dear sweet Rebecca," he said, his words falling softly against her hair as he kissed her. For a moment, they clung to each other awakening in the early morning sunshine from the nightmare year. Plunged under the darkest currents, they emerged from below the depths of distance and of separation. Caleb clung to his lifeline, to his anchor of all that was real. John said nothing for a minute, allowing them their reunion before saying,

"Rebecca, we better leave."

"Oh yes, John. This is Caleb."

He nodded, his sunny grin sliding over his face. They stood and walked to the edge of the forest.

"Caleb, I know where we can go. Where we will be safe," she said.

John looked at her, nodding his agreement.

"Go," John said, "They may be back soon."

Rebecca looked at him, the man who had saved both her and Caleb.

"I thank you," she said, but the words sounded too small. Under the arching tree, as Caleb stood beside them, she embraced John. Lord Furton, if he were still alive, would have said that she was acting in a way not befitting a lady. He would have used it as evidence of her wanton ways. But, Lord Furton had never understood the important things in life. The word love had no meaning to him and friendship rang empty.

"I am sorry that it could not turn out as you wanted," she said to John.

With the look of the man standing on the deck under the blazing sun, in those days long ago, he said in his easy way,

"Ah, but it did. You are happy. You are free. That is what I desired."

"Where will you go?" she said.

"Wherever the wind may take me," he said, with a twinkle of sea air in his eye and a tip of his hat.

"Thank you, truthfully, from both of us," Caleb said, not knowing their full story but, sensing that John had been a true friend to both.

John nodded and they watched as he left to seek his own life and to find his own rivers to cross. Rebecca took Caleb's hand in hers and faced the west. They would at last, after all that had happened, with benefit of friends and brother, with the devotion of true love and the unfailing faith in each other, be able to fashion a life of their own. The Caleb and Rebecca that stood together now were not so unlike the two who had planned to run away in England.

This time, though, Caleb did not hesitate. Sometimes, life must simply be grasped and lived. Problems might come tomorrow, but today there was only the promise of what they had long awaited. Caleb didn't ask her any of the practical questions that had seemed so important last summer. The answer to all of them was already holding his hand. This time, there would be no silver plates buried in the river to fund their future, but there was something far more valuable: the golden promise of freedom across the river.

Book Club Questions

1. Rebecca relates her life to *Romeo and Juliet* and Caleb relates to Dante's *The Divine Comedy*. What book from the classics most resembles your own life?
2. What do you think is the greatest lesson that Rebecca learns? What is the greatest lesson for Caleb?
3. What did you enjoy most about the story? Was there any part you could identify with?
4. Who or what do you think is the villain of this story?
5. If you could ask any character in the story a question, what would you ask?
6. What do you think of the title? Is it multi-layered in meaning?
7. What most surprised you?
8. What does the reoccurring motif of stars represent throughout the various sections of the story?
9. What does the inclusion of Caleb's watch throughout the chapters signify?

Acknowledgements

Thank you for choosing to read this book! I remain grateful to those who believe in my writing, to my family, friends, fellow writers, and readers. I enjoy hearing from my readers and you can email me at Megan@MeganEasleyWalsh.com. To learn about my upcoming releases, visit me at www.MeganEasleyWalsh.com.

About the Author

Megan Easley-Walsh is an author of historical fiction, a researcher, and a writing consultant and editor at Extra Ink Edits. She is an award-winning writer and has taught college writing in the UNESCO literature city of Dublin, Ireland. Her degrees are in history-focused International Relations. She is American and lives in Ireland with her Irish husband. She is the author of *Flight Before Dawn*, *What Edward Heard*, and *North Star Home*.

CPSIA information can be obtained
at www.ICGtesting.com
Printed in the USA
LVHW041438070119
603018LV00008B/184/P

9 781366 227300